Mermen & Magic

DANGEROUS WAVES

L.M. BROWN

Books by L.M. Brown

Mermen & Magic

Forbidden Waters
Tempestuous Tides
Dangerous Waves

Heavenly Sins

Between Heaven & Hell
Between Good & Evil
Between Life & Death

Sexy Snax

One Perfect Wish

Single Titles

To See the Sky
My Boyfriend's an Alien

Dangerous Waves

ISBN # 978-1-78686-056-9

©Copyright L.M. Brown 2016

Cover Art by Posh Gosh ©Copyright 2016

Interior text design by Claire Siemaszkiewicz

Pride Publishing

Published in 2016 by Pride Publishing, Newland House, The Point, Weaver Road, Lincoln, LN6 3QN, United Kingdom.

Pride Publishing is a subsidiary of Totally Entwined Group Limited.

Prologue

Kai waited impatiently for his over-protective mother to make her decision. He tapped his fingers on the water, causing little splashes.

"You're definitely running a fever." His mother frowned as she removed her hand from his forehead.

They had come to the surface of the ocean for her to better check his temperature. Most of the rest of the clan remained under the water, though they would all be coming to the island the following evening, on the night of the summer solstice. The mating season had arrived and all mermen and mermaids would be swimming to land for the biannual task of breaking their fevers by having sex in the way that gave them the most pleasure.

Kai could hardly wait to join them for the first time.

"You haven't been swimming in the hot springs, have you?"

"No! I'm hot because of the mating fever, I know it."

Kai's mother gave him a skeptical glance. "Your brothers were both several seasons older than you when they first got their fevers."

Kai's stomach sank. His mother didn't seem to want him, the baby of the family, to grow up. Surely she wouldn't make him ride out the mating fever under the ocean instead of letting him join the others on land.

"Maybe you're unwell," she suggested. "Those fruits we ate last night weren't quite up to the usual standard."

"They were fine. I told you, it's the mating fever."

"I don't know…"

"Mama, please. Let me come to the island."

"But you're so young. It *can't* be the fever yet."

"It is. I know it." Kai continued to pester his mother until eventually she slapped at the water before throwing up her hands in despair.

"Which mermaid do you intend to spend the night with?" she asked, in a tone of resignation.

"Um."

"What's the matter, Kai?"

"I've been talking to Tal and he invited me to be with him."

"A merman?" His mother stared at him in surprise. "Why didn't you say anything before? I thought you liked Adva. She's a sweet young mermaid."

"She is, but she doesn't have what I need."

"You have no idea what you need yet. You've never had a mating fever."

"I know I want a merman."

"And you've decided on Tal?"

"I think so."

Kai's mother sighed and shook her head. "Are you sure? He's not the most sociable of mermen. You need someone who'll take care of you for your first time."

"Tal will. He's been nice to me."

"Very well, but please be careful."

Kai punched the air in triumph when his mother gave her consent and slipped back beneath the waves. He scanned the surface and spotted Tal a short distance away. He waved him over and swam to meet him.

"What did your mother say?" Tal asked. "Will she let her baby come play with the big boys on the island?"

Kai wrapped his arms around Tal's neck. "I'm not a baby and I don't need permission. Now, how about you tell me what we're going to do tomorrow night?"

Tal tugged Kai under the water, kissing him hard as they sank below the surface.

Kai was about to repeat his question telepathically when suddenly he couldn't see Tal or the world around him.

He could feel Tal's lips pressed against his mouth, and his hands on his body, but everything else had gone dim.

His awareness of the world vanished, and when his vision returned, he found himself somewhere else entirely. A city under the ocean stretched out before him. Buildings in various states of disrepair surrounded him, and mermen and mermaids swam past without seeming to notice his presence.

He scanned the area, searching for Tal and the rest of his clan. He couldn't see anyone he recognized among the crowd.

"Excuse me!" he called out, but no one responded to his call.

He swam toward the nearest mermaid, intending to ask her where they were, but before he reached her, a human appeared directly in front of him. He was so shocked to see a regular human so far under the water he nearly didn't realize she was staring right at him. She wore a long, flowing gown of white gauzy material. The matching headdress glistened with jewels. Kai had never seen such a being before.

"This way, Kai."

"How do you know my name?"

The woman smiled at him and waved him toward one of the larger and better kept buildings.

He tried again to get her attention. *"Where am I?"*

"Follow me. Let me show you your new home."

"I have a home already."

"That was your home before."

"Before what?"

The woman smiled again and took his hand, guiding him through the archway. *"Before you became one of my chosen."*

"Chosen? What do you mean?"

"You are my new Oracle."

Kai had no idea what the woman was talking about. What did she mean by Oracle, and what did it have to do with him?

"This is my temple. I'm the Atlantean Goddess of Prophecy. My name is Cari."

"I don't believe in gods and goddesses."

"It does not matter whether you believe in me or not, I'm as real as you are. This temple is the home of the Oracles and as soon as you come to Atlantis, it will be your home too."

"How many Oracles are there?" Kai couldn't see anyone in the temple. The place appeared to be deserted.

"There are always three of you. You are my new Oracle of the present."

"What exactly is an Oracle?" Kai felt a little ignorant, as though he should already know the answer to his question. Cari didn't seem to mind his asking and smiled as she explained.

"An Oracle is a merman or mermaid who has been gifted with the power to see visions. You can, if you wish, see anything happening anywhere in the world. The other two Oracles see the past and the future respectively. I have brought you here for the moment to show you what your future holds."

"What if I don't want to come to Atlantis?"

"The ocean is a dangerous place, especially for an Oracle."

"I've survived well enough until now. My clan is a strong one and I'm going to be a warrior with them. I'm already undergoing training for how to handle a spear."

"As an Oracle you are more vulnerable. You must come to Atlantis if you wish to remain safe."

"Why can't I be an Oracle and a warrior with my own people?"

"Because the price you pay for being an Oracle is your sight. The only time you will be able to see is when you are in human form. Under the water you will be blind, except when you're in the midst of a vision."

Kai wasn't sure he believed her, yet he recalled the horror of his vision vanishing. He didn't want to be blind, but if he retained his sight when he had legs, there was one obvious solution to the problem. "Maybe I'll just go live on land instead."

Cari shook her head. "Atlantis is the safest place for you. The *other Oracles will welcome you. They are mourning the loss of their present Oracle and know you are coming here."*

"How can they know, when I've not even agreed to this?"

"Because Ula, my Oracle of the future, has already seen your arrival. You will come to Atlantis and take your rightful place here."

"My mother might have something to say about your plans for me." If anyone could get him out of this mess, his mama could.

"Your mother can say whatever she wishes. Her arguments will make no difference. Your clan will deliver you safely to the city, where you will begin your new life. I would advise you to begin your journey to Atlantis immediately."

Kai wanted to argue, but the temple vanished and Cari with it. He could feel Tal's arms around him as he kissed the merman he intended to spend the solstice with. He would have been relieved, except he couldn't see Tal. Everything was black. His sight had gone, just as Cari had told him it would.

"What's the matter?" Tal asked. *"Why aren't you kissing me back?"*

"Take me to land."

"Tomorrow night is going to be so much fun."

"No, now." Kai tried to keep the panic from his thoughts, but something of his fear must have bled through to Tal.

"What's wrong?"

"I need to go to land. I need to…"

"Need to what?"

"I need to see."

"See what?"

"Anything."

Tal pulled away from him and Kai felt his hand on his face. *"You're blind?"*

"Please, take me to land. She told me I could see again when I take human form."

"She? What are you talking about?"

"She said she was a goddess and I'm an Oracle. I need to go to

land."

"An Oracle? Oh no! Let me look at you."

"What is it? What are you looking for?"

"You have the mark of the trident on your inner arm."

"How did that get there?"

"It means you've been touched by a god, or, I guess in your case, a goddess."

Tal stopped touching him and Kai reached out blindly, trying to figure out where he had gone. He had never felt so helpless in his life.

"We need to go back to the clan. They'll know what to do."

"I have to go to land." Kai tried to recall the way to the island so he could swim there on his own, but his lack of vision had him disoriented and he had no idea which direction to take.

"I don't think that's a good idea. Oracles don't leave the ocean. It's forbidden."

"Cari never mentioned anything about that."

"It's not common knowledge outside Atlantis – or the sunken city, as most of the mer call it."

"How do you know about it?"

"My clan, my original clan that is, took sanctuary in the sunken city. I left because mermen aren't allowed to have intercourse with other mermen there, but many of my people stayed, including my brother. From what I've heard from others who have visited the city, he became a guard to the Oracles and he fell in love with Ula, the Oracle of the future. It was when the next mating season arrived he discovered the Oracles are never allowed on land."

"What about during the mating season?"

"Not even then."

Kai had heard more than enough. He had no intention of staying in mer form during the mating season. He hadn't finally convinced his mother to let him go to land, only to have some goddess forbid him. As a grown merman, he was perfectly capable of making his own decisions. "If what you're saying is true, I won't go to Atlantis. I'll just stay here with the clan."

"I don't think you have much choice. The Oracles have always lived in the sunken city. Even those like you, who come into their powers in other parts of the ocean, always go to live in Atlantis."

"There's a first time for everything and I don't want to go there. It sounds more like a prison than a home."

"In some ways it is, though the city is the safest place in the ocean, especially for a blind merman. The perimeter is protected by sea dragons and they keep all the sharks and other monsters of the waters at bay. They also hide the city and its inhabitants from any humans who venture too close to the boundaries."

Kai didn't care how safe Atlantis was. He didn't want to live as a prisoner in a place where he couldn't even see his hand in front of his face. He would fight anyone who tried to make him go there. He wasn't a helpless child. He was an adult now and he had ambitions of becoming a great warrior.

"I won't go!" he insisted.

* * * *

Three months later, when Kai arrived at Cari's temple, he was still arguing with his parents and the rest of his clan.

"Welcome, Kai," a female greeted him. "I'm Ula, the Oracle of the future. Let me show you to your quarters."

Kai shook off Ula's hand irritably.

"Ah," Ula said. "Cari warned me you weren't happy about your new calling."

"I won't stay here," Kai told her. "I'd rather take my chances in the ocean."

Ula sighed and patted his arm. "I understand, more than you know. But before you make your choice to swim away from your destiny, there's something you should see."

Kai's vision returned, and he stared at the elderly merman struggling to rise from his sleeping sponge. "Who's he?"

"Panos is the Oracle of the Past, though as you can see, he's quite unwell and I've seen for myself his end is near. Would you like to see the merman who'll replace him?"

Ula didn't give Kai time to respond. A moment later they were in another part of the city, where two young mermen swam swiftly through the crumbling buildings. A third, older, merman struggled to keep up with them. He appeared to be some kind of guard.

"Prince Finn, you come back here right now!" the merman shouted.

The two youngsters ignored his order and continued on their way.

"Which one will be the new Oracle?" Kai asked.

"Delwyn, the prince's companion."

"He seems very young."

"He's four years younger than you."

"He doesn't seem old enough to be an Oracle."

"Delwyn is older than I was, when I came into my powers."

Kai swam closer to the two silver-finned mermen, but just when he reached them the vision changed once more. Now he saw Delwyn older, probably around the age Kai was now.

"He's a handsome young merman," Ula commented. *"And he's going to need you as he takes his first steps as an Oracle."*

The vision ended and Kai returned to the darkness he had almost become accustomed to.

Three mer, each blessed with powers that seemed more like a curse, and Kai, whether he wanted it or not, was one of them. He let the temple servants — his prison guards — guide him to his chambers.

As he curled up on his sleeping sponge, his biggest regret was failing to persuade Tal to take him to land, even if it had just been for the one solstice. The pain at the height of the solstice had been excruciating and the thought of going through the same experience all over again next mating season made him feel sick.

Kai tried not to dwell on the reality of the life stretching before him. If he did, he suspected he might just swim for the nearest shark and put an end to his misery. Instead, he thought about Delwyn, who he had briefly glimpsed in a vision. The young merman had been swimming with Prince Finn and had no idea his life would soon change forever.

Chapter One

Cari sipped her drink, savoring the sweet nectar of the gods. The secret ingredients of the nectar had been stolen long ago from the Greek pantheon, and in her opinion was the best acquisition the Atlantean gods had ever made.

Her quiet contemplation was rudely interrupted by the arrival of the most powerful goddess currently awake. Medina, Goddess of Love, appeared in the garden amid flashes of lightning and a flurry of pale pink silk robes.

"Ah, there you are." Medina didn't bother waiting for an invitation. She sat on one of the cushioned chairs and helped herself to a drink. "This modern world is so vast, don't you think?"

"The world itself is the same size it's always been. There are merely more humans inhabiting the planet than there used to be." Cari wondered what Medina wanted. She doubted it was a pleasant chat about the changing times. She didn't bother to ask, Medina would reveal the reason for her visit in her own good time.

"Have you been to Greece recently?" Medina inquired.

"Yes. I enjoy eating Greek cuisine in its home country."

Medina waved her hand in dismissal. "You can keep the food. Have you seen what's become of the temples?"

"Times have changed. The old gods are no longer worshipped as they used to be. It's not just Greece. The Roman ones, the Norse, so many of them are mostly forgotten in these modern times. Only scholars of history even know their names, and they don't truly believe."

14

"The people have forgotten us. Even in Atlantis they don't recall us. Most of the mer call the place the sunken city."

Cari shrugged. She had long since resigned herself to never enjoying the power which came from having thousands of followers. Unfortunately for Medina, the goddess of love had been sleeping for centuries and had only recently awoken. Cari supposed it had been a shock for her to find what had become of the world they had once known.

"If they were to remember," Medina continued, "our powers would eclipse those we once had. Imagine the benefits of being worshipped by even a fraction of the current population of this new world."

Although Medina's tone was mostly wistful, Cari detected a sense of purpose there too. The goddess of love was never going to be happy with merely a handful of followers.

"How it is you didn't sleep like the rest of us?" Medina asked. "What kept you in this realm?"

"My followers were not composed of Atlanteans alone," Cari replied. "Many of the mer already believed in me on that fateful day. Even though they didn't worship me in my temple, they had seen the power of my Oracles with their own eyes."

"The mer believed in me too," Medina pointed out impatiently. "I still slept."

Cari knew what Medina asked. She had a few ideas about why some had slept and others had remained in the world, though they were only theories. "You'll recall you performed some powerful magic in the weeks before you slept?"

Medina tapped her lip. "Are you talking about the little spell I put on Caspian?"

Cari snorted. "*Little* spell? Yes, I *am* referring to that. It would have taken a lot out of you to put a love spell on a god as powerful as Caspian."

"It shouldn't have taken that much power to put him under the influence for less than a day."

"Had you done other magic on other gods in the days

15

leading up to our fall?"

"Yes, of course, the gods often came to me for assistance with matters of the heart." Medina huffed. "So, are you saying my good deeds are the reason I was too weak to stay awake?"

Cari ignored the remark about good deeds. She was certain Caspian didn't see her meddling that way. "It's as good a theory as any."

Medina took a sip of nectar. "So, now you choose your trio of Oracles from amongst the mer."

"Yes."

"Interesting."

Cari frowned at the direction the conversation was taking. "We all needed followers to stay in this realm."

"And lucky you, the mer were ready to fall at your feet. Rather a shame you couldn't have warned the rest of us so we could take similar precautions."

"I didn't know what would happen."

Medina laughed in obvious disbelief. "The Goddess of Prophecy didn't see the biggest disaster to befall our kind before it happened? Forgive me if I don't believe you."

Cari glared at her uninvited guest. "You know as well as I do, our powers are useless within the temple of another god. I could not see what would happen. If I'd had any idea, don't you think I'd have done everything in my power to stop it?"

Medina nodded and lowered her eyes. "Whatever our differences, I know how much you care for your brother."

Cari took another drink and wished it were something stronger. "What transpired weakened me too. It nearly drained me to appoint new Oracles."

"Humph."

Cari waited, her patience wearing thinner by the minute, wondering what Medina wanted from her. She tapped her manicured finger on her glass, subtly hinting for the goddess to get to the point.

"Your current Oracles are all untouched," Medina

commented.

"Yes, I know."

"You used to take most of your Oracles to your bed," Medina continued. "The men at least. Are you losing your touch, or don't you like the idea of letting a half-human fuck you?"

"I'm not prejudiced against the mer. I've invited some to my bed over the years, just not my Oracles."

"Is there any particular reason why not? What's changed since I was last here?"

"The Oracles are forbidden to have sexual relations with anyone. Not that any of the present ones would accept an invitation from me anyway, both Kai and Delwyn are what humans these days call gay."

"What?" Medina's jaw dropped and she placed her glass on the table with a shaky hand.

"You heard me," Cari replied. "They're homosexual. It's really not so unusual."

"That's not the part I'm shocked at. You've forbidden the Oracles to enjoy sexual pleasures?"

"Yes."

"Why?"

"It would appear the power of sight carries down through the generations now."

"It never used to, did it?"

"No."

"Then how did that happen?"

Another question Cari didn't have an answer for, though again she'd had plenty of time to formulate her own theory on the matter. "I suspect it was a side effect of my mother's interference with the mer physiology."

Medina snorted in a thoroughly unladylike manner. "Your mother seems to be at the bottom of all our troubles, doesn't she?"

Cari smiled softly. "Oh, I think there's plenty of blame to be left at other doors as well."

Medina grimaced. "So, because the powers you gifted on

the Oracles are hereditary, you've forbidden them to have sex."

"It's for the best."

"To live without love is never for the best."

"The descendants were discovered to inherit more than one gift if there were two or three different Oracles in their line."

"Ah, now I see what the problem is. If a humble little mermaid or merman could see more than you intended they might rival your own powers. Only *you* are permitted to see everything. Rather selfish of you, don't you think?"

Cari bristled at the accusation. "Many years ago there was a mermaid who did see all. She saw the past, the present and the future and was driven crazy by the visions. She didn't even live to see her first mating season. We imposed the rule to prevent the same thing happening again."

"I'm surprised it wasn't already too late. How many mer had powers by the time this was discovered?"

"A great many, I'm afraid. Relations were banned for all of them so each line ended with them."

"Could you not have simply removed their powers?"

"I tried, but it didn't work. My Oracles are appointed automatically. When one Oracle dies, another comes into their powers without my doing a thing. When I undid the original spell, my appointed Oracles lost their powers, but those who had been born with the powers retained theirs. The law was the only option. I cast my original spell for the final time."

"The final time?"

Cari sighed. "I cannot undo the magic and start over. As you have already seen, we don't have the followers we used to, or the powers our believers instill in us. I think I would have the strength to remove the powers of the present Oracles, but I wouldn't be able to cast the spell again."

Medina nodded. "Yet I still don't like the idea of your Oracles being unable to love, especially considering they are mer, and as you know, go into heat twice a year. Surely it's painful for them."

"They have learnt to cope with the solstices."

"And how do they *cope* with a life without love?"

"They know it's for the best."

Medina waved her hand and a vision appeared in front of her. Cari recognized the two mermen at once, Kai and Delwyn, her Oracles of the present and past. They were under the water, where they stayed, and Delwyn had curled up in Kai's arms. They were stroking and kissing. It was nothing Cari hadn't seen before.

"They are not soulmates," Medina commented. "Although they are close, their souls don't cry out for each other."

"That would be a good thing," Cari replied. "Were their souls bound, it would make their solstices even more unbearable."

"Then you admit they struggle on the solstice nights?"

"Yes, of course they do, as does any merman or mermaid who doesn't find relief in the mating season."

"You don't think it's wrong to stop your Oracles finding love?"

Cari stood and stalked toward the vision, shattering the image as she approached. "It's not ideal, but right now there's nothing to be done about it."

"Kai's soulmate will soon be on his way to Atlantis, and Delwyn's is already there."

Cari used her powers to see into the future. "Oh, damn."

"You see him?" Medina asked.

"They must not meet. It would make Kai's mating seasons unbearable."

Medina laughed. "No one can avoid their fate. Surely you, of all people, know that?"

"Destiny is not a set course. You must help me to stop them meeting."

"Must?" Medina rose and glided over to Cari. "I am the Goddess of Love and the only thing I must do is right this wrong you have inflicted on your Oracles."

"You can't interfere!"

"Of course I can, and I will."

With a gloating smile Medina vanished.

This was not good at all. Cari didn't need Medina meddling in the lives of her Oracles. They were protected in Atlantis and it was where their powers were most potent. They could *not* be allowed to leave.

* * * *

The heat of the sun warmed Dax's bare back. He hadn't moved from his spot on the sand in nearly an hour. Most of the clan had congregated a little way down the beach, but he was reluctant to join them. He knew he was simply putting off the inevitable, yet he couldn't seem to help himself.

Nearly three years had passed since he had parted ways with the clan he had grown up with. In that time he had traveled with any clan who would let him. Most merpeople he came across happily welcomed him into their group, though there was the occasional tight-knit clan who were reluctant to let him travel with them for more than a few days.

Dax had been with the current clan for nearly eight months, but the time drew near when he would have to move on. Like so many small communities, they talked about traveling to the sunken city, the most secure colony of merpeople in all the oceans. His original clan had decided to go there, and considering the dangers of the oceans, Dax couldn't blame any leader for making the decision to seek sanctuary there.

Unfortunately for Dax, the laws of the sunken city were strict and rigorously upheld, and one in particular made his skin cold and his fins shudder. There were no same sex relations allowed by those who chose to reside there. As a merman who found pleasure with other males, Dax had no choice except to bid farewell to any clan who chose to seek refuge in the sunken city.

Cale, the scout who had been sent to the city in advance,

had returned earlier in the day. Dax didn't need to hear what he had to say. He knew the report he would give all too well. It would be the same as the one from the last clan's scout, and all the ones before.

Malka, the leader of the clan, had been in seclusion with the scout ever since his return. Dax knew from previous discussions that Malka already leaned toward the idea of moving to the sunken city. She had been in charge since her mate's death ten years ago, and although she had kept the clan together, from what Dax had heard and seen, she had grown tired of the continuing struggle some time ago.

As soon as she made the announcement to swim to the sunken city, Dax would part company once more and seek out another clan to travel with.

"Dax!" Keshet's shout startled a nearby bird. Dax lifted his head and smiled as his lover approached.

"Any news?"

Keshet nodded as he dropped down onto the sand. "Malka has ordered everyone here to the island by dusk. She's going to make an announcement."

Dax sighed. He hadn't spoken to Keshet about the law in the sunken city yet. He guessed now was as good a time as any.

"What is it?" Keshet asked. "Do you think they won't want our clan in the city?"

"Where's Gilad?" Dax replied, avoiding the question for the moment. Their other lover should hear what he had to say too.

"He was relaxing in the rock pool last time I saw him. Do you want me to fetch him?"

Dax stood and brushed the sand from his body. "No, let's go to him. It'll be quiet there."

Keshet frowned and furrowed his brow. "You want to fuck?"

Dax chuckled. He couldn't blame Keshet for the conclusion he had come to. Usually when the three of them spent time alone together sex was their favorite activity. Dax would always be grateful for the way Keshet and Gilad, the only homosexual mermen in the clan, had invited him to join them. Even though the two mermen had been in an established relationship for several years, they hadn't hesitated to assure him they wouldn't let him suffer through the solstice alone.

"You know you don't have to wait until the solstice if you want a little relief," Keshet continued as they slipped away from the beach. "Gilad and I are happy to have you join us whenever you want."

"I don't wish to intrude on your time alone too much," Dax reminded him.

"It's not an intrusion. You know both of us would consider making this thing between us more permanent?"

"I know, but I'm a selfish merman. I want someone all of my own. I don't like to share."

Dax caught Keshet's roll of the eyes. "You don't seem to be doing a bad job of sharing, if you ask me."

"I do what I must to survive the solstice without the pain that comes with abstinence."

"Is that all we have together?"

Dax shrugged. "You and Gilad have a connection, a closeness, something special."

"I love him.

"Yes, and he loves you."

Keshet smiled and a dreamy expression spread over his face. Dax had no doubt about his two lovers' feelings for each other. A part of him wished he shared those tender feelings, but he didn't, and no matter how good the sex was with the two of them, Dax knew he never would. His heart wasn't involved. He suspected it never had been.

They found Gilad right where Keshet had said, reclining in the rock pool, his orange fins mostly hidden beneath the water. Gilad grinned up at Keshet, barely casting a glance at Dax. Keshet climbed into the pool, transforming into his mer form and swimming into Gilad's arms. They kissed languidly as they wrapped their arms around each other.

Dax could tell he had been momentarily forgotten and he stifled a twinge of envy.

"Aren't you going to join us?" Gilad asked once they had parted.

"Dax has something he wants to talk to us about," Keshet explained.

Gilad's face lit up with a bright smile. "He's decided to join us permanently?"

"No." Dax immediately shut down that line of conversation. "It's about the sunken city."

"Has Malka made a decision yet?" Gilad asked. "Most of the clan are eager to go there, especially if it means safety for the youngsters."

Keshet answered before Dax could say a word. "It's not been announced yet, but I think we all know we'll be heading to the city before the next solstice."

"It's the best decision for all of us," Gilad said. "Even when a clan has been traveling for as long as ours, it's no good upholding the nomadic traditions when the result is there's no one left to do so."

"I think we all know what she'll say," Dax agreed. "The scout will no doubt be reporting to her that the sunken city will welcome us there, they always do."

"What do you mean?" Keshet asked.

"My first clan reported the sunken city welcomes all mer there, and so has every clan I've traveled with since."

"You've been with a lot of clans, haven't you?"

"A fair few," Dax replied. "They all eventually seek shelter in the sunken city. I'm sure Malka will be doing the same soon enough."

Keshet gazed at him steadily. "You won't be coming with us, will you?"

"No."

"Why not?" Gilad asked. "Surely the city would be safer than traveling the oceans on your own?"

"That's what I want to talk to you about," Dax explained. "There's something you need to know about the laws of the sunken city."

"Yes?" Keshet prompted when Dax struggled to find the words to break the bad news to his lovers.

"Sexual relations between two mermen, or two mermaids, are strictly forbidden," Dax finally blurted. "None of us would be allowed to have sex together if we were to go there."

"But what about on the solstice?" Keshet asked. "My mating season fever breaks when another merman takes me."

"And mine breaks when I fuck another merman," Dax added. "That's why I've not gone to the sunken city and I never intend to. My clan was a small one and, try as I might, I couldn't find my release with a mermaid. I suffered through several mating seasons without release until Kyle, my first male lover, reached maturity."

"Where's Kyle now?" Gilad asked. "Surely he didn't go to the sunken city if he needed a merman to break his fever?"

"He had no choice," Dax explained. "When his father died in the final shark attack that decimated our clan, he became leader of our people. He made the only decision he could for the safety of everyone."

"Couldn't he have left the city after seeing your people to safety?" Gilad asked. "Why would he want to stay there if he couldn't break his fever?"

"He wouldn't have left his family." Dax had no doubt Kyle would have stayed in the sunken city, no matter the cost to himself. He was that sort of a merman, and his selflessness was one of the reasons Dax loved him. He just wished he had told him as much before he'd left. Instead, he had convinced Kyle all they had shared together was a mutual need to get off during the solstice. Perhaps sex was all it had been for Kyle, but Dax knew his own feelings had run a little deeper.

"Perhaps you could come to the sunken city with us and see whether Kyle is prepared to leave with you now?" Gilad suggested.

"He'll have settled into his new life after all this time."

"How long has it been since you saw him?" Keshet asked.

"Nearly three years."

"Well, there you have it," Gilad declared. "That's plenty of time for his people to build lives in the city and for him to swim away with the love of his life."

Dax laughed and shook his head. "I'm not the love of his life. We just used each other during the solstice. We never even sought each other out the rest of the year."

"I bet you wanted to," Gilad teased. "You enjoy sex way too much to be celibate all but two nights of the year."

Dax ducked his head to avoid the knowing gaze of his lovers. They were right, of course. Dax had never been with Kyle outside of the mating season, but he had been tempted. Only Kyle's youth, and the niggling doubt about his lover's feelings for him, had stopped him from being with him every night of the year.

"If you're right about the city, then perhaps it's not the right place for us," Keshet suggested. "The three of us could travel on after we reach the city, and perhaps bring your Kyle along for the journey."

Dax couldn't prevent his smile at the idea of the four of them starting a new clan. Maybe he would travel to the sunken city after all. He could at least see Kyle and his other friends before making his decision.

* * * *

Kai, Delwyn, and Ula swam into the quarters of Justin, heir to the throne of the sunken city, and his lover Lucas. They had been invited over for dinner and Kai looked forward to the break from their normal routine.

As Oracles they spent most of their time in their temple, and although they sometimes ventured out to the market or the temples of other immortals, they never traveled past the boundaries of the city.

Ula and Delwyn spent most of their days secluded in the

temple. For Delwyn it was a chance to study the old texts and writings on the walls of the building. Ula meanwhile chose to hone her skills in music-making with a variety of shell-made instruments. Kai had no interests in the ancient inhabitants of the city and had no talent for music or other restful pastimes. Of the three of them, Kai found his imprisonment the most confining, and escaped the temple whenever he could, though a guard always escorted him wherever he swam. More often than not, Kai chose to swim to the barracks, using his powers to see the trainees going through their drills. His dream had been to become a warrior, yet now that had been dashed upon the rocks. His spear had been taken from him before he'd arrived in the city, his mother convinced he would do himself harm with the weapon.

Kai spent most of his days in boredom and restlessness, watching others live out his dreams, forever wondering what might have been, had he not been inflicted with the curse of being an Oracle.

The opportunity to leave the temple, even if just for an hour or two, was one he never missed.

Kai didn't need to use his powers to see their ever-present guards with them. Under the pretext of escorting the blind mermaid and mermen, the guards watched them constantly whenever they left their home in Cari's temple. Kai tried hard not to think of the temple as their prison, but he found it almost impossible to do so.

Justin, recently blind, still struggled with traveling about the city, but Kai was pleased to see he had become more adept at navigating his own suite of rooms.

Today Justin was telling them how he and Lucas had met. Kai had heard some of the tale before, but he was always happy to hear the story again. The knowledge that Justin and Lucas were allowed to be together in the sunken city gave him hope that one day another law might be changed, the one stopping the Oracles from enjoying the pleasures of love.

"*I guess Medina isn't so bad,*" Justin said. "*Though getting on the wrong side of her is definitely not recommended.*"

Kai chuckled. The Goddess of Love certainly had a temper, as Justin had learned the hard way.

"*You're quiet this evening,*" Delwyn commented, his voice in Kai's head concerned. "*Are you well?*"

"*Just thinking.*"

"*About what?*"

"*We all know the old Atlantean gods and goddesses are waking, yes?*"

"*What of it? It's not as though the mer worshipped them. Why should their rising make any difference to us?*"

"*Maybe if we did go to them things would be different,*" Kai suggested. "*What if we were to go to the Goddess of Love and ask her for help?*"

"*Help with what?*"

"*Finding love, of course,*" Kai replied.

Delwyn sighed. "*Finding love isn't the problem. It's the whole being trapped underwater during the mating season. Falling in love with someone will only make our situation worse.*"

Kai knew Delwyn made a good point, yet he couldn't help wondering whether Medina might be able to assist in that regard too. From what Justin and Lucas had told them, the goddess was extremely powerful. Could she be the answer to their problem?

Chapter Two

The following day, Kai swam up to the entrance of the temple of Medina, Goddess of Love, his ever-present bodyguard at his side. He didn't know the name of the guard. He had long since decided not to bother asking. These days, the palace changed their protectors so frequently it seemed as soon as he met one, another had taken his place. At least they were, for the most part, cooperative, bowing to the requests of the Oracles. It made their imprisonment a little more bearable.

"You can wait outside," Kai told him.

The guard didn't question him. Kai used his powers to quickly check he had left before focusing his attention on the statue of the powerful Goddess of Love.

He wondered whether this was a good idea or if he should leave well enough alone. Justin and Lucas had told him all about their own dealings with the temperamental goddess, and the last thing he needed was to get on the wrong side of her. On the other hand, what did he have to lose? The situation of the Oracles couldn't get much worse. "*Medina,*" he called, his projected voice low, so it didn't carry outside the temple.

The place remained as silent as it had for so many centuries. The temple had recently come back to life, with crumbling stones repairing themselves and colorful murals restored to their former glory. The salty water no longer seemed to erode the building as it once had. Consequently, most of the merfolk preferred to avoid Medina's temple, even more than they did the rest of Atlantean gods' temples.

"*Medina,*" he tried again.

"I'm here," Medina replied. *"And what brings one of Cari's Oracles to my temple?"*

Kai used his powers again to see the goddess for himself. She was as beautiful as he remembered from Justin and Lucas' marriage ceremony. Her long, dark hair flowed about her in waves each time she moved her head. The clothing she wore was the same as depicted in the carvings on the temple walls. An ankle-length, gauzy gown that barely covered her body and was designed to draw the eye to her ample bosom and slim waist.

Medina smiled and held out her hand. *"Come sit with me."*

Kai swam to her side and settled on the steps. She seemed to be in a good mood, at least. Maybe if he stayed on the right side of her he wouldn't fall afoul of one of her curses.

Medina chuckled. *"I rarely curse anyone,"* she said. *"My goals are to help lovers find each other and to keep them together for the rest of their lives."*

"You can read my mind?"

"Yes. All gods and goddesses can read the minds of those who are in their presence. I can also hear the thoughts of any man or woman when they are thinking about love or lust."

Kai flushed and hoped Medina hadn't heard his thoughts about her body.

"I heard them and am flattered you like what you see. But I'm not what you need, am I?"

"No. I don't know exactly what I need, but I'm pretty sure it's a man." He wondered if he had insulted her.

"No, I'm not offended. Now, what can I do for you?"

"Maybe I should leave. If Cari were to hear me…"

"No god or goddess can see or hear events in the temple of another, unless they are standing within it."

"Cari is the Goddess of Prophecy. She can see everything."

"Everything except what happens in the temple of another. You have no need to worry about her hearing anything we say here."

Kai relaxed a little. The last thing he needed was one goddess angry with him because he had approached another.

"Now, what can I do for you?" she asked again.

"I was wondering if you could help the Oracles find love like the other mer do."

Medina was so quiet Kai had to check she hadn't disappeared. The goddess frowned and tapped her lower lip with the painted nail of her index finger.

"I am aware of the law regarding Oracles and sex and I must say I don't approve of it. As you know, you mer are very sexual beings. Forbidding you from taking pleasure with others is the worst type of cruelty. It seems it is up to me to put this travesty right, but your Goddess of Prophecy will be working against us, unless..."

"Unless what?"

"It will take a great deal of power, but I may be able to shield your actions from her visions."

"You can do that?"

"I think so," Medina replied.

"Then you can help us?"

"I believe so. Now, let's see what we can do to find you your merman." Medina patted his arm. *"Give me a moment to locate him for you."*

Kai waited, wondering who Medina would find. Would it be Delwyn or another man entirely? Deep down, he suspected the merman for him would be someone else. Delwyn's heart was already broken and it would take more than Kai to put those pieces back together.

"Do you wish to see him?" Medina asked. *"He's a most handsome merman and not so far away."*

"He's not in the sunken city?"

"No."

Then it wasn't Delwyn. Kai's nerves increased and his heart began to race. *"Yes, I'd like to see him."*

Even though Kai had not triggered a vision, his sight was restored to him by the goddess for just long enough to get a good look at the handsome merman.

He had a silvery blue tail and fins and light green hair that was just long enough to fall into his eyes. Kai could see his frustration as he shook it out of his way. He carried a spear, and although there didn't appear to be any predators in sight, he seemed to be ready for action at any moment. His chest was smooth and well defined. He was well muscled and Kai could see the barely restrained power the merman had.

Kai's heart rate increased as he thought of coming face to face with the warrior.

He could have watched him all day, but all too soon the vision ended and Kai returned to darkness.

"Did you like what you saw?" Medina asked. *"Do you want him to show you the pleasures to be found between two mermen?"*

Kai nodded. *"But how can we when it's forbidden?"*

"Forbidden fruit can be far sweeter than any other kind."

"You can get permission for the Oracles to go to land?" Kai asked.

"How about we concentrate on getting you to land first?" Medina suggested. *"I can't change the law – that's something only your king can do – but I can give you the opportunity to take charge of your destiny."*

"What do you mean?"

"To find a great love, such as that which I am giving you, risks must be taken. You will have to leave the city."

"But we're watched all the time."

"I see no guards here now."

"He's just outside. I can't pass the boundaries of the city."

"Then you don't want love as much as I thought you did."

The temple went silent again, and this time when Kai checked to see if Medina was still there, he found her gone.

"Medina?"

"You've changed your mind so quickly?" the goddess replied.

"If I leave, I'll be deserting Ula and Delwyn."

"Their loves are already in Atlantis. They have no reason to go elsewhere to seek them."

"Are you sure?"

"I'm the Goddess of Love. You can take my word for it. Now, back to your own quest for love. Your lover is on his way to

Atlantis already. Meeting him will not be a problem. Winning his heart, that will take some effort."

"No love at first sight then?"

Medina laughed. "Lust at first sight, maybe. Unfortunately your merman has had a lot of loss in his life and his heart will not be easily surrendered. You must be careful not to give him your body too soon."

"Why not?" Kai tried to dampen down the disappointment of going even longer without enjoying the experience of sex.

"If you give yourself to him too early you will only ever have a brief taste of his body, but if you wait until he gives you his heart, he will be yours forever."

"How will I know when the time is right?"

"That will be for you to judge."

Kai didn't like the sound of that. Being kept so isolated from other merfolk meant he had little to no experience in matters of the heart. How could he judge another man's feelings when he didn't even know how to recognize his own?

"One more thing you must remember," Medina said. "Don't let Cari know of our discussions. I doubt she would approve."

"She'll be furious if I leave the city."

"I will do my best to shield you from her visions, but you must help me by being careful not to let her know what you plan until it is too late to stop you. Remember not to speak of this inside Cari's temple, or she will hear you for certain. In fact, I would suggest you do all your plotting here in my own temple. It's the one place I know for sure she won't be able to hear you."

Kai experienced a twinge of guilt at his deceiving the Goddess of Prophecy. He hoped she wouldn't be too angry at what he had done, or at least that she would understand why. He told himself he didn't have a choice. This was his one chance at finding happiness, and he had to grasp it.

When he left the temple he found his guard waiting outside. He didn't question what Kai had been doing inside the building. His job was to observe and report to the liaison to King Nereus. None of the guards generally stepped in to stop the Oracles from doing anything, yet Kai knew if he swam too close to the boundaries that would change.

Kai let his guard guide him back to his prison. He hoped the merman Medina had shown him arrived in the sunken city soon.

* * * *

The sunken city was a day away when Malka decided the nearby caverns were a suitable place to rest before they tackled the final stretch of the journey.

Dax found a small alcove in which to sleep, and curled up on the hard rock. The scout had spoken of soft sponges on which to sleep in the city, and he hoped the following night would be far more comfortable than this one.

He tried to block out the noises of the rest of the clan who were similarly tossing and turning.

Since he had slept in far more uncomfortable places over the years, there was no reason at all why he couldn't sleep, yet slumber continued to elude him.

Dax knew he dreamed when he saw them. Two mermen entwined on one of those luxurious sponges.

They kissed and leisurely touched each other, stroking their fins as they both quivered with obvious desire.

Dax drifted closer to the couple and as he drew nearer he realized the two mermen were blind. He had met the occasional blind merman before — getting on the wrong side of some of their more aggressive neighbors could sometimes result in the loss of sight either on a temporary or permanent basis. However, from the easy way the two mermen touched each other, Dax guessed they were long used to their sightless existence.

Neither merman spoke, or if they did, their words were privately communicated. Dax supposed that was as it should be, yet he couldn't help wondering what they said. Did they whisper words of love, or were they telling each other all the wicked things they wanted to do together?

Dax's heart rate increased as he imagined the dirty talk that might be passing between the two lovers.

They were both handsome and young, with firm bodies and shining scales. The younger of the two had silver fins and short dark hair. The older had jade fins and hair tinged a lighter shade of green. Even though the silver-finned merman had the more unusual coloring, Dax felt drawn toward the other. Something about the way he moved held Dax entranced. He wanted the strange merman to touch him the way he stroked his lover. The idea of a blind merman tracing every inch of his body with his nimble fingers turned him on, even trapped in his half-fish form as he was right now.

"Beautiful, aren't they?" a female asked.

Dax couldn't look away from the erotic sight in front of him, even to satisfy his curiosity as to who had spoken.

"You want him to touch you like that, don't you?" the woman asked. *"Or perhaps you would enjoy the experience of him learning every inch of your body with his tongue. Doesn't that sound delightful?"*

"Yes." Dax shivered as he watched the two mermen roll across the sponge, the silver-finned merman ending up on the bottom as the other merman rested on top of him. Had they been on land he would have been straddling his lover, but with no legs in their current form all he could do was rest on top of him.

The younger merman groaned and whined, sounding as though he were on the brink of a climax, if only he possessed the organ required to come.

"They cannot find fulfillment in their current form," the woman explained needlessly.

"I'm a merman. I know this."

"Would you like one of them for your own?"

"What do you mean?"

"I think you know. If you want one, just say so and I'll make it happen."

Dax didn't understand, though he supposed since he was

dreaming things didn't have to make sense.

"Say the word and he will be yours," the tempting voice whispered into his mind.

The two mermen on the sponge kissed again. Their soft noises of pleasure became more vocal as their passion rose. They clung to each other as they strained toward a peak they could not reach.

"Yes," Dax whispered as he stared into the sightless jade eyes of the merman who held his rapt attention.

Dax sat up with a cry of pleasure on his lips. For a moment he couldn't remember where he was and fancied he still watched the two mermen on their sponge. He wondered from what depth of his mind the erotic dream had sprung. He had never considered himself a voyeur, far preferring to participate in sexual activities rather than watch others doing so. Yet, his blood had quickened to the sight of the two mermen together.

He left the cavern and the rest of the sleeping clan, intending to swim off his restlessness and push aside the strange and unsettling dream. Still he couldn't help wondering if the two mermen he had seen did exist somewhere in the vast oceans of the world. Were they even now finding pleasure in each other's arms?

He was so lost in his thoughts he almost didn't see the woman standing in his path. For a moment he questioned his vision and his sanity. How could a human be standing here on the seabed?

"Ah, but you assume I'm human," the woman said. Dax recognized her voice immediately and realized he must still be dreaming.

"I'm not a dream," she said. *"Nor have you slept at all this night. Everything you just witnessed is real. The two mermen are alive and well and you will meet them very soon."*

"Who are you?"

The woman smiled. *"My name is Medina and I'm here to answer your prayers."*

"Prayers?"

"Oh yes, I forgot you are mer. You don't worship gods and goddesses."

"Is that what you are? A goddess?"

"Yes. I heard your prayer – or your wish if you prefer – to have someone of your own to love. To enjoy a special relationship with another merman, the one who makes you complete."

"You can read my private thoughts?"

"When they pertain to love, lust, and sex, I can read the thoughts of every man and woman in the world." Medina stepped closer, the waters apparently no obstacle to her. *"You will have what you desire, my young warrior."*

Medina didn't wait for Dax to respond. She vanished from the ocean in the blink of an eye, leaving Dax to wonder whether he had lost his mind entirely.

Chapter Three

The sunken city loomed ahead of them. It was bigger than Dax had expected. The sprawling streets, lined with dwellings that had once housed humans, stretched out in every direction from the center of what had once been an island.

"This way, this way," Halcyon called as he waved the group toward him.

Dax followed his companions, keeping to his place near the back of the group. He glanced at Gilad and saw he no longer touched Keshet. It seemed they didn't intend to take any chance of running afoul of the law.

"This is our marketplace," Halcyon explained. *"It's where you'll come to trade for rare food, trinkets or whatever you have or need. For day to day food, we rely on sea fruits, which we grow here in the city and also outside the boundaries. If any of you would care to join the gathering teams, come and see me once you've been housed and I'll see you're assigned to a group. The city is growing right now, and we need every set of hands we can get."*

Malka stared about her with clear interest. *"You say the city is growing? Do you have room for us here?"*

Halcyon nodded firmly. *"There are plenty of houses empty at the moment, and we're clearing out the rubble from more every day. Many of the residences have been empty a long time, so we want to make sure they're safe before we let anyone move into them. Again, if you have any strong mermen who want to help with the work, let me know. As soon as a house is clear we've got someone ready to move in."*

"It sounds as if you're quite busy at the moment."

"Word about the new change in the law is beginning to spread. Many clans who had decided against settling here have returned."

"A law change?" Malka asked.

"The law regarding sexual relations between mermen and mermaids of the same gender," Halcyon explained. "The king repealed the law forbidding such relations, and the result is a lot more clans are not only visiting the city, but choosing to settle here too."

Dax checked on Gilad and Keshet. They still weren't touching, but they had moved closer to each other.

"And what about the mating rituals?" Malka questioned. "Has the law regarding the compulsory participation in those also been changed?"

Halcyon shook his head. "King Nereus does not see the need to change the law since most merpeople are not only willing, but eager to participate on the nights of the solstice."

"There are many merpeople out there who come from clans where permanent mates are the norm. When one loses a mate, it isn't always easy to move on and give yourself to another."

"I sense you speak from experience?" Halcyon had a sympathetic expression on his face, but Dax knew their liaison didn't have the power to alter the law.

"I have been leader of this clan since the loss of my mate. I have taken no other merman as my lover since my mate's death."

"If you choose to stay here in the city, you'll be expected to participate in the mating rituals," Halcyon told her firmly. "Unless you can convince King Nereus to alter that law too. You won't be the first to raise the issue with him, though I should warn you, no one else has managed to convince him to change things."

Malka scowled and gripped her spear tightly. "Please explain to me why I should dishonor my mate by participating in these rituals."

"The rituals are set in place to ensure the survival of our race. Our numbers are falling and the pregnancy rate is worryingly low. All mermaids in the city are expected to try to conceive by way of the mating rituals."

"And how exactly do mermaids who lay with other mermaids expect to manage such a miracle?"

Halcyon shifted slightly and seemed momentarily lost for words.

"They can't, can they?" Malka pressed on. *"Nor can two mermen together conceive a child. You tell me the law has been changed to allow those who need the touch of their own gender to be together on the nights of the solstice. Yet, those of us who do not wish to lay with another at all are expected to do so."*

"I don't make the laws."

"I am well aware of that fact. I'm just rather confused as to why one law is changed while the other remains. It hardly seems fair."

"The law change has come about due to King Nereus's heir."

"What about the heir?"

"Justin is a merman who prefers the touch of men."

"Ah, now I see." Malka nodded and her smile turned cold. *"Because if affects the king's own son the law is changed. If this Justin were to lose his mate – I presume he has one – maybe the other law might be changed too."*

Halcyon gripped his spear and pointed the tip at Malka's throat. *"That sounded much like a threat against Justin's lover."*

"Did it?"

"Yes. And if I come to hear you've even look at Lucas with ill intent I'll tear you apart and feed you to the sharks."

Malka raised her own spear. *"You could try. I wish to be taken to your king immediately. I'd like to hear him try to justify this travesty."*

Halcyon glared at Malka one last time before he turned to the rest of the clan.

"Whilst Malka is requesting sanctuary at the palace, and raising her concerns with the king, please feel free to swim around the market and talk to the citizens of the city. They'll all answer any questions you have."

Halcyon swam away with Malka, leaving the rest of them to wander the market and explore.

"Malka didn't seem happy about the mating rituals," Keshet commented. *"I wonder whether she might decide against staying*

here."

"*You could always stay here and leave the clan,*" Dax pointed out. "*Especially since the law has been changed so you and Gilad can be together.*"

"*Our clan is our family. Where Malka goes, we go.*"

Dax understood the sentiment, even if he didn't share it. He wondered whether, if he had to make the choice, he would go with the clan or stay in the sunken city. He guessed his decision would depend on Kyle.

"*Dax!*"

The female voice in his head was one he had not heard in a long time, yet the soft tones were as familiar to him as his own thoughts. "*Lynna?*"

Dax twisted round, looking in every direction for the green fins and long, curly blonde hair of Kyle's younger sister. He spotted her swimming toward him with a young merbaby strapped to her back.

"*I thought it was you,*" Lynna squealed as she barreled into him. "*I can't believe you're here!*"

Suddenly, she smacked him hard with her tail.

"*What was that for?*" Dax complained as he swam out of her way in case she struck him again.

"*You swam off without saying goodbye,*" Lynna told him.

"*I said goodbye to Kyle.*"

"*I'm not Kyle.*"

"*Obviously.*"

"*You should have said goodbye.*"

"*And give you the chance to talk me out of leaving?*" Dax laughed, knowing Lynna wasn't really angry with him, or at least not enough for her to hold a grudge. "*Now who might this little mermaid be?*"

Lynna reached behind her to unfasten the delicate-looking netting holding the merbaby in place. "*This is Maurissa. She's nearly two now and eager to be swimming all over the place.*"

"*Do you know who her father is?*" Dax asked, only realizing how it sounded after the words had left his mind. From the narrowing of Lynna's eyes, she wasn't happy with the way he had phrased the question.

"*Subtle, Dax. Really subtle,*" Gilad teased.

"*I didn't mean to be so blunt, but we all know what the mating rituals mean for mermaids. Go to land and spread your legs for any merman who wants to plant his seed there.*"

Lynna whacked him with her tail hard enough to send him crashing into a nearby vendor stand filled with necklaces made out of shells. He scrambled to apologize as Lynna berated him. "*I'll have you know not everyone in the city is like that. Most of us choose one partner and stick with them. Xane is sweet and he's the only merman I've been with.*"

"*Do I get to meet this Xane?*"

"*Not if you plan on insulting him too,*" Lynna snapped.

Dax laughed and swept Lynna into his arms. "*I've missed you, darling. You're still the prettiest mermaid in all the oceans of the world. Now, where's that handsome brother of yours?*"

Lynna's brief smile vanished from her face at the mention of Kyle. "*He's not here.*"

"*Let me guess. He decided against living in a city where he wasn't allowed to love who he wants?*"

"*Not exactly.*" Lynna cast a quick glance around, before drawing Dax away from the crowd. He could tell her next words were only for his mind. "*He's been banished to the land of humans.*"

"*What?*"

"*He fell in love with the king's son, and when the king found out he banished him.*"

"*I thought Halcyon said the heir had a male lover.*"

"*That's the new heir. It was all rather strange and I don't know everything that happened. Kyle became involved with Prince Finn, and when they were caught, Kyle was banished to land. The prince disappeared some time after, then a few months ago the king announced he had a new heir and Justin – he hates being called Prince Justin – moved to the city and was married in the way of humans to Lucas, Halcyon's younger brother.*"

"*Ah.*" That explained their liaison's hostility to Malka at the perceived threat to Lucas. "*And the king changed the law* for Justin, but not for Finn?"

"Yes."

"That seems rather harsh."

"I know, but no one except the king knows exactly what happened. Perhaps he has his reasons."

"Maybe. How long is it since Kyle was banished?"

"A little over two years."

"And Maurissa is nearly two years old?" Dax realized Kyle had never seen his neice.

"I can't leave the city, not with Maurissa so young, but if you happen to come across Kyle – I'm sure he will have returned to the ocean once it was safe for him to do so – please let him know he can come back here."

"Can he come back?" Dax asked. "Even though the law has been changed, it doesn't necessarily mean he would be allowed to return."

Lynna's expression became one of disappointment. Dax wished he had simply agreed to her request, knowing there was little chance he would ever see Kyle again.

"What about the rest of the clan?" he asked in an effort to change the subject. "How's your mother?"

"She decided she didn't want to participate in the mating rituals and left before the first solstice."

"On her own?"

"No, she departed with a few of the others in a similar situation. I've heard nothing from any of them since."

Dax didn't like the sound of this. He had believed his clan would remain in the city, safe from the perils of the oceans. Instead Kyle had been banished to land and other members of the clan were out there, probably struggling to survive.

"Have you any idea which land mass Kyle went to?"

"No. But Calder, the leader of the guards, will know which direction he went in."

"I'll have to ask him. Whether he can come back here or not, I'm sure he'll want to know about his niece and all the rest of your news."

Lynna flung her free arm around his neck as she kept a

firm grip on her daughter. *"Thank you, Dax. You be sure to tell Kyle we've not forgotten him."*

Dax realized, after Lynna had given him directions to her home and swum off, he had already made his mind up not to stay in the city, at least not right away. He wondered how many of the clan would be leaving with him, or whether he would once again be facing the dangers of the oceans on his own.

* * * *

Dax found the leader of the city guards easily. He heard Calder before he saw him. The merman shouted orders to his recruits as he instructed them in their drills. Dax hesitated at the edge of the group. Those spears looked far sharper than his own pitiful weapon, and he didn't like the idea of being stabbed with one.

One of the recruits spotted Dax hovering and pointed him out to the leader.

"You here to join up?" the auburn-haired merman asked. *"I'm Calder, leader of the guards. We're not exactly short of recruits these days, but we can always use someone who knows what to do with his weapon."*

One of the mermen nearby snickered and Calder glared at him.

"I'm not here to join up, at least not right now," Dax replied. *"My name's Dax and I'm searching for an old friend. His clan came here a couple of years ago."*

"Did your friend join the guards?"

"I don't know. His sister seemed to think you'd know which way he went when he left here."

Calder appeared rather doubtful. *"Who's your friend?"*

"His name's Kyle. His sister said the king banished him. Something about getting involved with Prince Finn."

Dax could tell immediately Calder knew who he was talking about. At least he remembered him.

"I remember Kyle. He did join the guards and young Finn took

an immediate liking to him. The prince hired him as his personal bodyguard before he'd even finished his training."

Dax smiled. Calder's words didn't surprise him at all. Kyle was an easy merman to like. *"Do you know where he went when he left here?"*

"I don't know where exactly, only that he traveled northeast to the land of humans. It was two years ago now. He could be anywhere."

"Northeast." Dax nodded thoughtfully.

"That doesn't mean he's there now," Calder warned him. *"If he's living among humans he could be anywhere in the world. You've seen the flying machines the humans have. They can travel from one continent to another without ever setting foot in the ocean."*

"Or he could have traveled by boat," one of the recruits piped up as he swam over to join them. *"I'm Marin. Welcome to the barracks."*

Dax nodded a greeting to Marin. He had never seen a merman with two-toned fins before, yet this merman clearly had them. The tail itself was pale blue, while the fins were a blue so dark they were nearly black. When he drew near, Dax noticed he also had mismatched eyes. Marin was definitely one of a kind.

"Did I tell you to ease up on your drills?" Calder asked, with a glare at Marin.

"No, but since you seem to have forgotten your manners, I thought I'd come over and introduce myself."

Dax couldn't quite hide his startled expression at the way Marin spoke to his superior. Calder, however, didn't seem surprised or even particularly annoyed. He shook his head and smiled with obvious fondness at the younger merman.

"It's all right," Marin whispered loudly. *"You're allowed to flirt with me now, remember?"*

Calder laughed and Marin wrapped his arms around him, kissing him hard and brief on the lips.

"Marin!" Calder scolded, but there was no venom in his tone. *"Just because the law has been changed, it doesn't mean*

you have to throw yourself at me in front of strangers. What must Dax think of us?"

"Dax doesn't mind," Marin replied cheekily. *"Kyle and I talked quite a lot while he was here and Dax's name definitely came up in the conversation, and pretty frequently too."*

"Oh." Calder raised an eyebrow in Dax's direction. *"Then Dax and Kyle were…"*

"Lovers," Marin supplied. *"Just like we are, baby."*

Calder's grimace returned. *"Don't call me that, especially not in public."*

Marin laughed and Dax felt the familiar pangs of envy. He wondered why all the handsome mermen always seemed to have found someone to love, while he drifted along, letting the currents carry him wherever they liked, always alone.

"Kyle made it to land," Marin explained after he had finished teasing Calder. *"He came back briefly, before leaving again to return to the land called England."*

"Do you know where England is?"

"Only that it's northeast of here and took many weeks to swim to. You wouldn't be wise to try to make the journey alone. You'll be traveling through dangerous waters."

"If the clan I came here with decides to stay here, I won't have a choice."

"You could stay here," Marin suggested. *"Now that relationships between two mermen are no longer forbidden, you'll find plenty of mermen here who would be eager to get to know you better."*

Dax grinned. *"I don't doubt it, but I have to make sure Kyle is well and I know his sister wants me to take him her news as well."*

"Lynna's a sweetheart," Marin commented. *"Have you met Xane yet?"*

"Not yet."

"You'll terrify him." Marin swam back to the recruits with another grin over his shoulder. *"If there's one merman in the city who would make a worse guard than me, it's Xane."*

Dax narrowed his eyes at the thought of Lynna being

protected by such a weak merman.

"*Xane is a good merman and he'd never let anything happen to Lynna,*" Calder assured him.

"*Did I just project my thoughts without meaning to?*"

"*No, I'm just good at reading faces. Don't worry about Lynna. She's in the safest place in all of the oceans of the world and I keep an eye on her too.*"

"*You do?*"

"*Kyle was a friend. Watching over his baby sister is the least I can do. Now, there's one more thing you can do to try to track down Kyle, and that's pay a visit to the Oracles.*"

"*Who are the Oracles?*"

"*They're one mermaid and two mermen who have been blessed by the gods. They see visions of the past, the present and the future. You'll need to get permission from King Nereus to approach them, and it'll rather depend on his mood as to whether he'll grant you access. If he does, you'll only be allowed one question, so consider it carefully.*"

"*I've never heard of mer being able to see visions.*"

"*There are only the three of them, and they all live here. They're blind, except when they're having a vision. Ula sees the future, while Kai sees the present and Delwyn the past. They'll be able to tell you where Kyle has been, where he is now, and where he'll go in the future.*"

"*Then I have to see them as soon as possible.*" Calder's words about the Oracles being blind reminded Dax immediately of his strange dream of the two blind mermen touching each other on the soft sponge bed. Could he have been seeing Kai and Delwyn? If King Nereus gave him permission to see the Oracles, he guessed he would find out soon.

"*Just be warned,*" Calder continued, "*the land of humans is strange to all of us, even the Oracles. What they say may not be particularly helpful.*"

"*I still have to try.*"

Calder nodded. "*I wish you all the best in your search. And if you ever change your mind about joining the guards, just come and speak with me. I'd be interested to see how you handle the*

spear you carry."
"I will, and thank you."

* * * *

Dax found the palace with ease. He hoped he wasn't going to be in trouble for wandering off from the marketplace, first to the barracks and now to the palace. A few inquiries confirmed King Nereus was still holding his audience. A queue of half a dozen mermen and mermaids lined up by the stone columns. Apparently there was some holdup with the king. Dax had a suspicion who might be taking up King Nereus' time. Malka would fight her corner as long as she could, then for a while longer. He wondered when Malka would finish her campaign.

Several of the waiting merpeople swam off, declaring they would return another day, rather than wait any longer.

Dax held his place until, finally, Malka swam out of the room ahead, a wide grin on her face. He guessed she had won her argument. He wasn't surprised.

Malka stopped by Dax briefly and confirmed her victory, before swimming back toward the marketplace, leaving Dax to wait in line.

After Malka's departure the rest of the mermen and mermaids entered and departed the king's audience chamber relatively quickly. Some exited with scowls, others with smiles. Dax couldn't tell from their expressions what sort of a mood the king might be in.

When Dax entered the audience chamber he expected to find the king alone. Instead the king was accompanied by a handsome blond merman who appeared strangely tanned compared to the rest of the merpeople. It was almost as if he had spent far more time on land in the sun than under the waves.

"Good day, what brings you to our city?" King Nereus asked.

"My clan has come to seek sanctuary here," Dax began.

"Another, that's two in one day. You're the leader of your

clan?"

"No!" Dax shook his head vehemently. He was no leader. *"My clan leader has already been to see you today. Her name is Malka."*

"Ah. Yes. *I can see your Malka being quite an interesting addition to the city. But she has already secured our hospitality. You don't need to ask for sanctuary separately. She spoke on behalf of all of you."*

"I know. I come to you on a different matter."

"Yes?" King Nereus appeared politely curious.

"Malka's clan is not my birth clan. My own clan came to the city a few years ago and I hoped to speak with the leader — a close friend — again. I've been told he's left the city."

"Not everyone chooses to stay here."

"He planned to, but, er…"

"But what?"

"I'm told he has been banished to land."

"Ah. Then there is nothing I can do to direct you to where he is."

"I hoped the Oracles might be able to assist me."

"The Oracles are not at the beck and call of every merman who wants an answer to their questions. Their visions tire them greatly."

"I didn't know that."

"That's all right. Though now you see why I cannot permit you to see them."

"Is there anyone else who might be able to help me track down Kyle?"

Something in the king's face changed, though Dax wasn't sure if this was good or bad.

"What is it, Father?" the blond merman asked. Dax had almost forgotten he was there. Only when he spoke did Dax realize the merman was blind. Had he been wrong in his guess that the Oracles were the ones he had watched in his dream? Maybe this was one of the Oracles? Calder hadn't mentioned one of the Oracles being the son of the king, but perhaps he had not thought he needed to.

There followed a brief exchange of expressions between King Nereus and his son. They were clearly communicating privately. Dax wondered what they were saying.

"Perhaps I've been a little hasty," King Nereus finally said. *"Justin here has reminded me Kyle fell afoul of our old law forbidding relations between two mermen."*

"A law that is no more," Justin added. *"If you should find Kyle, perhaps you might pass on this message to him. He is free to return to Atlantis, along with his lover, should he wish to do so."*

Dax felt a wave of gratitude for the king and his son. The idea of reuniting Kyle and Lynna gave him a warm feeling.

Justin smiled in Dax's direction. *"Kyle and Prince Finn were in the best of health when I last saw them. They were living in England, an island northeast of here. I suspect they are still there and doubt they will want to return to Atlantis. But please pass on the message and tell them I thank them once again for their hospitality to Lucas and myself."*

"Can you give me directions to England?"

"I'm afraid not. I took little notice of the route, leaving Lucas to guide me."

"I'm sorry," Dax offered. *"That was a thoughtless question."*

Justin laughed. *"I lost my sight after my arrival in Atlantis. I had perfect vision on the journey here. I just took little notice of my surroundings. My partner, Lucas, will be able to assist you."*

"Where can I find him?"

"He'll be visiting with his family around this time. But why don't you join us for dinner this evening?"

"Aren't you dining with the Oracles this evening?" King Nereus questioned.

"I'm sure they won't mind Dax joining us. All three of them are most appreciative of being in the company of a handsome merman."

King Nereus gave his son a smile, albeit a little forced. Dax had a feeling he wasn't entirely comfortable with talk about mermen ogling other mermen. He guessed, with two sons who favored their own sex, the king would have to get used to it.

"I'd be delighted to join you," Dax replied. *"I look forward to meeting Lucas and the Oracles."*

King Nereus gave him a stern glare. *"Just remember what my decision is regarding your questioning of the Oracles. Don't take advantage of my son's hospitality."*

"Father, you know sometimes the Oracles have no control over their powers. The most innocent question can trigger a vision."

"I realize that, but no direct questions which are designed to bring forth a vision are to be asked."

Dax nodded. *"I understand and will abide by your decision. If Lucas is able to direct me to England anyway, there's no reason for me to bother the Oracles at all."*

Chapter Four

The merman who met Dax at the archway to Justin's chambers was a stranger to him.

"You must be Dax," he greeted him warmly. *"I'm Lucas. Won't you join us?"*

Dax swam in behind Lucas and found he was the last to arrive. The three Oracles reclined on sponges, laughing at something Justin was telling them. As Dax drew closer he caught the end of an amusing story about something called an aquarium.

The female Oracle, who introduced herself as Ula, was one of the most stunning mermaids Dax had ever seen. Her long aquamarine hair floated about her, and her pink lips stretched into a wide smile. Her pale blue fins were similar in color to Dax's own, as were her eyes. At least, her eyes matched his in color — like all of the Oracles she was totally blind.

Dax recognized the two male Oracles immediately. They *were* the two mermen he had seen in his dreams the night before. He wondered if they were actually lovers, or near enough to it, or whether what he had seen had been nothing more than his imagination. Then he saw the younger of the two mermen touch the older in a way that told him everything he needed to know. They light brush of fingers against fins, which might have been accidental, considering their lack of sight, seemed instead to be deliberate and designed to tease.

"This is Delwyn, and next to him is Kai," Lucas said, pointing to each merman in turn. *"Everyone, this is Dax, a newcomer to the city."*

"One who won't be with us for long," Ula commented with a smile. *"You're intending to leave in search of your clansman, yes?"*

"I hope so. I've been told Lucas knows the way I must go, so provided he gives me directions I should be able to leave within the next few days. I just want to catch up with those of my clan who have stayed here first."

"I'll be happy to tell you the way," Lucas replied. *"Justin tells me it's Kyle you're searching for."*

"Yes. From what Justin said earlier, I understand you met him."

"Yes. He was kind enough to open his home to me during my brief visit to land. He was very happy there."

Dax frowned. *"How can any merman be truly happy living among humans?"*

"He has built a new life for himself. You will see for yourself when you find him."

"I hope to convince him to return here with me."

Lucas' expression was one of doubt.

"You think he won't want to come here, even after he finds out the law has changed?" Dax couldn't believe Kyle wouldn't jump at the chance to return to his sister and meet his new niece.

"He has a new life and has found love in England."

"With a merman."

"A merman who has no love of the sunken city, and also with a human man."

"What do you mean?" Dax thought he understood Lucas's words, but he wanted to be sure he was hearing what he thought he had heard.

"Kyle has two lovers, one of whom is human."

"That doesn't sound like Kyle," Dax replied. *"He never took more than one lover at a time."*

"When he was with you," Delwyn commented quietly.

"You think I should leave him to get on with his life, don't you?"

Delwyn shook his head. *"You should see him for yourself, of* course, just don't try to force him into returning here if he does not wish to do so. He has to live the life he was meant to."

"As do you," added Ula. "Your life and that of Kyle's may overlap in places, but you must follow your own course."

"You've seen my future?" Dax asked. He wasn't sure he wanted to know the answer, yet something in Ula's tone beckoned him to ask the question.

"I have seen a glimpse. What you desire is close."

Dax couldn't stop his gaze wandering to Kai. The jade green eyes couldn't see him staring, though he could tell from Lucas' smile that he had caught the telling glance at the merman.

"Let's eat and I'll let you know the landmarks to watch out for on your way to land," Lucas suggested. "And maybe by the time we're done, Kai here will have found his tongue."

Dax chuckled at the teasing and the dark blush that spread across Kai's face and neck.

"He's normally quite chatty," Delwyn piped up. "I can't think what has him speechless."

"I can," Ula added with a cheeky grin of her own.

"Like I can get a word in edgeways with all of you," Kai replied as he snatched up a piece of fruit and popped it into his mouth.

"How can you see where the food is?" Dax questioned.

"It's in the same place every time we eat here," Delwyn explained. "The servants are very good at that. And Kai will be using his powers to see around him as well."

Dax realized the Oracles were quite adept at dealing with their blindness. He noticed Justin wasn't finding it quite so easy to locate the food on the table. He missed the bowl the first time and appeared grateful to Lucas when he put a plate into his hand.

"Justin hasn't been blind for long," Lucas explained. "He still swims into the columns now and then when he doesn't have me to guide him."

Justin laughed. "And try as I might, I can't keep Lucas at my side every minute of the day, though it's not for lack of begging."

"I told you, you need to get accustomed to doing things for yourself again," Lucas scolded affectionately.

After a while the conversation tapered off and they enjoyed the best sea fruits Dax had ever eaten. They were sweet and succulent and he couldn't find any mark on them to indicate any other creature had tried to nibble on them before they had been gathered by the merpeople.

"The food in the sunken city is the best in all the oceans of the world," Lucas said.

"I still miss pizza," Justin complained. "And burgers and chips."

Lucas smacked Justin lightly on the arm. "Quit whining and enjoy the harvest. It's much better for you than the stuff you ate on land."

Everyone laughed as Justin continued to bemoan the lack of various foods, none of which Dax had ever heard of.

When they had finished eating, Lucas went through the directions to England several times, making Dax repeat them until he was sure he knew the way.

"You really shouldn't make the journey alone," Lucas said.

"You did," Justin reminded him.

"And there were reasons I was sent on my mission alone," Lucas reminded him. "That isn't the case here and Dax should consider traveling with a clan if he can. There are many dangers in the waters between here and his destination, as I'm sure you remember."

Dax sat up straighter. "I'm a warrior in my clan. I can take care of myself."

"You should still travel with others if you can."

"I've often traveled alone. I've survived everything the ocean has thrown at me so far."

"There's always a first time."

"I'll think about it."

The six of them continued to talk long after they had finished eating. Of all of them, Kai appeared to be the quietest. He didn't say much, but when he did everyone listened to him. Even Ula, who had a sharp wit and an even sharper tongue, listened when Kai had something to say. Dax found he liked the sound of Kai's voice in his head.

Delwyn was in the middle of telling a story about one of his visions of the distant past when the room trembled around him.

Delwyn stopped talking and grabbed Kai. Lucas and Justin also reached for each other. Dax had felt the earth move before, but never quite like this. A crack appeared along the wall across from him, and for a heart-stopping moment, he thought the columns would come crashing down around them.

Then the tremors stopped as suddenly as they had begun.

"That was the strongest yet," Ula said.

"Do you get a lot of those here?"

"Not until recently."

Dax frowned. *"Has something happened to cause them?"*

"The Atlantean gods are waking up. The tremors are a sign another one is about to join us."

"You believe in gods?"

"They are as real as you and me."

"Do you know one called Medina?"

Justin snorted, and Lucas appeared uneasy at his question.

"What do you know of the Atlantean Goddess of Love?" Ula asked.

"Is that who she is?"

"Yes," Ula replied, *"but you haven't answered my question."*

"I dreamt of her," Dax explained. *"Or at least I thought it was a dream. Now I'm not so sure."*

"If you dreamt of her, with no knowledge of her existence, it's more likely she visited you."

"Did she curse you?" Justin asked.

"I don't think so. She didn't mention a curse. Should I be worried?"

Lucas shook his head. *"Not everyone who meets Medina goes out of their way to irritate her. Believe me, you'd know if you'd been cursed."*

Dax breathed a sigh of relief, then he and Lucas checked

the chamber for damage. A couple of guards swam in to check they were all safe, and everyone decided now would be a good time to bring an end to the evening. The guards escorted the Oracles back to their temple and Dax left to go to Lynna's home outside the palace. She had been kind enough to offer him a place to stay, and although Xane had stared at him in terror, he didn't argue with his mate's decision.

* * * *

Kai couldn't sleep. No matter how hard he tried to shut down his thoughts, his mind remained too active. In his visions of the present, which he had been deliberately triggering during the meal far more frequently than he normally would have, Kai had seen Dax and been within touching distance of him for the first time. The warrior was the most handsome merman he had ever seen. His heart had pounded so loudly he was sure everyone present must have heard the thumping.

"Are you asleep?" Delwyn asked, as he swam down onto the sponge and settled into the spot beside him.

Kai moved to the side to give Delwyn a little more room. *"No. Can't you sleep either?"*

Delwyn brushed his fins against Kai's tail and snuggled into his side. *"You were quiet this evening. Is something troubling you?"*

Kai winced as Delwyn gave voice to his thoughts. *"Not exactly."*

"Is it Dax?"

"What makes you think that?"

"Because you were talking and laughing perfectly normally until he joined us. Then you went so quiet I wondered if you were having the longest vision ever."

"I was just lost in my thoughts a little."

"Thoughts about Dax?"

"Maybe."

"He is extremely handsome, and strong too."

"You've been using your powers to see him?"

"Yes, of course. It's not as if you weren't doing the same thing all through dinner. I just had to wait long enough for our meeting to be in the past."

Delwyn ran his hand down Kai's chest, tracing the muscles, until he reached his abdomen and the jade scales of his tail. Kai could tell he had something else to say, yet he seemed to be struggling to find the words.

"Are you going to leave me?" whispered Delwyn, the thought barely audible in Kai's mind.

For one horrified moment Kai wondered if he had been projecting his most secret thoughts for Delwyn, and the Goddess of Prophecy to hear. *"Why do you ask?"*

"Because when I saw you and Dax at dinner he could barely take his eyes off you, and you used your powers far more than usual."

Kai responded by pulling Delwyn closer and drawing him into a soft kiss. *"You worry too much. We're prisoners here, and just because a handsome merman joined us for dinner, it doesn't mean our positions have changed. We still can't leave the city."*

"If we could go to land, would you be with me properly?" Delwyn asked as they explored each other's mouths with their tongues.

"Of course I would," Kai replied, telling Delwyn what he knew he needed to hear. He spoke the truth, at least in part. Even if he had a lover of his own, Kai would never leave the sweet young merman nestled in his arms to suffer through the solstice alone. Any lover Kai took would have to understand that, as long as Delwyn didn't have a merman of his own, they came as a package deal. It was a shame Delwyn's heart had long since been given to another. The lost Prince Finn had been his first love, and his departure from the city had left a hole Kai couldn't fill. Delwyn's heart had been broken and Kai wasn't sure anyone had the power to fix it. Delwyn rubbed up against him and their fins

tangled together. Kai's heart rate quickened as their kisses became more passionate. When Delwyn finally pulled away, he rested his head on Kai's chest. *"You're sweet to lie to me the way you do."*

"Hey," Kai chided. *"I would* never *leave you alone while I found pleasure with someone else. Unless you had someone too, I would make sure the merman I'm with knows you come with me. It's the two of us, or none at all."*

"You might not have a choice," Delwyn pointed out. *"If something happens to take you from me, you have to follow your heart. Don't let the merman of your dreams get away because of me. If he wants you and only you, don't let me stand in your way."*

"Let's not worry about things which may never happen."

Delwyn was quiet for so long Kai thought he had gone to sleep. It came as a surprise when he heard Delwyn's voice in his head once more. *"Do you think Dax is handsome?"*

"You've seen him for yourself."

"I know, but I want to know whether you think he's handsome."

Kai smiled. *"Yes, I thought he was attractive. Now try to go to sleep."*

"Not a chance," Delwyn replied in a teasing tone. *"Why would I want to go to sleep when this conversation is just starting to get interesting?"*

"Because it's late."

"Dax looked a very powerful merman," Delwyn continued. *"One who knows what to do with his cock."*

"Delwyn!"

"Are you going to deny it?"

"You don't know anything about Dax. He could be as untouched as you."

Delwyn snorted. *"Like any merman with a choice would go through a single mating season without losing his virginity. Do you think he has a lover at the moment?"*

"I've no idea, and it isn't really any of our business."

"I could find out for you."

Kai laughed out loud. *"You're terrible, you know that."*

"Let me go see." Delwyn stilled in Kai's arms, a sign he was deliberately triggering a vision to see into the past. He returned to the present a few minutes later. *"Hmm, do you want to know what I saw?"*

"You're a tease, you know that, right?"

"Yes. But you didn't answer my question."

"We both know you won't be able to resist telling me everything you saw for more than a few minutes."

Delwyn dragged Kai into a sitting position and wrapped his arms around Kai's neck. He trailed kisses down his shoulder as he spoke. *"He and Kyle were lovers before Kyle came to the city."*

"I could have guessed that myself."

"True, but you don't know the details of who liked to do what to whom."

"Did you ever think it might be rather intrusive to spy on people while they're having sex?" Kai pointed out, not for the first time.

"I have to get my fun somewhere," Delwyn muttered. *"It's not as if we can go play in the sand ourselves."*

Kai supposed he couldn't blame Delwyn for the way he used his powers. When all he could see was the past, who could criticize him for wanting to see those who were happy and taking pleasure with each other? If sometimes he went a little too far, Kai wasn't going to be the one to stop him. He was pretty sure King Nereus would have something to say about how they used their powers if he were to discover the truth, but Kai would never betray Delwyn's trust, just as Delwyn kept Kai's secrets.

"What else did you see?" Kai whispered, giving into the temptation, as Delwyn no doubt knew he would.

Delwyn laughed and snuggled closer. *"He likes to be the one to take his lovers."*

"Hmm?"

"Do you think you'd enjoy being taken by him?" Delwyn asked. *"His strong body bending yours to his will. His thick cock pushing into your arse while he wraps his hand around your*

shaft."

Kai groaned at the vivid images popping into his mind at Delwyn's words. It wasn't an Oracle vision, but his imagination was just as overpowering.

"*Do you ever wonder what your trigger might be?*" Delwyn asked.

Kai and Delwyn had come into their Oracle powers before experiencing their first mating seasons. Virgins both, they could only speculate as to what form of sexual activity would break their fevers on the night of the solstice.

"*Would you like to be the one to pound into Dax?*" Delwyn teased. "*A warrior merman at your mercy. All that strength, bound to your will. An experienced merman like him, begging on his knees for you to give him what he needs.*"

"I doubt he'd be impressed with me," Kai replied with a sigh. "*Although we seem to be of a similar age, he's not likely to be enthralled with the pitiful talents of the oldest male virgin in the sunken city.*"

"*If he's the one for you, he'll be happy to show you what to do.*"

Kai wasn't so sure. Patient wasn't a word he would use to describe Dax. He seemed to be the exact opposite. He had made it abundantly clear he was eager to leave the city as soon as possible.

Delwyn ran his hands down Kai's arms and wove their fingers together. "*I wonder about my trigger all the time, but especially during the solstice. Sometimes I wonder what it would be like to bury myself in someone else, so we can't even tell where one of us ends and the other begins.*"

"Really?" Kai asked. "*I thought you'd prefer it the other way around.*"

Delwyn sighed. "*I don't know. Sometimes when I watch the one being taken it seems kind of painful. After so many mating seasons without relief, I've had more than my fair share of pain. But I may not have a choice if that's what I need to break my fever.*"

"If the merman you're with cares for you, he'll make sure it's good for you. I'd do my best not to hurt you."

"I know you would." Delwyn went quiet for several minutes before he spoke again. *"Kai, what happens if we both have the same trigger and can't come because we need the other inside us?"*

It took a moment for Kai to realize what Delwyn had meant, and when he did, he couldn't help chuckling. *"We're prisoners here, with no real possibility of setting foot on land, and you're worrying about what would happen if we both need another merman coming inside us?"*

"But what if…?"

"Hush, you silly merman. Stop worrying about things that will likely never happen."

Delwyn sighed again. *"You're right, as always. It doesn't matter if we have the same trigger, because you're going to leave with Dax and fall in love with him, and I'm going to be stuck here until I die of old age or sexual frustration."*

"Are you an Oracle of the future now?" Kai teased.

"No."

"Then stop worrying and let's go to sleep."

Kai knew Delwyn didn't seriously believe Kai would leave with Dax. There had been other handsome visitors in the past, and Delwyn had said much the same thing about them. He was merely grumbling at their life and had no idea Kai was already thinking about how his escape might come about.

They curled up on the sponge together. Kai didn't have the heart to send Delwyn back to his own sponge, and the truth was he liked feeling the other merman in his arms.

Delwyn fell asleep fairly quickly, but Kai worried long into the night. Could he truly leave Delwyn behind while he sought out love? Part of him was terrified at the choice which lay before him. The rest was eager to get to know Dax, and if it meant leaving the city, he knew he would have to do so, or else risk losing his chance at love.

Whatever his decision, he couldn't make it alone. He owed Delwyn the truth. Discussing the dilemma here was out of the question, but perhaps if he asked Delwyn to come with him to Medina's temple they could talk things through there.

* * * *

It didn't take much for Kai to persuade Delwyn to come with him to Medina's temple. In fact, Delwyn was eager to have company on his exploration of the newly restored building. He pestered Kai every moment of the short swim, but Kai refused to tell him the reason for his request. Delwyn would soon understand why it was so important they only talk in Medina's temple.

"Here we are," Delwyn announced, after Kai had shooed their guards out of the door. *"Now are you going to finally tell me why you wanted to come here? You don't usually show any interest in the ancient gods."*

Kai smiled at Delwyn's gentle chiding. The youngest Oracle loved to immerse himself in visions of the past, yet when he tried to talk to Kai or Ula about what he had seen, the other Oracles could barely keep their interest for more than a moment or two. The past held little joy for them, and they struggled to show enthusiasm for whatever Delwyn wanted to share with them. Hearing about the past just wasn't as exciting as seeing it, like Delwyn did.

"I came here a little while ago," Kai said. *"I called Medina to ask her for help."*

"Help with what?"

"Finding love."

Delwyn snorted. *"Finding love isn't the problem. It's being able to act on it."*

"I know. That's why I came to see her. She told me that to find love I would have to leave the city."

Delwyn, already pale from the years spent so far beneath the surface of the ocean, whitened even more. *"You're leaving?"*

"I don't know yet. She showed me the one I'm supposed to be with. It'll take time to win his heart, and he's leaving soon."

"It's Dax, isn't it?"

Kai nodded. *"I won't leave with him if you don't want me to."*

"I could come with you?" Delwyn suggested. *"Maybe my love is out there, waiting for me to swim into his arms."*

"Medina said your love was already here in the city."

Delwyn ducked his head. *"When are you planning on leaving?"*

Kai swam over to him and pulled him into his arms. *"I won't go if you want me to stay."*

"I'd be a horribly selfish merman if I let you lose the love of your life by keeping you here."

Kai felt awful for even thinking about leaving Delwyn behind, yet who knew when he might get another chance to seize love with both hands. If he didn't take the risk, he may not have a second opportunity.

"It won't be forever," Kai promised. *"I'll be back before you know it, and maybe you'll have found your great love while I'm on my travels."*

"I doubt it," Delwyn muttered. *"No one even gets to see us these days. All this talk about preserving our powers so we can focus on finding a solution to the population crisis means King Nereus will let even fewer approach us than he already did."*

Kai didn't know what to say. Delwyn was correct and there didn't seem to be any indication of things changing any time soon.

Delwyn shook his head and pulled out of Kai's arms. He seemed to dispel his morose thoughts and shot Kai a mischievous grin. *"So, have you any idea about how you're going to seduce Dax?"*

Kai grimaced. *"I wish I did. What do I know about seduction?"*

"About as much as me," Delwyn replied. *"How did you seduce Tal before you came into your powers?"*

"We never actually made it to land," Kai reminded him. *"And I didn't have to seduce him. He did all the chasing. I have no idea how to make a merman fall in love with me."*

Delwyn swam down onto the steps and awkwardly took a seat. Kai wanted to help him navigate the room, but by now he knew better than to try. Delwyn patted the stone beside him. *"Come here and let us try and figure something out before you flipper off into the sunset with him."*

Kai joined Delwyn and sighed. They sat in silence for several long minutes. *"So, any ideas?"* Kai asked.

"I've got nothing," Delwyn replied. *"Who do we know who might be able to give you some tips?"*

"More to the point, who do we know who won't betray us?"

"No one," Delwyn said. *"Even if someone is trustworthy, King Nereus could read their minds just as easily as he does ours. If he were to come and ask me about you, I couldn't hide the truth from him."*

"Maybe I shouldn't go with Dax. Not that he's even agreed to take me with him yet. He may decide having a blind merman in tow is more trouble than its worth."

Delwyn gave Kai a quick one-armed hug. *"If he doesn't take you with him, he's a fool. And if he doesn't fall madly in love with you before you've passed the city boundaries then he's even blinder than we are."*

"I'm fairly sure it'll take longer than that to win his heart. What if I'm not up to the challenge?"

Delwyn punched him on the arm, a little harder than was strictly necessary. *"He's probably halfway in love with you already. All you'll have to do is plant one of your fin-curling kisses on him and he'll be head over tail for you."*

Kai chuckled. *"My kisses are that good?"*

"Do you think I'd kiss you as much as I do if you were awful at it?"

"I guess not."

"You need to have some confidence in yourself," Delwyn scolded. *"If you doubt yourself when you're with Dax, he'll never find out how amazing you are."*

Kai had no doubt Delwyn was right, but having confidence was easier said than done. He wondered whether he was up to the challenge.

Chapter Five

Although Dax had intended to leave the city as soon as possible, he found himself agreeing to stay longer when he saw the damage to Lynna and Xane's home after the trembling of the earth.

One of the walls had caved in completely and the central column was dangerously near to collapse as well.

There was no question of Dax sticking around to help with the repairs. Dax and Xane cleared out the rubble and set about rebuilding the wall and reinforcing the central column.

By the end of the second day, everything seemed to be patched up as much as they could manage. Hopefully, the repairs they had undertaken would prevent any further damage if another quake happened. Realistically, from what the Oracles had said, it wasn't a question of *if* another one would happen, it was *when*.

Dax was exhausted by the time he finally fell onto the soft sponge in the spare sleeping chamber of Lynna's home each night.

Dax made up his mind to leave the following day and curled up on the sleeping sponge, determined to get a good night's sleep before he set off. Unfortunately, Dax had no sooner closed his eyes than the room began to shake, this time even more violently than it had during the dinner party. Again, the tremors stopped as suddenly as they had begun.

Maurissa cried out from the next room, and Dax hurried to check the rest of the family were safe. A quick glance at the newly rebuilt wall revealed it was still standing, so at least the damage this time appeared to be minimal.

Lynna and Xane had woken, and Lynna had Maurissa in her arms, trying to settle her down.

"Are you okay?" Dax asked. *"Is anything broken?"*

"Just a few dishes," Xane confirmed. *"I'll fetch us some more from the palace in the morning. They have plenty in the stores ready for distribution to new residents."*

Dax swam out of the building and looked down the street. Several other mermen and mermaids were doing the same.

"The entrance to the temple of the Oracles has been blocked," a merman swimming into the street called. *"We need every merman we can spare to help shift the rubble."*

Dax didn't hesitate to join the volunteers. They swam as fast as they could for the temple. Dax didn't know where to go, so he simply followed the others.

* * * *

Kai could feel Delwyn shaking even though the earthquake was over, at least for the moment. Kai hoped Ula was all right. Her quarters were situated on the far side of the temple. She had insisted on keeping those so she didn't accidentally intrude on the two mermen during one of their more intimate moments. Kai tried calling out to her, but she was too far away to hear him. He used his powers to see her immediately after the quake and could tell she was safe, but trapped in the darkness.

"We should try to reach Ula," he said, hoping a set course of action would be enough to shake Delwyn out of his current state of anxiety.

Delwyn seemed to collect himself. *"Yes, we should find her. Which way do you think would be best?"*

"I'm using my powers to see which routes are clear and which are blocked. I think we'd be best going through the main hall."

"Then let's go."

Kai let Delwyn take his arm, and guided him out of the room. Although it could be draining to use his powers continually, seeing what was right in front of him wasn't anywhere near as tiring as seeing something happening on the far side of the world. He could do this quite easily for several minutes at a time.

"*Ula?*" he called out, as they drew nearer to where she should be. "*Call out if you can hear me.*"

The corridor leading to the servants' quarters was completely blocked. He hoped they were safe. Since their quarters contained an underground tunnel to the palace he hoped they had escaped that way. They at least had their sight to help them. Ula was Kai's first priority. The Oracles watched out for each other. It was the way things had always been and the way they always would be. Only another Oracle knew what it was like to live with the burden they carried. They were more than friends. They were family.

* * * *

When Dax and the other merpeople arrived at the temple, he could see what had happened. The building next to the Oracles' home must have been in a sad state of repair already. The wall had collapsed and the falling rocks had gathered in front of the entrance, blocking anyone from entering or exiting the temple.

Dax felt a wave of terror wash through him at the thought of his new friends, and especially Kai, being injured. He wondered when he had started thinking of the Oracles as his friends. He had only met them once. He brushed the thought aside. Friends, acquaintances, or whatever he chose to call them, he didn't want to think of them hurt or worse.

The mermen gathered together and began to move the smaller rocks first. Dax recognized Calder, Marin, and several other guards, all of whom were helping with the heavy lifting. Lucas was there too, along with Justin who, while he couldn't help move the rubble without placing himself in danger, provided both encouragement and nourishment for those doing the hard work.

It took many hours before a gap big enough for a merman to fit through was made.

Marin, one of the smallest and slightest mermen in the rescue team, volunteered to swim through the narrow opening and search for the Oracles.

"What happens if an Oracle dies?" one of the nearby mermen asked another.

"Another merman or mermaid gets their powers and loses their sight. It's usually one who's about to hit puberty. Don't worry, there'll always be three Oracles."

Dax frowned at the casual attitude toward the loss of another life. It was as though they didn't see the Oracles as merpeople. They were just the Oracles, beings with powers to see visions, not mermen and mermaids with lives to enjoy. They didn't even refer to them by their names. Dax wondered if they even knew them.

Ula appeared first, swimming out of the rubble. Calder took her arm and guided her to Justin. She was shivering violently and Dax could tell she had been terrified.

"She should have seen it coming," one of the mermen commented with a nudge to his companion, who snickered in response.

Dax glared at them and hurried over to Ula. *"Are you okay?"* he asked.

Ula nodded. *"So is Kai."*

"And Delwyn?"

"Yes, he is well, but I know it's Kai you are most anxious to hear news of, isn't it?"

Dax's face heated at the knowledge that Ula had read him so accurately. *"Are you sure they're safe?"*

Ula smiled and nodded. *"I used my powers to see their immediate futures and they both have one. That means they must be safe, or else I'd see nothing at all."*

Dax breathed a sigh of relief and turned back to the rescue effort.

* * * *

"*Kai? Delwyn?*" The voice in Kai's head came from near the main entrance, away from Ula's chambers.

"*We're here,*" Kai called back. "*We're heading to Ula's chambers.*"

"*Ula's safe. She's out here. Come on. This way. Before the roof collapses on top of you.*"

Kai breathed a sigh of relief that Ula was out of danger. He changed his course and tugged Delwyn toward the exit and safety. He pushed Delwyn out of the temple first, then followed behind him. It was a tight squeeze to get through the gap, and for one awful moment, Kai thought he might get stuck, but he managed to push himself to freedom. Once they were out of the danger zone he stopped using his powers and let the mermen who had come to their rescue guide him the rest of the way.

"*This way,*" Calder said. "*We'll take you to the barracks. That building is far more secure than the rest of the city. You'll be safe there until we can find somewhere else for you to stay while the temple is undergoing repairs.*"

Kai let the leader of the guards guide them to the barracks. Dax appeared as if he might go with them, but there was still a lot of work to do clearing the rubble, and after patting Kai and Delwyn on the shoulders he carried on assisting, leaving the Oracles in Calder's care.

When they arrived at the barracks they found the place deserted.

"*Most of the guards are over at the temple,*" Calder explained. "*Only the ones guarding the sea dragons didn't join in the rescue of our Oracles.*"

Delwyn swam onto one of the sponges and curled up. Ula did likewise. Kai, however, wasn't tired at all. He had grown up believing he would become a warrior and now he was here inside the barracks that housed the best warriors in the oceans. He wished he could have had a different future, one where this was his home, and not the temple. He wanted to be the one doing the guarding, not being protected.

Kai used his powers to see the room and its contents. There were plenty of spears lining the walls, along with a few tridents. Kai went to touch one of the latter, but Calder stopped him before his fingers touched the handle.

"I wouldn't pick that up if I were you," he warned. *"We've had to take the tridents out of commission. Save for King Nereus' personal trident, they aren't to be used."*

"Why not?"

"We need to figure out how to work them properly," Calder explained.

"Don't they work in the same way as spears?" Kai asked. *"Just with three prongs rather than one."*

"They aren't just for stabbing at things," Calder replied. *"There are those who can conjure sea-fire with them, which makes them much more dangerous, especially since we don't know why some can manage it, while others can't. Prince Finn did it first, and while his shot would appear to have been something of a fluke – he never managed it again – others have been more successful. Unfortunately, one of our guards was badly burned in a training session when his opponent accidentally conjured the sea-fire. It was decided afterwards the tridents should not be used until we know more about how they work."*

"Can I help study them?" Kai asked, trying not to let his eagerness show too much.

"Have you handled a weapon before?" Calder asked.

"Yes, but it's been a long time. I'd love to be able to help. It'll give me something to do to pass the time."

"You'll be back in the temple within a few days," Calder assured him.

"I know, but I can carry on working with the trident there. It's not as if I have anything better to do."

Calder went quiet and Kai used his powers again to see his expression. The sympathy he saw on the older merman's face annoyed him more than he wanted to admit. He didn't want pity, he just wanted to be like everyone else.

"Here." Calder picked up one of the tridents and passed

it to Kai.

He expected to feel something powerful when he gripped the staff, but all Kai felt was eagerness.

"Well, it looks as though you aren't going to be blowing anything out of the water with it today."

"How can you tell?"

"Because it's not glowing and nothing is shooting from the prongs."

Kai smiled and jabbed the trident forward a time or two. *"I wanted to be a warrior when I was younger."*

"Me too," Calder replied. *"There's nothing like getting the better of a shark or two to really get your blood stirring."*

"I wouldn't know about that," Kai said. *"I had a rather protective mother and never got that close to one."*

Kai sighed and put the trident back in its place. What was the use in dreaming about becoming a warrior? That hope had been stolen from him along with his sight.

"Go get some sleep," Calder said. He pointed towards the sleeping sponges. *"Tomorrow we'll go and assess the damage to the temple and see if we can find you rooms in the palace until the repairs are complete."*

Kai swam down onto the nearest sponge and curled up. He didn't care if the whole temple was in ruins. Not that it made any real difference. The king would just find a new prison to keep his precious Oracles in.

* * * *

"It's going to take some time to make the temple safe again," King Nereus announced. *"We need to closely examine all the neighboring buildings, as well as the temple itself, to ensure this does not happen again. The safety of the Oracles is of great importance, therefore you will be allocated suitable quarters within the palace."*

Kai heard Delwyn sigh. Of all mermen, the Oracle of the past knew better than most that the home of the royal family was just a more luxurious prison. Prince Finn had always hated being confined to the palace, and Kai didn't relish the thought of being stuck there himself.

"This is not to your liking?" King Nereus asked. *"Do you have somewhere else you'd like to stay?"*

"No," Delwyn replied. *"We're just sorry to lose our home, even temporarily."*

Kai gave him credit for sounding convincing. He wasn't sure he could have managed it.

"Of course, of course." King Nereus appeared sympathetic, but Kai knew they hadn't fooled him. Most of the inhabitants of the city were blissfully unaware that King Nereus could read the thoughts of any merman or mermaid who had sworn allegiance to him and the city. Kai wished he was still ignorant of the fact himself. Unfortunately, the Oracles were all well aware of the truth, which meant they could hide nothing from their king that the merman truly wanted to find out. Kai tried to keep his thoughts under control. If he didn't think about Medina or Dax at all, maybe King Nereus would never discover his guilty secret. Even though he hadn't done anything wrong, if the king caught even a hint of his desire to escape, their guards would be tripled, and any hope of winning Dax's heart would be lost forever.

They left the king's audience chamber and allowed the guards to escort them to their new quarters. Kai left the palace at the earliest opportunity, swimming to the temple to see just how bad the damage was. His personal guard swam at his side.

When he arrived at the temple he could see the efforts at clearing the fallen rubble were still underway. Many of the guards from the barracks were hefting stones to the side. Kai wanted to help them, but as soon as he got too close, his guard stopped him with a hand on his arm.

"Better stay back. You wouldn't want to get in their way."

Kai nodded and swam to the side. Yes, that's all he would ever be in such a situation. In the way. A burden.

"Hey, Kai, nice to see you again."

Dax's voice in his head was a welcome distraction from

his depressing thoughts, and Kai used his powers to see where the merman was so he could swim over to him.

"I thought you'd have left by now?" Kai said. *"You were most eager to go searching for your friend."* He didn't reveal he had been checking in with Dax via his visions and knew very well he had been helping with the repairs, first at Lynna's house, then at the temple.

"I am, but all hands are needed in the city at the moment. Kyle will just have to wait. Where are you staying while the temple is being repaired?"

"We've been allocated quarters in the palace."

"You don't sound too happy about it."

"It's fine."

Dax took hold of his arm and pulled him to one side. Kai drew in a sharp breath as his pulse quickened at the merman's touch.

"How would you like to have dinner at Lynna's house?"

"You're asking me to dinner?" Kai couldn't hide his surprise. Maybe he was already seducing Dax without even realizing it.

"Lynna would love to hear how Kyle is getting on. You could tell her."

Ah, there it was — the catch to the invitation. It wasn't an offer because he wanted to spend time with him. Dax just wanted him to use his powers. *"I'm not supposed to have visions without permission from the king."*

"But you do, don't you?" Dax teased. *"How else could you turn to me the moment you heard my voice in your head?"*

"That's different."

"How so?"

"Because seeing what is right in front of me takes very little energy, provided I moderate my use of the power. Seeing Kyle, so far away, is much more draining."

"Oh, I didn't realize."

"That's all right. Most mer don't know how our powers affect us."

"I'm sorry I asked. You don't have to use your powers, but the

offer of dinner still stands."

Kai smiled. Dinner without catches he could accept. *"Where's Lynna's residence?"*

Dax gave him directions and Kai let him get back to work clearing the debris. He used his powers for a few minutes to watch him easily push a boulder aside. Dax was such a strong and handsome merman, Kai couldn't help wondering how it might feel to be overpowered by such a man.

* * * *

Lynna greeted Kai and his guard with a bright smile and several apologies for the mess in her home. With a two-year-old merbaby she had her hands full, and the upkeep of the residence wasn't a high priority.

Kai assured her he couldn't see anything in her home that wasn't perfect. It took her a moment to realize he meant it literally, and he assured her he was only trying to set her at ease.

"There's no need to be nervous," he told her. *"I'm just a regular merman, albeit one without a working set of eyes. It's kind of you to invite me here."*

"I believe I'm the one who invited you," Dax reminded him. *"Have you met Xane?"*

Kai shook his head and used his powers to see Lynna's mate hovering nervously at the far side of the room. *"You work in the palace, yes?"*

"Yes," Xane replied quietly. He held his daughter in his arms as the little toddler struggled to swim away toward a floating toy just out of her reach.

Kai smiled to try to put the merman at ease. He wasn't sure he succeeded.

"Let's sit down to dinner," Lynna said as she gently guided Kai toward the banquet she had prepared.

"Are you expecting more guests?" Kai asked, when he saw how much was laid out before them.

"No, but Dax eats enough for three," Lynna replied.

Beside him, Dax choked and Kai chuckled at the teasing. Lynna and Dax might not have been blood related, but they certainly interacted like a brother and sister. In some ways, their relationship reminded Kai of his own with Ula. Family in the heart, if not by blood.

Kai gestured to his guard who lingered in the doorway. "My guard…"

"He's welcome to join us," Lynna said as she drew up an extra sponge.

"I've already eaten," the guard replied. "I'll just wait outside the door."

"Are you sure?"

"Quite." The guard bowed and swam outside.

Lynna looked around the room, distress clear on her face at how the merman must have perceived the place.

"Don't be offended," Kai told Lynna. "The guards are discouraged from becoming too close to their prisoners in case we convince them to allow us more freedom than the king would like."

"You really see yourself as a prisoner, don't you?" Dax asked.

"It's what I've been since the moment I arrived in the sunken city. I'd give anything to be able to swim away from here and never come back."

"Why don't you? Apart from the guards, what's keeping you here?"

Kai thought about it for a moment. He didn't dare tell him the truth—that he had every intention of leaving with Dax as soon as the opportunity arose. Instead, he gave him a partial truth. "Ula and Delwyn are my family. I wouldn't want to leave without them."

"I guess one Oracle sneaking out is doable, but three might be pushing it."

"Getting even one of us out of the city wouldn't be easy."

"I take it you've considered the possibility."

"Of course I have, but I don't see a way we could manage it." Kai wondered if he was saying too much. Even though they were only speculating, as he and the other Oracles had done many times before, it was still dangerous. He cursed himself for not being more careful.

"You could use one of the tunnels out of the palace," Xane suddenly said, joining in the conversation. *"There are many of them, and not even the king knows about them all."*

"The only problem would be losing our guards to get into the tunnel in the first place," Kai pointed out. He really should put an end to this conversation. *"It doesn't matter anyway. Speculating on escaping is all we ever do. None of us would actually leave the others."*

"Never?"

Kai picked up a piece of fruit in an attempt to avoid the question. Since his visit to Medina's temple he had thought about little else. While it remained true he still hated the idea of leaving the other Oracles, and Delwyn in particular, he was slowly becoming accustomed to the idea. Delwyn's selfless attitude had helped a lot with that. Kai wondered if he should have spoken to Ula too, but had decided against it. Delwyn would tell her what had happened when it was too late for anyone to stop him.

Leaving the city was a scary prospect, yet Medina had been adamant, that if he were to win Dax's heart it would come at a price. Kai hoped he could go through with it.

No one brought up the topic of Oracles leaving the city again during the rest of the meal, and Kai thought the subject had been forgotten, at least until he found himself alone with Dax.

"What if you could leave the city?" Dax asked. *"Would you take the risk?"*

"It's pointless to discuss such things."

"But would you?"

Kai knew it was too dangerous to talk about matters here, not where he didn't have the protection of Medina shielding his plotting from the other gods. *"Meet me at Medina's temple later tonight."*

"Huh?"

"Medina's temple, do you know where it is?"

Dax shrugged. "I'm not sure, but I can find out. Why do you want to go there?"

"I'll explain later."

"Why can't you explain now?"

"Just meet me there," Kai said. "I should be returning to the palace," he called out to Lynna. "Thank you for your hospitality."

He hoped Dax did as he asked. If there was any possibility of leaving the city with the merman, Kai needed to talk him into it now, before Dax went on his way, leaving Kai behind, to wonder about what might have been.

* * * *

Dax found out from Xane where Medina's temple was located, and set off for the building as soon as his hosts had turned in for the night. He had no idea what time Kai expected him to arrive, but he didn't mind waiting for him. He was extremely curious to find out why Kai wanted to meet him.

When he approached the temple he saw Kai's guard near the doorway. He gave him a passing nod and entered the building. He found Kai inside, stretched out on the steps in front of Medina's statue. The merman didn't seem to be using his powers and didn't appear to be aware Dax had arrived.

"Hello, Kai," Dax said, as he approached the merman.

"You came?" Kai swam into a sitting position and grinned widely.

"Of course I did. I'm eager to know why you wanted to meet me here."

"It's safer here than my own temple," Kai explained.

"Lynna's home is structurally sound, as is the palace."

Kai shrugged. "I wanted to speak to you privately."

Dax was a little confused. All mermen were able to communicate privately to others without projecting their thoughts to everyone in the vicinity. The only reason to really be alone together was when a couple wanted to explore each other's bodies without others watching them. He didn't get the impression Kai had sex in mind. Although Dax felt attraction to the merman, Kai had given no indication the feelings might be reciprocated. It also wasn't as if his manner right now was particularly flirtatious, or if it was meant to be, Kai had no talent for flirting.

"*I have a proposition for you,*" Kai said, in a very businesslike manner. "*I want you to take me with you when you leave the sunken city.*"

"*Excuse me?*"

"*I want to go with you when you leave. You* are *leaving to find Kyle, aren't you?*"

"*Yes, but you can't be serious.*"

"*Why not? We talked about it at dinner.*"

"*Hypothetically, not on the basis of taking you with me on what might be a dangerous journey.*"

Kai tried to hide his grimace, but Dax caught it anyway.

"*You have to see it just isn't practical.*"

"*You were the one who asked me if I'd ever leave, remember?*"

"*Yes, I remember, but I only asked because I was curious, not because I planned on inviting you to come with me.*"

"*Why are you making it sound such a preposterous idea?*"

Dax rolled his eyes, thankful Kai couldn't see him. "*You're blind, not to mention a prisoner, as you've pointed out to me several times over dinner.*"

"*I might be blind, but I'm not helpless. I can help you find Kyle.*"

"*I thought using your powers to see so far away was draining?*"

"*It is, but I could do it, if you'll take me with you. As we get nearer I'll be able to see him for longer periods.*"

"*I thought you said you wouldn't want to leave the other Oracles. What's changed your mind?*"

"*I did.*"

Dax jumped at the sound of another voice in his head. He spun round to see Delwyn entering the temple behind him.

"*You remember Delwyn?*" Kai asked.

Dax shook his head, though not in response to Kai's question. *"Please tell me you're not suggesting I smuggle two Oracles out of the city?"*

"No," Delwyn said immediately. *"As much as I would love to escape this place, even for a day or two, this isn't my journey to make."*

Kai frowned as Delwyn spoke. Dax had a feeling Kai wasn't entirely happy to be leaving Delwyn behind.

"And how do you plan on us getting past the boundaries of the city? Do you know where the secret tunnels Xane spoke of are?"

"No, but after I left Lynna's I asked Delwyn about them. He knows where to find at least one of them."

"And how does he know about secret tunnels even the king has no knowledge of?"

Delwyn smiled. *"I can see back in time to when the city was built. I have more knowledge about the city than anyone else alive."*

Although Delwyn seemed to be stating a fact, rather than boasting about his knowledge, Dax wasn't convinced. Still, now the idea of taking the sexy young merman with him had been planted in his mind, he was finding it deliciously tempting.

"Meet us back here at the same time tomorrow," Kai said. *"And if you can get a couple of spears from the barracks that would be ideal."*

"I have my own spear already."

"One which is nearly rotted through," Kai pointed out. *"The ones in the barracks are blessed by the gods and will last far longer. Just tell Calder you're thinking of joining the guards and ask for a couple of spears to get the feel of them."*

"He'll believe me?"

"Yes."

"And stealing doesn't bother you?"

Kai snorted. *"One of the primary jobs for the guards is protecting the Oracles. The spears will be used for exactly that purpose."*

"You have a uniquely sneaky way of viewing things."

Kai laughed and swam right up to him. *"If we're going to escape the city without being caught, sneaky is a fine quality to have, wouldn't you say?"*

"I haven't agreed to take you along yet," Dax reminded him. The words sounded hollow and he knew he was a heartbeat away from agreeing to Kai's crazy plan.

"But you will."

"What makes you so sure? I don't know if I want to be traveling for weeks with a blind merman to take care of."

Kai appeared hesitant for a moment. *"If you don't bring me along, I won't be able to help you find Kyle."*

"I can probably find him well enough on my own, thanks to Lucas' directions."

"Can you? I think I saw Kyle and his lovers packing up their belongings when I saw them earlier today. It looked to me as if they might be moving to a new location."

"What? Is that true?"

"Maybe. Maybe not. But can you afford to risk it by leaving me behind?"

"That's blackmail."

Kai grinned and Delwyn chuckled. *"Then you agree to take me with you?"*

Dax had a feeling he was being played. *"Damn it."*

If Kai and Delwyn had slapped their hands together in victory, they couldn't have made it more obvious they had won him round. Dax was cornered and he knew it. It looked as if he had no choice. He was going to take Kai with him on his journey to the land of humans. He wasn't sure whether to be excited or terrified. Right now he was settling on a bit of both.

"Say nothing about what we've discussed," Kai warned him. *"And don't speak of our plans unless you are here in this temple."*

"What's so special about this place?" Dax glanced around. Although the temple appeared to be in a better state of repair than much of the rest of the city, it didn't seem particularly special.

"This is the temple of Medina, the Atlantean Goddess of Love,"

Kai explained. *"She will protect us on our journey."*

Dax snorted out a laugh which he tried, rather unsuccessfully, to hide when he realized Kai was perfectly serious.

Kai glared at him until he got his mirth under control. *"Don't believe me if you wish, but don't talk of our plans, not even to me or Delwyn, outside of this temple."*

"Very well, but if the whole basis of your plan to escape this city involves the protection of a mythical goddess, I would suggest you come up with a new one before we meet again."

"I'm not relying on Medina to get us out of here, but anything we talk about in here will not be heard by the other immortals, including Cari, who the Oracles are bound to serve."

Dax wasn't sure he wanted to delve into the intricacies of the various gods and goddesses of the city. Merpeople didn't have a religion, and that was fine with him. He didn't see any need to start believing in the powers of ancient human gods who, as far as he could see, had never done anything for his people.

"When are you planning on leaving?" Kai asked.

"I intended to set off in the morning, but, if I'm taking you with me, I wonder if it might be better to wait a while, plan things out a little."

"I agree, but we shouldn't wait too long before leaving. The longer we linger, the more chance there is our plans will be discovered. All it takes is one stray thought in the presence of king and our chance is lost."

"Are you in the presence of the king a lot?"

"More than I like to be at the moment," Kai admitted. *"King Nereus has the power to read the thoughts of any merman who has pledged allegiance to him and the city."*

"I've not made any pledge to him."

"But we have," Delwyn said.

Kai nodded. *"We'll leave in a few days. It'll give you time to get the spears and for Delwyn to scope out which route is the best for us to use."*

"You're serious? You're really going to go through with this?"

Kai folded his arms across his chest. *"Do you agree to take me with you?"*

"It's not like you're giving me much choice in the matter," Dax replied. He tried to soften the words with a smile, before he recalled neither of his companions could see his face. He wondered what he was letting himself in for. He did a quick calculation of how long it was until the next mating season and smiled to himself. The mating season would be upon them long before they reached the land of humans, which meant he would be spending the solstice with Kai. The thought was enough to make his heart race. He hoped Kai was as eager for his touch as he had appeared for Delwyn's in Dax's dream. He would have to wait and see.

* * * *

The next day Dax found Gilad and Keshet in what Keshet excitedly informed him would be their new home. With plenty of work still to be done to clean the place up, Dax wasn't sure what he was so happy about. Surely they could have found a better place to stay?

"I know it doesn't look like much," Gilad said. He always had been able to read Dax far too easily. *"But it's close to the barracks as well as the palace."*

Dax turned to Keshet. *"You're joining the guards?"*

"Yes. I talked to Calder, their leader, this morning. I tried to talk Gilad into trying out too, but he insists he's too clumsy with a spear."

"I'd be lethal to all the other guards as well as myself if I joined up."

Keshet rolled his eyes. *"Calder suggested Gilad be paired up with a merman called Marin for training. I got the impression Calder considers Marin to be the worst recruit the city has ever seen."*

Dax chuckled. *"I met both of them shortly after we arrived, and Marin would agree with Calder's assessment."*

"You went to the barracks?" Gilad asked. *"Does that mean*

you're going to stay? We have plenty of room here for the three of us."

Dax shook his head. *"I only visited there to ask about Kyle. I'm going to be leaving in a few days."*

Gilad couldn't hide his disappointment, but he didn't try to argue with him. Dax knew he wouldn't. Gilad and Keshet didn't need him hanging around with them. They had each other, and anyone could tell that was all they needed.

"You probably shouldn't go swimming away on your own again," Keshet said. *"It's a dangerous ocean out there. You're lucky you've managed to survive this long with all the clan-hopping you do."*

"If no one else is leaving, I won't have a lot of choice." Dax didn't mention the possibility that he wouldn't be leaving alone. If word got out he was even considering stealing away one of the Oracles he would be thrown into the palace dungeons until the ocean froze over. Not that he thought either of his lovers would betray him, but it was better to be safe than sorry. There was also the fact that taking a blind merman with him would do nothing to allay their fears for him. It would be more likely to increase them.

Chapter Six

Kai looked over the food at the marketplace, using his contemplation of the harvest as an excuse to use his powers more than he normally would. Delwyn hovered beside him, waiting for the signal — a nudge from Kai — to lead him to the temple of the Goddess of Sea Creatures. Delwyn had assured him the most unused tunnel in the temples beneath the city was hers. If Kai and Dax were to escape the city undiscovered, this would be their best chance.

All they had to do now is wait for Dax to enter the temple before them. They had done all their plotting in the Goddess of Love's temple, meeting several times over the last few days to go over the finer details. Kai hoped they hadn't been observed. If they had been seen lingering around Medina's temple in the company of a newcomer to the city too often, it would raise far too many questions.

Dax had already been to the temple opposite them and hidden the blessed spears behind one of the columns. He had also stashed a small supply of food. It wouldn't be enough to last their entire swim to land, and would probably be gone in a matter of days, but they had decided speed would be of paramount importance in their initial departure. Stopping to search for food would be too risky until their journey was well underway.

Dax approached the temple from the far side of the market. He swam alone and didn't seem to be in a hurry. He appeared cool and collected as he played the part of a merman simply going about his daily business, stopping at stalls, greeting other mer and stopping to chat on the way.

Kai glanced at their guards, who were conversing

privately with one of the nearby stallholders. The pretty young mermaid flirted with the two mermen, and from the familiar way she touched them, Kai suspected she had known them both intimately.

It would be so easy to slip away from them and dart for the temple, yet Kai didn't dare. If anyone spotted him making a dash for freedom the guards would keep a much closer eye on them from then on. They had just one chance and Kai had no intention of blowing it. He didn't want to risk Dax losing patience and leaving the city without him. Kai was actually a little surprised the merman had waited this long before beginning the search for his friend.

"We're going to take a swim in the old temple," Kai called to the guards, pointing at the structure.

"What for?" the nearest guard asked. *"Delwyn must have read all the stories on all the walls by now."*

Delwyn's fascination with the past had been their excuse for spending so much time in the various temples around the city. To avoid suspicion they had been visiting most of those which remained structurally sound.

Kai shrugged and smiled. *"You know Delwyn."*

The guards nodded and swam over to join them.

"You can always wait here," Kai suggested. *"The temple is only over there. You'll see us when we come back out."*

"We're not supposed to let you wander off on your own."

Kai tried to keep smiling, though he suspected his face showed more of a grimace. He hated being treated like a child.

"Well, come on, let's go check them out," Delwyn declared with over-the-top enthusiasm. *"Maybe today we'll find out whether the Atlantean politician with the boil on his arse ever got his cushion, or whether his speech had to go on indefinitely."*

Kai snickered. He could tell Delwyn was making this up, even though the guards seemed convinced. They had to be two of the more gullible amongst their ranks. They hadn't even asked how Delwyn could read the stories when all he could see was the past. Kai knew he'd looked into distant times and had read the stories when they'd been freshly written, before time and the ocean had taken their toll on them. Reading the stories was also something Delwyn could do almost as easily from their quarters as he could in the temple. The single advantage of triggering his visions in the temples themselves was that it took a little less effort the closer he was to the murals, which meant he could read for longer and, of course, it got Delwyn out of their prison for a while.

"We'll just wait outside," the second guard said, before swimming back to the mermaid.

The first guard was less lax in his duties, and at least followed the two Oracles to the entrance of the temple. He declined to enter the building with them and settled down nearby to wait.

"And there are two of the more stupid mermen in the city," Delwyn commented.

"I hope they don't get into trouble when I leave," Kai said.

"I'll make sure Otus gets the blame."

"Which one is he?" Kai asked.

Delwyn sighed. *"You really should at least try to learn their names, you know. Otus is the one sitting outside."*

Kai had never liked that particular guard. He had an arrogant air to him and often made comments about the demeaning task of babysitting the Oracles. *"I'm surprised they didn't both just carry on flirting with the mermaid on the stall."*

"Otus has no interest in her. He's a lover of men."

"He is? How do you know that?"

"It's common knowledge in the barracks."

"Is he the type you'd want to be with if we could go to the island?" Kai hoped Delwyn had better taste.

"Hardly!"

Dax appearing round the corner put an end to their conversation. He glanced over their shoulders to check they were alone. *"Your guards?"*

"Outside."

"How long do you think we have before they come in here to find out where you are?" Dax asked.

"Not long enough," Delwyn replied. *"We're in the middle of the city and the tunnel out is long and winding. Chances are you won't have reached the end of it before they're in here checking on us. Otus isn't the most patient of mermen at the best of times and he'll soon be bored waiting."*

"Then we should go now," Kai said. *"Where are our supplies?"*

"I have them here." Dax swam behind a column and emerged a moment later holding two spears and a net of food.

Kai took one of the spears from him. Dax seemed a little reluctant to hand the weapon over.

"Where's the entrance to the tunnel?" Dax asked. *"I've hunted all over and I can't find one."*

Delwyn gave them a smug smile. *"Do you see the carving of the octopus on the arm of the throne?"*

"Yes."

"Press against each of the legs in a counter-clockwise order, starting at the bottom. That will reveal the entrance. After you're in there, I'll press them again in reverse order to close the door again."

"How in the world can you know that?" Dax asked as he did as Delwyn told him. The stone back of the throne dropped down slowly, revealing a narrow passage under the room.

"This is the route the goddess's priests used when they wanted to avoid the main entrance."

"Seems rather inconvenient, if you ask me."

"For us, yes, but not for them. Only the goddess and her priests knew of this tunnel."

Kai smiled at Delwyn's words. The merman truly did know more about the city than anyone else alive.

"Are you sure you won't come with us?" Kai asked. *"You could get into just as much trouble as the guards might."*

"No, my place is here," Delwyn replied. *"I'll be perfectly well. The king wouldn't dare harm one of his precious Oracles, no matter what we do."*

"I'll keep an eye on you, and if you're wrong, I swear I'm coming right back to you."

Delwyn smiled. *"I know you would. Now let me kiss you one last time before you go on your big adventure."*

Kai hugged Delwyn and pressed their lips together. He meant the kiss to be chaste — after all, the supposed love of his life hovered right beside them. Delwyn had other ideas though, and deepened the kiss with a loud groan.

"What are you doing?" Kai asked him privately.

"Seeing if your Dax is the jealous type," Delwyn replied mischievously. *"I think he might be."*

"You're a terrible tease," Kai scolded.

"Ah but you love me really."

Kai pulled out of the kiss and chucked Delwyn under his chin. *"You take care of yourself and Ula. I'll be back before you know it."*

Delwyn sighed. *"Only return if you have to. If you have to choose between your love and me, choose him."*

"Are we going or not?" Dax interrupted their private conversation.

Kai nodded and swam into the tunnel ahead of Dax. All too soon, the entrance closed behind them, leaving Delwyn to try to give them as much time as possible to escape.

They had been swimming down the tunnel for barely five minutes when the ground began to shake around them.

"Not now," Kai cried.

The earth took no notice.

Even though it would be dangerous to use his powers to see anything other than his own surroundings, Kai had to check that Delwyn was safe. He breathed a sigh of relief when he saw him swimming rapidly out of the building, barreling into their guards.

"Hurry," Dax ordered, taking charge and grabbing Kai by the arm, dragging him swiftly down the tunnel.

All Kai could do was hope the chaos of the earthquake gave them a good head start. It was a small hope, especially when their guards had been trained to protect them, and would even now be hurrying into the temple, only to find one of their charges missing.

The end of the tunnel was some miles away, but finally they found the exit, just past the city boundaries. The continuing chaos, following the latest earthquake assisted their escape. Kai swam as fast as he could, not daring to look back. His fear of the king's guards catching them eased the more distance they put between themselves and the city.

Kai used his powers to check in on Delwyn again. He could see he was safe and, while the guards had soon figured out that Kai wasn't inside the temple, they hadn't found the secret passage.

The guards were clearly questioning Delwyn, who repeatedly pointed to his eyes, obviously reminding them he was blind, so how could he have seen where Kai went when the earthquake began?

Kai smiled at Delwyn's smooth way of dealing with the guards. It wouldn't work with King Nereus, of course, but his best friend was giving them as good a head start as he could.

Kai came out of his vision of Delwyn to check where he and Dax were now. Still too close to the city.

"Not that way." Kai grabbed hold of Dax's arm and brought him to an abrupt halt.

"This is northeast."

"The gathering grounds are right ahead of us. We could be seen."

"I thought you were blind. How can you tell what's in front of us?" Dax asked, his voice laden with suspicion.

"I can see the area in visions. We should head east for the moment. That's the quickest way to bypass the grounds."

Another glimpse of Dax and his surroundings told Kai his escort was far from convinced.

"We don't have time to argue," Kai told him. *"The next team of gatherers is already on their way here."*

"I don't see them."

"I'm an Oracle. I see far more than you do, and I'm telling you they're on their way right now, so we need to swim east before they arrive here and we're spotted."

"It'd be quicker to go across the grounds and stay ahead of them."

"If they catch up with us there's nowhere to hide in the gathering grounds. It's all open space. We have to go east. There are plenty of rocks and caves in that direction for us to hide in."

"I don't hide from my enemies," Dax argued. "I'm a warrior, not a coward."

"The gatherers aren't your enemies, they're my people and I don't want them hurt. Now come on, we need to hurry." Kai could see, in his vision, the mermen heading their way. Although they weren't swimming particularly fast, the gatherers gained on them while he and Dax hovered in place.

Without waiting for Dax to respond, Kai swam sharply to the right, heading for the nearest rock face, slipping behind it with ease. When he used his powers to see Dax, he saw he was finally following. He ducked behind the rocks just in time. The sound of the gatherers swimming nearer grew louder. Kai hid himself in the rocks, thankful his dark green fins blended into the background, concealing him quite well. Had Delwyn been with him they might have been spotted. His bright silver fins could be seen from a mile away.

"I guess we're going east," Dax said, though he didn't sound happy about the prospect. "How much time is this little detour going to add to our journey?"

"Not as long as a stay in the palace dungeons would," Kai snapped back. "Kidnapping an Oracle could get you thrown in there for years."

"I've not kidnapped you! You wanted to come with me."

"I know, but I hope you appreciate my point. Punishments in the sunken city are harsh and you wouldn't escape the king's justice if the guards caught you with me."

"Then I guess we'd better be careful not to get caught."

"Which we can do by heading east," Kai replied. *"Now come on and let's move. There's a long way to go."*

Kai caught a quick glimpse of Dax's expression of annoyance before he retreated to the world of darkness once more. Even though he only looked right in front of him, using his powers so much was tiring. He hoped once they had safely passed the outer boundaries of where the merpeople of the city ventured, he could refrain from using them as much. To use them almost constantly, as he had been doing since leaving the city, simply wouldn't be possible. Already, the ache at his temples warned him he was overdoing things, and there would soon be a price to pay.

They swam in silence for a while. Kai wondered whether Dax would object to him taking his arm to guide him. He wanted to ask, but he didn't want his question to be taken the wrong way. After deliberating for a while, he decided against asking and instead concentrated on using his hands and fins to navigate his way through the rocks and clusters of seaweed. Since he had been blind for so many years, Kai had become quite adept at finding his way about the temple and its surrounding area. He could make his way to the marketplace, the palace, and various other places around the city without any assistance. The guards who accompanied him whenever he left the temple were more to keep an eye on him than to help him find his way. This was the farthest he had ever been without his sight since his arrival in the city. He hoped his other senses would compensate for his lack of vision. Or if they didn't, that Dax wouldn't mind Kai clinging to him as they continued their journey to land.

"I think we're clear of the gathering grounds now," Dax commented, after they had been swimming for several hours. *"Nothing would ever grow out here."*

Kai used his powers to survey their surroundings. *"You're right. We can probably carry on in a northerly direction now."*

Dax looked around him. *"I think I recognize this area. There's* an island nearby a clan I used to travel with used occasionally."

"Any island this close to the sunken city is probably used by the city's inhabitants as well," Kai pointed out. "We should carry on swimming."

"I never saw anyone from the city while we used the island."

"That doesn't mean they don't use it. It's safer to carry on. There'll be plenty of islands between here and our destination if you want to stretch your legs."

"There aren't many in this direction. Just a few, and they're inhabited by humans."

"They can't all be."

"Mostly, though there are parts we can swim to where humans can't walk. The islands around the city are the only ones with no humans on them. It's almost as if they haven't discovered them, even though their flying machines have traveled overhead many times."

"Perhaps they've been hidden from humans, just like the sea dragons hide our city from anyone who approaches."

"Perhaps," Dax replied right as his stomach growled unexpectedly.

Kai chuckled. Maybe they should take a short break.

"I've not eaten in hours," Dax explained sheepishly as he bit into one of the sea fruits and placed a second in Kai's hand. "Maybe we should have picked some more food from the gathering grounds before we decided to bypass them."

"There are plenty of other food sources," Kai told him. "We won't starve before we reach land."

Dax continued to grumble. Kai ignored him and headed in the direction they needed to go. They still had some fruit and visions of the next few miles of seabed revealed plenty of seaweed to chew on. He had eaten some in the past, before he became an Oracle, but couldn't recall the taste. Curious, he swam for the nearest patch and picked some, stuffing it into his mouth. He tried not to grimace at the bitter flavor. The last thing he wanted to do was give Dax a reason to start complaining again. Unfortunately, when Dax followed his example, his first bite of the seaweed immediately set him off.

"This is foul. We can't live on this for the duration of the journey."

"Surely you've eaten seaweed before when you've been traveling?" Kai asked.

"The clans I've traveled with have always remained close to islands with vegetation, and when traveling, have enough sea fruits with them to last the duration of the swim."

"I thought we decided to take as little as possible, or it'll slow us down?"

"We did." Dax sighed.

"The seaweed isn't so bad," Kai argued. "It'll keep us alive at least. Seaweed sustained our people for centuries before we learnt to harvest the sea fruits."

"There's a reason we stopped eating the stuff as well," Dax complained. "Why should we stomach this when there are far better options available to us? There are all sorts of fruits and vegetables on the island."

Kai took another bite of his seaweed. His intention was to argue his case again, but when the seaweed stuck in his throat and he began to cough, he knew it would be no use.

"The island…" Dax said. "If we wait until dark we should be safe enough."

Kai wondered whether he should remind Dax he wanted to find his friend in England as soon as he could. Even though the island wasn't too far away it would add nearly a day to their journey to linger around in the water, waiting for the sun to go down.

"Very well," Kai agreed. "You go to land and I'll wait down here."

"Don't be ridiculous. You have to come with me. Not all of the food on land will taste as good after it's been brought underwater."

"It's safer for me in the water," Kai said. "I'm happy to carry on eating seaweed. You're the one insisting on having a banquet on land."

"I just want to eat something that's not revolting seaweed that isn't fit for sharks."

"Sharks don't eat seaweed," Kai pointed out. *"Why don't you eat another of the fruits we brought with us? Isn't that why we brought them? So we could swim as far away, as quickly as possible, without stopping for supplies?"*

"There may be places on the journey when there's nothing to eat at all. We should save the fruits for emergencies."

Kai supposed Dax had a point, but he still didn't relish the idea of going to land so close to the city. *"We shouldn't take unnecessary risks."*

"It's not much of a risk. Most of the mer will be in the city working on the repairs caused by the last earthquake."

"I suppose, but — "

"Don't be so stubborn." Dax waited as Kai thought things over. *"It's not as if it's the mating season yet. I'm not asking you to spread your legs for me."*

Kai ducked his head to avoid Dax's gaze. The handsome merman clearly wasn't as attracted to him as Kai was to the warrior. He wondered what would happen when the mating season *did* arrive. If the timescale for the journey was accurate, the mating season would be upon them long before they arrived in the land of humans. He tried not to think about what would happen then. They had only left the city a matter of hours ago. He had enough problems to contend with right now, without adding to them by worrying about things like whether or not Dax thought him handsome, and just how he planned to go about seducing him.

Still, Kai couldn't help wondering whether Medina had made a mistake. According to her, Dax was his soulmate, so surely there should be some attraction there. If there wasn't, how could Kai convince Dax to fall in love with him?

They found a place to rest, and Kai spent the time trying to think up an excuse to avoid going to the island. He still hadn't come up with one when Dax nudged him on the arm. *"Come on, it should be dark by now."*

Kai's body told him the same thing. All merpeople could instinctively tell the time of day, even so far under the ocean there wasn't a hint of daylight above them. He guessed he was going to the island after all.

Chapter Seven

It had been a long time since Kai had stood on his legs. He hoped he didn't make a total idiot of himself and fall flat on his face the moment he tried to walk. He doubted Dax would be impressed with him stumbling about like a toddler in the sand.

He held onto Dax's arm as they swam upward, Dax guiding him through the water at a steady and firm pace. Although Kai had seen Dax in his visions, the glimpses had been brief and they had been moving too swiftly for Kai to study him properly. He supposed if they must go to land at least he would be able to check him out thoroughly.

Kai wasn't sure how long they had been swimming, but it didn't seem like any time at all before they broke through the surface of the ocean. His head pounded from using his powers so much during their escape. It would be several hours before he could summon the strength to bring forth another vision. He would have to wait until he had rested a while before checking on Delwyn again.

"There it is," Dax said. "Right where I said it would be."

Dax's voice sounded different in Kai's ears from how he'd heard it in his mind. Something in his tone sent shivers down his spine. He tried to shake off the feeling and concentrate on the problem at hand, the problem being that Dax had swum off ahead of him, leaving Kai with no idea which way to go. He tried to force a vision of his surroundings, but he was completely drained. All his efforts produced was an even greater pounding in his temples.

"Where have you gone?" Kai shouted, hoping Dax hadn't swum out of earshot.

The waters shifted around him when Dax returned. "What's the matter? You haven't changed your mind about coming to the island, have you?"

"No, but I can't see which way to go without you to guide me."

"I thought you Oracles have your vision when you're not underwater?"

"We have our vision when we take human form," Kai clarified. "Right now I'm as blind as ever."

"Oh. Sorry."

"Don't worry. A lot of people don't realize how our powers work."

Dax took his hand and placed it on his shoulder. "Hold on tight and let's get you to land so you can fend for yourself for a while."

Kai yanked his hand away and resisted the urge to smack Dax round the head. "Don't bother yourself with worrying about me. Just point me in the right direction and I'll swim there on my own."

"Don't be stupid, I've guided you this far..."

"With thoroughly bad grace, judging by your last comment."

"I didn't mean it like that."

"I don't care how you meant it, just show me the direction to go in."

Dax huffed loudly. "Are you going to be this difficult for the whole of our journey?"

"Well, that depends."

"On what?"

"On you," Kai snapped. "If you continue to treat me like a nuisance then yes, I'll probably be difficult. Now which way?"

"Oh fine, suit yourself," Dax muttered.

Kai let Dax move him round in the water. He felt a slap to his rear.

"That way," Dax said.

Kai resisted the urge to smack Dax with his tail, and

swam in the direction he now faced. The sooner he was on land and able to 'fend for himself' the better. He didn't want to be a burden on anyone, and had always tried to be as independent as possible. Although it had been difficult when he had first lost his sight, over the years he had managed to get by with relatively little assistance. This was actually the first time he had truly struggled. He knew Ula and Delwyn found things far more difficult than he did. Seeing the future and the past didn't exactly help when living in the here and now. At least Kai had been able to do most things for himself, thanks to his powers.

He swam in what he hoped was a straight line and eventually felt the water change around him. The pull of the tide toward the island became more pronounced. He let the waves carry him in, and when he felt his fins brush the wet sand, he realized he had made it. One final surge, and he flopped down onto the beach.

Using his arms, he dragged himself out of the surf, and when his fins were clear of the water, he rested while they dried off. He didn't need to see his legs to know he had taken human form. He knew the moment he saw the stars twinkling in the sky above him and the edge of the nearby tree line.

Dax walked a little farther down the shore. He had his back to him, so Kai took the opportunity to scramble to his feet. Thankfully he didn't fall over, though it did feel quite strange to be walking again.

His legs seemed a lot longer than they had been the last time he had used them, and he guessed he must have grown quite a bit taller in the years since he'd come into his powers. He glanced down at his groin. His legs weren't the only things to have undergone a growth spurt. His cock had definitely not been this size the last time he had seen it. He touched the flesh and drew in a sharp breath as it hardened beneath his light touch. He stroked himself again, marveling at the way his body reacted to the stimulation. At least it still worked after being out of use for so long.

How had he forgotten this?

"There's some fruit bushes over here," Dax called.

Kai jumped as his traveling companion shouted him over. He let go of his cock, but not quick enough too late to stop Dax seeing what he was doing.

"If you want to play with yourself, make sure you wash your hands before handling the food," Dax warned.

Kai flushed with embarrassment. *Terrific.* Now Dax must have the impression he was so sexually frustrated he couldn't even wait until he was alone to touch himself.

His erection vanished as swiftly as it had come. He washed up in the surf before wandering into the trees, searching for something that might pass for food. He found a bush laden with berries and picked a few. They tasted delicious and quite different from the sea fruits that were the main sustenance of the merpeople of the sunken city. Kai had vague recollections of eating something similar before.

Kai could see Dax through the trees. He took the opportunity to study him while the other merman was nicely engrossed in tracking down food. He wished they had come to the island in daylight, so he could see Dax properly. He didn't know how long Dax planned on remaining on land, but now they were here, Kai rather hoped they would stay until after the sun rose in the morning.

"How long are you planning on staying on the island?" he called.

"Bored already?" Dax shouted back.

"No, just wondering."

"I think it'll be safer to sleep here than in the water," Dax said as he approached him, his arms laden with a variety of fruits. "If we leave at first light we should be safe enough. I think we're alone here anyway. Certainly no one has been on this side of the island for a while. If they had, we wouldn't have such a fine feast here, would we?"

Kai took the offered food and stacked it in a neat pile on the floor.

"You did wash your hands like I told you to, yes?" Dax

asked.

Kai glared at him. "My hands are perfectly clean. I was just..."

Dax chuckled and gave him a nudge with his elbow. "I'm just teasing. And I know exactly what you were doing. Same thing every merman alive does when he comes to land."

"You weren't," Kai muttered.

Dax roared with laughter again. It was a nice sound, Kai thought as he smiled back at him. Perhaps now the immediate danger had passed he could concentrate on winning Dax's affections before they reached land and he was reunited with his old lover.

Kai studied Dax as they ate their fill. He wondered how strong the ties were between Dax and Kyle. Pretty strong, considering his recent actions. What other reason would a merman have for leaving a place of safety and swimming out into the dangerous ocean alone, just to find him? Kai suspected he had some stiff competition, and he wondered whether he was up to the challenge of winning Dax's heart. Medina seemed to think so, but Kai wasn't so sure.

"You look as if you want to ask me something," Dax commented, around a mouthful of orange.

Kai ducked his head. "It's probably none of my business."

"Okay."

Damn. Kai hadn't thought Dax would take him at his word and simply let the matter drop. He had hoped he might press him to ask his questions, or at least not sound quite so disinterested in what he had to say.

Dax grinned at him. "Oh, go on and ask, you nosey mer."

Kai glared at him. "I'm not nosey."

"Yes, you are, but I don't mind. I have no secrets to hide."

"None at all?"

"No. Why, do you?"

"Not really. My life is pretty boring. We Oracles don't get out much."

"Well, maybe you'll have some adventures to share with the others when you get back home."

"Perhaps."

"So, what did you want to ask me?"

"I was just wondering what the deal was between you and Kyle."

"We're from the same clan."

"I know, but you seem pretty determined to track him down and yet you've not even asked about most of the others who came to the city."

"Kyle's a friend."

Kai raised a brow in question. "And the rest of them?"

"Fine, Kyle was my lover. Is that what you wanted to hear?"

Kai didn't let on he had already been informed of this fact by Delwyn. He wanted to know how close they had been, whether it was merely sex or if Dax's heart had been involved. Was Dax's eagerness to track down Kyle because he wanted to continue their relationship? Was Dax in love with Kyle? There were so many questions he wanted answers to. "Do you think Kyle will want you barging back into his life?"

Dax laughed. "I'm not going to jump on him and demand he opens his legs for me, if that's what you're asking. I just want to check he's doing okay. He's been banished to the land of humans. He's never lived among them before, and for all I know he could be dead."

"He's not, I promise."

Dax smiled. "And is he leaving for parts unknown?"

Kai ducked his head. "No. He seemed quite well settled in his home when I last checked in on him."

"Then you *were* lying about what you saw?"

"A small untruth, which I hope you'll forgive me for. Kyle really is well."

Dax shook his head. "I forgive you. I guess I can understand your eagerness to escape the city, and that might call for a little stretching of the truth."

"Thank you." Kai concentrated on his food for a few minutes before a horrible thought occurred to him. "You aren't going to make me go back, are you?"

Dax frowned at him. "I probably should, but I admit your company is preferable to making the journey alone. And I might need your help finding Kyle once we arrive in England."

Kai breathed a sigh of relief. The hard part — escaping the city — was over. Now all he had to do was convince Dax to keep him in his life long enough for them to find out whether they could have a future together. He just wished he had a clue how to accomplish that.

* * * *

Kai and Dax returned to the ocean the next morning, shortly before dawn. Kai was eager to depart the island. He wasn't entirely convinced no one from the city would come across them there. He also wanted to check in on Delwyn while still close enough to the city that the vision wouldn't drain him too much. Kai and Dax had slept a few hours on land and his powers were charged enough for him to manage a short vision. He knew he would have to preserve his powers for emergencies, but he considered this to be necessary.

As soon as he was in mer form, Kai concentrated on Delwyn while Dax waited patiently.

Delwyn hovered beside Ula in King Nereus' audience chamber. Justin sat at the king's side, but no one else was present.

King Nereus seemed as furious as Kai had ever seen him. Delwyn had a stubborn tilt to his chin and kept shaking his head. The king seemed to be concentrating on him, rather than Ula, which told Kai the king had used his mind-reading powers to determine who knew the truth about the missing Oracle.

King Nereus banged his trident on the floor and Calder entered the room. He bowed low before the king and left a few minutes later. Kai wished he could hear the voices of the mer he was watching, but one of the drawbacks of his powers was he couldn't hear any private telepathic communications. Still, he was sure King Nereus had enough information from Delwyn's mind to determine which direction Kai had gone and who he traveled with.

He wondered briefly whether he should have brought Delwyn with him, but knew if he had it would have increased the risk of their getting caught. Whoever had stayed behind to secure the tunnel after them would have been brought before the king, with the same result. Had the tunnel not been secured, the guards would have caught them before they even made it to the city boundaries.

Kai didn't see they had any other choice other than the one they had made. He just hoped their head start had been enough.

"What did you see?" Dax asked.

"We need to hurry," Kai replied. *"King Nereus already has the guards out searching for us, and now he knows which way to send them."*

"You were checking on Delwyn?"

Kai nodded. *"Yes, of course."*

"Oh."

"What is it?"

"Nothing, I just thought you were checking on Kyle."

Even though it would be draining, Kai considered a quick glimpse of the other merman might be in order. He closed his eyes and concentrated on Kyle.

Kyle sat on a comfortable-looking piece of human furniture. He rested his head on the shoulder of a strange man who Kai recognized as his human lover. Prince Finn was nowhere in sight, yet Kyle seemed to be quite content where he was.

"He's relaxing in the building I believe is his home on land."

"You saw him?" Dax asked. *"Just now?"*

"Yes."

"So, you can see anyone, just by thinking about them?"

"Nearly everyone."

"*And he was definitely well?*" Dax asked. "*Did he seem happy?*"

"*I think so. He's on land in a human building with one of his lovers. I couldn't see any more.*"

"*That's a bit vague. I doubt it would be enough information to find him once we reach land.*"

"*I never said my visions were perfect. I can see where he is right now, but it's not as though I can discover his exact location.*"

Dax grumbled under his breath.

"*I'll keep checking in on him and see if I can find any more clues to where he is,*" Kai said. "*I may get lucky and spot some big landmark that could help us when we get there.*"

Dax stopped his mumbling and seemed to be grateful. Kai couldn't help wondering though, what Dax planned on doing when he found Kyle. Did he intend to try to persuade him to return to the sunken city, and if so, what would he do if Kyle had settled in his new life on land?

With the guards less than a day away, it wasn't safe to linger near the island. They continued on their journey as swiftly as they could. Kai hoped his blindness didn't slow them down too much. They traveled north, and it wasn't long before Kai noticed the change in temperature. The drop wasn't drastic, but to a merman who had lived most of his life in the relatively warm waters of the sunken city, the chill was quite obvious. Dax didn't seem bothered by the colder waters, but since he traveled around a lot, Kai suspected he was accustomed to such things.

* * * *

They were passing over an ancient shipwreck when a vision came upon Kai so suddenly he didn't even spot the signs that usually gave him advance warning it was about to happen.

A rock formation he had seen to the west told him the vision was something happening close by. At first he didn't know what he was seeing. There were a few merpeople swimming nearby. They seemed to be traveling in a southerly direction, but there didn't seem to be anything untoward about them. There were certainly no city guards amongst their number. In fact they seemed to be nothing more than two families, with youngsters too, making their way through the oceans. For a vision to come upon him so quickly there had to be something more to see.

Concentrating as hard as he could, Kai cast about him for clues. He soon saw what the travelers had not yet spotted. Directly in their path were two circling sharks, and they didn't appear to be the friendly type, if there could be said to be such a thing when it came to sharks.

Kai snapped out of his vision and changed direction. Dax, who apparently took so little notice of his companion he hadn't even noticed he had stopped swimming, was some way ahead of him. *"Dax, this way!"* Kai called out, thankful Dax at least hadn't swum out of range in his eagerness to reach their destination.

"We need to head this way," Dax shouted back.

"There's trouble over at the rocks."

"All the more reason to carry on the way we're going."

Kai ignored him and gripped his spear. He hadn't actually had to handle one since he had become an Oracle. He hoped he remembered how to use it.

"Where are you going?"

"There are sharks nearby."

"What sharks? We've not seen any all day and even if we had, I don't see what use you'll be against them. If we spot any, I'll handle them while you stay out of trouble."

Kai bristled at the way Dax spoke about him. Did he think him so helpless he couldn't even protect himself? *"There's a family of merpeople, maybe two, heading south toward that large rock formation to our west. They're heading straight into a pair of sharks. We have to help them."*

"Surely they have warriors in the group?"

"I couldn't see anyone carrying a weapon, and there were children with them."

Dax finally seemed to understand the urgency of the

situation. *"I'll go head them off while you go hide in the shipwreck we passed a little while ago."*

Kai glared at Dax's rapidly retreating back. He had no intention of hiding like a child while someone else went into danger. As long as his powers were working he was perfectly able to see where he was going, what he was doing, and fight anyone or anything he needed to survive. Yes, it would be draining, but he considered the circumstances an emergency.

Ignoring Dax's orders, Kai resisted the urge to show the bossy warrior just how well he could handle himself by aiming his spear at him. Instead, he swam in the direction of the rock formation. He saved his powers until he was closer, conserving as much of his energy as he could. He would need all the sight he could muster if he hoped to battle the sharks alongside Dax.

Of course, the best scenario of what was about to happen was Dax would have reached the travelers in time to send them in a different direction, safely bypassing the sharks.

When he caught up with Dax, Kai realized this wasn't the case. Dax and one of the other mermen were fighting the first of the sharks. A second merman directed the rest of the group round the other side of the rocks.

Kai swam as fast as he could into the fight.

Dax spotted him as soon as he arrived. *"What part of hide in the ship didn't you understand?"*

"I can help."

"You're blind!"

"Not when I'm having a vision and right now I can see more than enough to help."

Dax ducked as one of the sharks snapped dangerously close to his arm. *"I can't concentrate on fighting and protecting you at the same time."*

Kai jabbed at the shark, forcing the creature to back up. *"I don't need protecting. I'm a grown man, not a child."*

"You're an Oracle. You must be protected."

Kai stabbed at the shark again, and when the second one

came for him, he used the other end of his weapon to knock that one back too. *"The king said the same thing, as did his father before him and all the kings of the sunken city. That's why they kept us imprisoned there — for our protection. I don't want to live in a prison, no matter how luxurious they make it. Now stop your arguing and help drive these monsters back to where they came from, so we can be on our way again."*

He didn't wait for Dax to reply. He joined the other mermen, and between them, they quickly dispatched the sharks.

Once the route had been cleared, the women and children swam to join them.

"Thank you for your help," the elder of the mermen said. *"I'm Garey, and this is my family. We can't thank you enough for coming to our rescue. Normally we scout ahead, but now that we're so close to the sunken city, well, I guess we started to become careless."*

Kai felt an uneasiness in his stomach. The guards were already searching for him. Had they heard Dax refer to him as an Oracle or had Dax kept his words privately between the two of them? Sometimes it could be a little difficult to tell. He sent a private thought to Dax to ask if his communication had been private and breathed a sigh of relief when his answer came back as a rather abrupt, *"Of course."*

It didn't mean there wasn't any danger, though. Chances were the king would be questioning any newcomers about whether they had seen a merman matching his description. Although his green coloring was fairly common amongst the mer, any lead would spur the guards on, eager to deliver him back to his prison.

"Is that where you're going?" Kai asked. *"To the sunken city?"*

"Yes, we've been traveling for a few months now."

"Why are you going there?" Dax questioned. *"Do you want to settle in the city?"*

"Yes. We've avoided it until now, but the change in the law

means my daughter and her mate can live there too." He gestured to two pretty young mermaids who were trying to keep the youngsters of the group from swimming off whenever their backs were turned.

"The law has changed, hasn't it?" one of the mermaids asked. *"We've traveled such a long way, we'd hate to find out the rumors were untrue."*

"No, the law has changed," Kai confirmed with a smile. *"The heir to the throne is a merman who has taken a male lover. The king couldn't alter the law for him alone. Things are changing in the sunken city every day."*

"For the better, we hope," Garey said.

Kai couldn't quite muster up as much enthusiasm as everyone else for the changes taking place in the city. Yes, it was wonderful that homosexual relations were no longer banned, but to Kai, who wasn't allowed any type of sexual relationship, the change in the law made little difference.

"Are you going to the sunken city?" Garey asked. *"If we travel together the rest of the way we shouldn't have any more trouble with sharks. We lost the spears we were carrying when we began our journey in another shark attack. And as you can probably tell, we aren't trained fighters like the two of you."*

Kai couldn't stop himself from preening a little, and he shot Dax a smug smile over his shoulder. Garey thought he could take care of himself, even if Dax was unconvinced.

"I'm sorry, we're heading away from the city at the moment," Dax replied. *"We're heading to land in the north."*

"Human lands?"

"Yes. We've got quite a way to go yet."

"But why would you leave the sunken city to travel to the land of humans? Surely it's safer for our kind in the protected city?"

Kai could tell Garey was worried there might be something they didn't know about the underwater kingdom. He reached out and patted his arm. *"It's nothing sinister. My traveling companion just wants to track down an old lover and let him know about the change in the law. I'm traveling with him since, as you know, it's much safer than traveling alone."*

"Ah, yes, of course. I'm just an old worrier. After so long living in dangerous waters, to find we can all live in the sunken city seems a dream come true."

"If they have room for us," the other merman commented.

"There are plenty of empty chambers both inside and outside the palace," Kai assured them. *"King Nereus will welcome you all."*

"Maybe we'll see you again when you return to the city?"

"Perhaps," Kai replied.

"You didn't give us your names," Garey said.

Kai replied before Dax could. *"This is Xane, and I'm Otus."*

Introductions were made, and thankfully for Kai, Dax didn't call him on his lies. He also had the sense to wait until they were on their way again before he brought up the subject.

"So, who's Otus?" Dax asked.

"Aren't you going to ask me why I gave false names?"

"Presumably so they don't know who we are if they're questioned about your disappearance when they arrive in the city. I noticed you used your powers most of the time too. Making sure you could shake hands with all of them and help keep the merbabies from wandering. Very clever and quite sneaky of you. If they're asked about a blind merman traveling in this direction they won't be likely to think of you."

"You noticed all that about me?"

"Yes. Why do you sound so surprised?"

Kai shrugged. *"I don't know. You just don't seem to be the observant type."*

Dax laughed. *"When it comes to handsome mermen, I notice everything."*

Kai didn't know what to say. After so long confined in the temple, he was unused to people paying him compliments. Dax saying he found him handsome meant a lot, and more importantly, it gave Kai hope he might be able to win the merman's heart.

"Now, since you insist on throwing yourself into the path of sharks, how about I teach you how to use that spear properly?"

The compliment was quickly forgotten at Dax's latest comment insinuating he didn't know how to take care of himself. *"I thought I handled myself perfectly well."*

Dax raised his hands and backed up. *"I never said you didn't, but you nearly lost your weapon twice in the shark attack."*

Kai wanted to argue, but the truth was he had fumbled a little. He'd never fought a shark before in his life. He thought he had made a pretty good showing. Something of his thoughts must have reached Dax, or he saw it in his face. Kai felt the pat of a hand on his arm.

"Don't look so down. You did good for your first fight. With a bit of training you'll do better next time."

The words might have been meant with the best of intentions, but the patronizing tone hit a nerve with Kai. He gripped his spear, and after using his powers to determine Dax's position, he disarmed him with one swift move.

"What did you do that for?" Dax complained, as he swam after his spear. *"I thought you'd want to learn how to fight properly."*

"Not if you're going to speak to me like a child. I'm not an idiot."

"That's debatable," Dax snapped. *"Only a fool would go up against two sharks with no idea how to fight them."*

Dax grabbed his spear and swam back to Kai. With another swift jab, Kai tried to disarm Dax again. This time Dax was ready for him and it was Kai's weapon that went astray. *"I think I've made my point,"* Dax said. *"Now, how about you start being reasonable?"*

Kai knew he was rusty and Dax made some valid points, but it didn't mean he had to like the way he spoke to him. *"Fine, you can show me a few moves and I can get some more practice."*

"It would be better if we did your training on land," Dax suggested.

"I don't see why," Kai replied. *"It's not we'll find any sharks on land. It would make more sense for us to practice in the water."*

"If you weren't blind, I'd agree with you. We'll find land and

go there. I think there's an island a couple of days from here that is mostly uninhabited."

Kai glared at Dax's retreating back and fought the urge to turn his spear on the merman again. If they ran into danger in the ocean he would be blind, surely it made sense to learn to fight in the same circumstances in which they would be in a real one. Unfortunately, Dax had no intention of listening to his opinions on the matter. He said they would learn on land, so on land it would be. Kai wondered if a day would ever come where Dax valued his opinion at all.

Dax wasn't sure this was a good idea, but if Kai insisted on putting himself in danger, the least he could do was try to teach him how to defend himself.

The first thing he decided was this would be better achieved on land, at least for the start. It would be less tiring for Kai if he wasn't forced to spend his energy by having visions at the same time. He knew Kai disagreed with him, but that was tough luck.

They swam to the nearest island, which was a little way off their course, but not far enough out to make a great deal of difference to the length of their journey.

When they reached the shore, it was clear the island had been visited by humans. There was a structure set back from the beach, although the poor state of repair suggested they had long since departed. Dax hoped they didn't come back any time soon.

They found a long, open stretch on the beach, where there was plenty of space to move, and Dax began his first lesson in teaching Kai how to defend himself. He hoped he was a fast learner.

Dax watched Kai check the balance of his spear and the tip. Dax could tell from the way he studied the weapon Kai had some training in such things.

"You look as if you know what you're doing," Dax commented.

"I had training as a youngster, before I became an Oracle.

111

I wanted nothing more than to be a warrior in my clan."

"Well, let's see how much you remember." Dax tossed his own spear from hand to hand with a grin.

Kai hadn't even taken his stance when Dax charged him. "A shark won't wait for you to ready yourself," he said.

Kai ducked and rolled out of the way, twisting as agilely as he did in the water. He swept his spear in a wide circle, causing Dax to jump back or be knocked to the ground.

Kai shot to his feet with a cry of triumph and ran at Dax, who barely moved out of the way in time to avoid being skewered.

"Not so close," Dax warned as he stumbled out of the way. "I thought I'd be safer on land, where you have your sight."

Kai laughed and turned the spear on Dax with lightning speed, holding it close to his throat. "Whatever gave you that idea?"

Dax wasn't worried. He was pretty sure he knew Kai well enough to know he wouldn't hurt him. He stood his ground, waiting for Kai to draw back the weapon.

Finally, Kai pulled away. He tested the spear again with a few sharp jabs to the air and shot Dax a wicked grin. The seasoned warrior had a sinking feeling Kai might not be such an easy opponent to defeat.

They sparred on the sands for nearly an hour, Kai disarming Dax as frequently as Dax relieved Kai of his weapon.

It had been a long time since Dax had actually trained with someone. After traveling the oceans as much as he had in the last few years, he had enough experience battling sharks and other predators. He found he enjoyed practicing with Kai far more than he had anticipated. It became especially obvious just how much when they fought up close. Without human clothes to conceal their bodies, there was no hiding his erection. Dax would have been mildly embarrassed if Kai hadn't been in a similar state of arousal.

Fighting had always set his blood rushing south nearly as

quickly as fucking did.

When Kai fell backward onto the sand, Dax drew in a sharp breath at the delectable sight spread out before him. He ran the tip of his spear down Kai's chest. Kai didn't try to pick up his own weapon, which had fallen a couple of feet away from them.

Dax stared down into Kai's green eyes. He dropped to his knees and reached out to touch Kai with his fingers, rather than his spear.

He was still a few inches away from his prize when he heard the sound of voices coming from the ocean behind him.

Kai shot up and stared over Dax's shoulder. "The guards!"

Dax nodded and put a finger to his lips. He pointed at the trees. Kai picked up his spear and together they ran for cover. There was no time to hide that they had been on the beach, but if they could make it back to the water they might be in with a chance. They must be less than a mile from the underground caverns Lucas had told them to watch out for. They could hide there until the guards had passed them by, then be on their way.

They wasted no time scrambling through the trees and bushes and returning to the ocean farther down the beach.

Kai used his powers to see the guards as soon as he took his mer form. *"They're all on the island now. I think they're just stopping for rest and food."*

"Have they seen our footprints on the beach?"

"Not yet. They're heading in that direction though."

"Then I suggest we swim quickly, before they return to the water."

"They won't know for certain it was us. Any mer could have used the island."

"You know we can't take the chance," Dax said. *"They're far too close for my liking."*

Kai agreed, and they continued their swim north. Dax encouraged Kai to hold onto his arm so they might travel faster. He hoped it would be enough.

Chapter Eight

"I thought we were heading this way?" Kai asked when Dax suddenly nudged him in a different direction to the one they had been traveling in since their departure from the city.

"There's an island about two hours' swimming this way," Dax replied. *"We'll stay there until tomorrow."*

"Another detour? I thought you wanted to get to Kyle as soon as possible? We've made good time in the weeks since we left the last island. Why stop now?"

"I do, but we won't reach the land of humans before tomorrow night."

"So?"

"It's the solstice," Dax replied. His tone made it clear he thought this should have been obvious.

"What difference does that make?" Kai asked.

"Are you serious?" Dax pulled Kai to a halt. *"You didn't think we'd be going through the solstice without having sex, did you?"*

"I hadn't really thought about it," Kai lied. Thoughts of what would happen on the solstice had been increasingly common as the mating season approached, but Dax didn't need to know that. Handsome though the merman was, his mind seemed to be set on only one thing, reconnecting with his old lover. Kai realized he had made little effort to seduce Dax during their journey so far. Yes, there had been the moment on the beach when he had thought Dax was going to touch him, but the untimely arrival of the guards had stopped him. Later Kai wondered if it had been his imagination. Perhaps Dax had simply intended to help him

to his feet.

Now the mating season was here, Kai remembered Medina's warning to him. If he should give Dax his body before he was sure of his heart, he would lose him. Unfortunately, Kai had no doubt Dax's heart was securely in his own keeping right now. Kai had no intention of risking losing him for a quick romp in the sand. As painful as the solstice would be, he couldn't let Dax take him. But what was he supposed to tell Dax about his decision? The truth was out of the question, unless he wanted Dax to think him a fool, or even worse, a manipulator.

"We'll go to the island until the solstice is over," Dax stated firmly. *"You and I will use each other to break the damn fevers, then we'll be on our way again."*

"Use each other?" Kai knew what Dax meant, but he still couldn't quite believe the merman could be so casual about sex. Didn't sharing his body with a lover mean anything to him?

"I need to take another merman to break the fever. I'm hoping your fever recedes when you're taken. You'll forgive me for saying so, but you do rather look like someone who would enjoy being on the receiving end."

Kai pulled his arm from Dax's loose grasp. *"You think to judge what I need by my appearance? What would you say if I told you I needed to ram my cock into your arse to break my fever? Would you be so eager for us to* use *each other then?"*

Dax grabbed hold of him again, but Kai used his tail to smack him sharply and push him away. *"You aren't going to use me this solstice or any other."*

"You'd rather suffer through the fever just to be faithful to Delwyn?"

"What are you talking about?"

"I saw the way he kissed you right before we left. Do you think he'll be moping around waiting for you to come back? No, he'll be up on the island the colony uses, getting what he needs from another merman."

"No, he won't."

"Of course he will. As soon as he realizes how bad the fever gets when he doesn't find his release he'll be begging another merman to take your place."

Kai smacked Dax again, this time sending him spinning through the water. *"You have no idea what you're talking about."*

"I've been through enough seasons without breaking the fever to know how bad it is," Dax argued. *"You have no idea of the pain."*

Kai swam away from Dax before he answered. *"I know more than you do. How many seasons did you go through without release? Four or five, perhaps? Try going through more than twenty, then speak to me again about the pain."*

"What do you mean, more than twenty?"

"Oracles are not allowed to engage in sexual relations," Kai explained. *"I came into my powers just as I hit puberty. I'm twenty-seven years of age and there are two mating seasons a year. You figure out how many times I've had to ride out the fever without release."*

"You're a virgin?" Dax sounded stunned. Kai hadn't anticipated he wouldn't believe him. He guessed Dax must have thought he had lots of experience before becoming an Oracle, or he didn't realize just how much of a prison the city had been for them. Kai supposed it was better he knew the truth now, rather than finding out when they were in the midst of a more intimate situation, assuming they ever were.

"As I said, sexual relations are forbidden for us. We aren't allowed to leave the city, for any reason."

"You're really a virgin?"

Kai smacked Dax with his tail again.

"And would you stop doing that! You know, for a blind merman, you've got a damn good aim with that thing."

"I'm the Oracle of the present," Kai reminded him.

"So?"

"So, I can see anything happening right now, including where you are."

"You know, when you describe it like that, it sounds like you aren't blind at all."

"Of course I'm blind, but when I use my powers I can see what's happening around me or anywhere else in the world. It's draining to use them all the time, but a glimpse now and then is enough for me to get by."

Dax snorted. *"And you choose to use your powers to perfect your aim when you want to assault me. Charming!"*

Kai swam away from Dax, and, after a quick glance to get his bearings, he swam for a nearby cave entrance. It didn't look particularly welcoming, but it would do as a place to wait out the solstice.

"Where are you going?" Dax called after him. *"The island is this way."*

"I'm not going to the island. I'd rather stay underwater."

"Are you completely insane?" Dax sounded closer, and when Kai took another glimpse with his powers, he saw he had swum up behind him. *"You would rather suffer down here in a filthy cave than have sex with me?"*

"Yes, that's right."

"But it's the solstice tomorrow."

"So you keep saying."

"Because you're not listening. I have no intention of going through a solstice without breaking my fever."

"Then I suggest you start hunting down some equally desperate merman to help you with the problem."

"Why would I do that when you're right here?*"*

"Because I've learnt to cope with the fever in my own way and I don't want to have sex with you."

"You're from a clan whose people stick to one mate, aren't you?"

"Yes. Not that they're my clan now."

"Do you think your precious Delwyn would refuse what I'm offering if your roles were reversed?" Dax questioned quietly. *"Or would he be swimming to land right now, as fast as he can, ready to spread his legs for me?"*

"Delwyn isn't mine and I have no idea what choice he would make. I'm simply telling you the decision I've made, and if you

want to have sex tomorrow, you need to find someone else, because it's not going to be with me."

"So, we're just going to writhe in pain in this cave, are we?" Dax asked.

"I prefer to meditate. I find a clear mind helps."

Dax didn't like the sound of meditation, though since he had never tried it, he could hardly argue it wouldn't work.

"Very well." Dax settled down in a sheltered spot on the seabed near the entrance to the cave. "This meditation technique had better work, though. I can't believe you'd resort to this when you have another option."

"It's served me well for more than twenty mating seasons. I'm quite sure it will get you through one if you just give it a chance."

"I'd still rather have sex."

"So you said, but you can at least give this a try."

Dax scowled as he picked at the nearby seaweed, passing some to Kai before eating his own share. This area of the ocean was desolate and the poor sustenance wasn't going to help his temper. Kai ate his meal slowly and without complaint. When they had finished eating he returned to the subject at hand.

"Firstly, if you're going to meditate enough to push the pain aside, you'll need to stop thinking about it all the time."

"That's a bit difficult to do when you're writhing in pain."

"You won't be in pain when you start meditating. Provided you keep your focus you'll barely feel the pain."

"It's the word barely that worries me. I don't want to feel any pain at all."

"You said you'd give this a try," Kai replied impatiently. "If you truly want to, you need to start working on your focus right now, rather than leaving it until it's too late."

"Let's just get on with this," Dax muttered. He closed his eyes and settled back against the ground. A sharp rock dug into his back. He moved aside a little, only to brush up against a prickly bush with some wickedly sharp thorns.

"Stop fidgeting," Kai chided. "You need to shut out the world around you and retreat inside your mind."

"My mind is telling me I'm uncomfortable and I'm going to be in agony soon."

Dax felt the sharp sting of a hand on his sensitive dorsal fins. "Stop complaining or I'll simply leave you to suffer through the solstice on your own. I'm not going to have you ruin my focus with your constant whining all night."

"You talk like it's not going to be complete torture to make it through the night anyway."

"It won't be torture if you try to focus."

"Focus, focus, focus," Dax mumbled. "If you tell me to focus one more time I swear I'll drag you to the nearest island by the tail fins and pound you into the sand."

Kai snorted. "No you won't."

"What makes you so sure?"

"Because you seem to be a decent sort of merman, and I don't think you'd actually go so far as to rape me or anyone else, not even on the solstice."

Dax grinned. "I love the way you think I'm talking about sex when I say I'll pound you into the sand. I could have been talking about pounding you with my fists."

"Like that's any better. And I don't believe you'd do that either."

"You think you know me so well?"

"I think I have you figured out."

"Oh yes? Do tell."

Kai went quiet and Dax opened his eyes to see his thoughtful expression.

"Well? What have you figured out?"

Kai nodded firmly. "You've been a loner for a while, always traveling from one clan to another because you don't want to make any firm ties. I think it's because of what you lost when the shark attack killed your father and tore apart your clan."

"How do you know about my father?" Dax asked.

"I asked Delwyn to take a look into your past before we left the city."

Dax chuckled. "And your snooping brought you to that conclusion. Didn't you consider that maybe I'm just a randy young merman who gets tired of his lovers quickly and has to *move onto the next clan when he runs out of mermen in the latest community?"*

"I don't think so. Before we left the city I saw you with your lovers from the clan who came to seek sanctuary. You didn't seem to be bored of them, or they of you. In fact I'd say they were quite disappointed that you planned to leave them."

Dax shifted uncomfortably, and this time it wasn't because of the rocks and plants getting in the way. *"Are you saying you spied on me in your visions before we left the city?"*

"Yes." Kai didn't sound even slightly apologetic for his actions.

"How often did you spy on me?"

"Just the once."

Dax wasn't sure he believed him, but rather than be annoyed at Kai checking on him with his powers, he found himself quite pleased. It seemed Kai had a little more interest in him than Dax had initially believed. If that was the case, maybe he could convince Kai to come to the island after all.

Pushing aside the thought for the moment, he returned to the initial topic of discussion, the ridiculous idea of meditation. He supposed he ought to try to focus, just in case he couldn't talk Kai round to his way of thinking.

It took nearly two hours before Dax felt focused at all, and even then he didn't think he would maintain his concentration as soon as the first wave of pain hit him.

"Does this really work?" he asked when he could bear the silence no longer.

"It does for me."

"What about the other Oracles? Do they meditate too?"

"No."

"Then how do they get through the damn solstice?"

"Delwyn retreats into visions of the past. He finds the further back in time he goes, the less connection he has with his own body."

"Really? How far back in time can he see?"

"I don't know." Kai sounded surprised. *"I never asked. I*

know he has seen times from when the sunken city was still an island above us. He has seen the gods and goddesses of Atlantis, as it used to be called, walking amongst the people of the city, whilst the merpeople were still the only human, or half human, inhabitants of the ocean."

"Aren't we the only human inhabitants now?" Dax had traveled many of the oceans of the world and while there were occasional human divers — who he made sure to steer clear of — he wouldn't say they made their home under the waves.

"Yes, but once, long ago, we shared the sunken city with the Atlanteans. Their gods gifted them with the ability to survive at these depths and we lived in peace for many years, sharing the ocean floor with them."

"What happened to them?"

"I'm don't know."

"Can't Delwyn see what happened in a vision?"

"No."

"Why not?"

"We don't know. He's tried. Of the three of us, Delwyn is by far the most curious. Yet, no matter how much he searches he cannot see why they left. He sees them here, then they were gone. Almost as though they vanished in the blink of an eye. He still pokes around that particular time period to see if he can discover what happened, but he's not found anything yet."

"What do you think happened to them?"

"I think the gods had something to do with their disappearance, but I don't know what."

"You talk about the gods as if they are real."

"They are."

"You sound pretty sure about that."

"It's easy to have faith in the gods when you've talked to some of them."

Dax chuckled, albeit a little uneasily. He hadn't forgotten his visit from Medina, though as time passed he was increasingly inclined to put it down to tiredness and too much imagination.

"The Oracles get their powers from the Atlantean Goddess of Prophecy," Kai explained. *"We have all seen her and spoken to her on several occasions."*

"You really believe that?"

"Of course I do. There are other gods and goddesses too, but many are currently asleep."

Dax edged away from Kai. *"Of course they are."*

"I'm not delusional," Kai assured him. *"I don't care if you believe me or not, I know they exist."*

Dax raised his hands in mock surrender. *"Fair enough. So now I know how you and Delwyn get through the solstice. What about Ula? She doesn't seem the meditating type."*

"She's not. She gets cranky and ill-tempered. She usually shuts herself up in her chambers and we stay out of her way as much as we can. Delwyn carved a sign for her door that says enter at your own peril *in the old Atlantean language. Since none of our people can read the old script, he and I are the only ones who know what it says, well, until now."*

"Your secret is safe with me."

Dax closed his eyes and tried to concentrate on meditating once again. The niggling in his gut reminded him the solstice was approaching. He had a suspicion Ula's method might be better for him. Shutting himself away and raging at the injustice of his position sounded far more like him than meditating.

Groaning loudly, he clutched his hair and tugged. He must be out of his mind, and if he wasn't already, he would be within a matter of hours.

"If this doesn't work, will you reconsider coming to the island with me?" he pleaded quietly.

"No."

"Is that a definite no?"

Kai smacked him again. *"You need to concentrate."*

"I am concentrating.*"*

Kai sighed and patted Dax's tail. *"It'll come naturally after a few years of practice."*

"A few years! I can tell you right now this is a one-off occasion.

Next solstice I intend to be surrounded by willing mermen and not stuck in the middle of the ocean with you."

"That's fine with me. I can't say I'm enjoying this particular journey as much as I thought I would either. The freedom is great, but right now the company could be better."

Dax tried not to be insulted. He'd never thought of himself as a bad companion. Most merpeople seemed to enjoy having him around. The idea that Kai didn't like spending time with him hurt more than he wanted to admit.

* * * *

Dax heard them before he saw them. Voices at the edge of his mind. It could only be other mermen in the vicinity. He checked to see if Kai had heard them too, but the Oracle was lost in his mind, concentrating on his mediation, rather like Dax should be doing.

"We have company," Dax told him, poking him in the tail fins to get his attention.

"I hear them."

"You do?"

"I'm blind, not deaf," Kai replied easily. He sat up and pointed to his left. *"They're in that direction. It's a clan of around a dozen mermen and mermaids."*

"You've seen them in a vision?"

"Yes. I wanted to check they weren't hostile before they reached us. Not all clans are welcoming of strangers. And during the mating season some of them might be a little too welcoming, whether you want them to be or not."

Dax knew Kai was correct. He had run across clans in the past when the need to break the mating fever had overridden everything else, including good sense. He hadn't stayed with such clans for long. Desperate as he was for release during the mating season, he would never force another merman against his will.

"Are they friendly?" Dax asked.

"I think so. They have youngsters with them, and aren't

carrying many weapons. They should probably have more than they do, truth be told."

"Any mermen who look like they might want a good fucking?" Dax asked.

Kai gazed out toward the direction the clan was located. *"Probably. There were one or two who touched each other rather more than those mermen who prefer females."*

"Then let's go greet them." Dax swam up from his place on the ground and waited for Kai to join him. *"What are you waiting for?"*

"You're just giving up on the meditation?"

"Of course. Just because you don't want me to fuck you, it doesn't mean no one else does. There's probably someone in this clan who'll be happy to have me take them. You might even find someone you like, if you give them a chance. Just because you have no interest in me, doesn't mean one of these mermen won't get your pulse racing and your cock hard."

"I'm not going to have sex with a total stranger."

Dax should have known what Kai's reaction to his suggestion would be. *"Well, I won't force you. But since it seems there are other options for me, I'm sure you won't mind if I go to the island with them. Unless you've changed your mind about joining me?"*

Kai scowled at him, making it clear he had no intention of changing his mind. Well, more fool him.

"You're going to just leave me down here on my own while you go fuck some stranger?"

Dax sighed. *"You're right. You should probably come to the island too. It'll be safer for you."*

"You're missing the point."

"Which is?"

Kai huffed. *"Never mind. You just go fuck your new friend and I'll wait down here with the sharks."*

"There aren't any sharks in the area," Dax replied automatically.

Kai gave a strangled scream and waved him away. *"The mer aren't coming in this direction exactly. You should go and meet them before they pass us by."*

Dax decided to take Kai at his word, even though he could tell the merman was furious with him. Right now, his priority was getting through the mating season, and if there was a willing merman nearby, he had no intention of missing the opportunity of gaining release.

Dax found the clan a short distance away. They were obviously heading to the island. He kept his spear lowered as he approached them. He didn't want to appear intimidating or risk being seen off by the clan's warriors before he had had the opportunity of introducing himself.

One of the warriors at the edge of the group spotted him first.

Dax raised his hand in greeting. The warrior directed his spear at Dax, clearly not intending to let down his guard until he knew there was no danger. He was a good warrior, cautious and brave at the same time. Handsome too, at least to Dax's eyes. He let his gaze run over the merman's sculpted chest and offered him a wicked smile.

"I'm Lyon," the merman said as he lowered his spear slightly. *"Are you alone?"*

"Practically."

Lyon raised his weapon again. *"Explain yourself."*

"I travel with one other. He's just over that way."

"These are dangerous waters to be traveling through, just the two of you."

"I know, but we're managing all right so far. Are you heading to the island?"

Lyon nodded. *"Yes, of course, it's the only land mass in the area where we can see through the mating season."*

"Would you like some company?" Dax asked, meaning generally, but not opposed to the idea of Lyon taking it personally either.

Lyon held his spear pointed at Dax's throat before running it lightly down his chest. The move could have been a warning, but Dax could tell it wasn't. This was an invitation to him, and he intended to take Lyon up on the offer.

He took hold of the end of the spear, careful not to touch the well-sharpened tip. *"Nice spear,"* he teased. *"One of the longest I've ever seen. Compensating?"*

Lyon laughed and withdrew his weapon. *"Maybe you'll find out, maybe you won't. What about your friend?"*

"What about him?"

"I don't wish to infringe on an established relationship, not even for the mating season."

Dax shook his head. *"We're just traveling together. I offered to fuck him, but he doesn't want me to."*

"We have several females in our clan who are without mates," Lyon said. *"Perhaps he'd like to meet them."*

"He prefers men," Dax replied.

"Then it's just you he doesn't want?" Lyon asked.

"Seems like it."

Lyon chuckled. *"Well, even if he has no interest in breaking his fever, perhaps he'd still like to meet us. The youngsters will be remaining underwater and the mothers will be taking it in turns to stay with them. Your friend is welcome to spend the solstice with them."*

"I'm sure he'll be delighted to do so," Dax agreed on Kai's behalf.

Dax led the clan back to where Kai waited for him.

"This is Lyon," he told Kai. *"Lyon, this is my traveling companion, Kai."*

"Kai, like the Oracle?" Lyon asked.

"Yes, but I hear he's much better looking," Kai replied with a laugh.

Dax could tell Kai was using his powers to prevent Lyon and the others from noticing his blindness. A merman who shared the name with an Oracle could easily be explained as a coincidence. A blind merman who shared the Oracle's name was too dangerous for them. Dax wished he'd had the presence of mind to give false names, as Kai had done before. Unfortunately, it was too late now.

"Dax tells me you don't plan on going up to the island," Lyon

said once introductions had been made and the youngsters had settled.

"No, but if he wants to go up there, I'm not going to stop him."

"I'm sitting right here," Dax reminded him.

"Yes, I can see that."

"Kai likes you," Lyon said privately to Dax. *"He has that look in his eyes that all mermen get when they desperately want to fuck another."*

Dax smiled. *"You're imagining things."*

"I know what I can see."

Dax didn't bother to argue with him. Lyon thought he could see something in Kai's eyes. What he didn't know was Kai wasn't looking at him in any way. He wasn't seeing him at all, save for brief flashes to make sure he played the part of a sighted merman convincingly. Something about Kai *not* looking at him made Dax wish he would.

* * * *

Kai was tired. Tired of swimming, tired of using his powers, and really, *really* tired of watching Dax flirt with Lyon.

It wasn't that he didn't like Lyon, he seemed to be a perfectly pleasant merman, and clearly he wasn't opposed to the idea of spending the mating season with Dax. Kai just couldn't shake the image of Dax fucking Lyon on a sandy beach.

Kai wasn't angry with Dax. He knew he had struggled with meditating, though Kai privately thought he hadn't tried very hard. It wasn't that he wished Dax to suffer through the solstice, he just didn't want him to spend the night with Lyon. He tried not to think about the reasons why he didn't want Dax and Lyon to spend the night together. It sounded too much like jealousy in his mind, and he had never been the possessive type before.

The temptation to say something biting to Dax was nearly too much. Kai decided that, rather than make a fool of himself, he would simply join the mermaids and youngsters. At least that way he wouldn't have to watch all those longing glances and tentative touches. He could imagine them instead, he told himself bitterly. Unfortunately, he suspected his imagination wouldn't stop there.

It was going to be the longest solstice ever. He had a feeling the pain of knowing Dax was on land, fucking Lyon, would be far worse than the pain of the mating fever. How was he supposed to win the heart of a merman who made it clear he was prepared to have sex with any willing merman?

Chapter Nine

Kai curled up on the uncomfortable rock. His fever ran high and the pain was almost unbearable. When the first stabbing sensation hit him, he wondered whether Dax was right. Was he just being stubborn in refusing to go to the island? Dax and the merpeople from the traveling clan didn't seem to think anything of having casual sex with each other just because it was the solstice. The merman Dax would be fucking tonight had even less connection with Dax than Kai did. Could Medina have been mistaken? If he had let Dax take him, maybe it would have been enough to convince him to give Kai his heart.

The more he brooded, the more he wondered if perhaps he should have taken Dax up on his offer. Turning down sex certainly hadn't helped.

Kai closed his eyes and hugged his aching stomach. His head pounded from using his powers, and he couldn't seem to concentrate long enough to fall into the meditative trance he knew would see him through the night and the following day.

While Delwyn lost himself in visions of the past to get through the solstice, Kai had never before used his powers in such a manner. The main reason was he had nothing in particular to focus on seeing, at least until now.

He knew he shouldn't do it. It was the same thing he scolded Delwyn for, and it would only make his headache worse. Yet the temptation lingered at the edge of his mind, and before he had even consciously made the decision, he was watching Dax on the island.

The mermen had found a secluded spot on the beach and

were stroking each other intently.

Kai watched them, unseen and unheard. He knew if he had been with them in body, and in his human form, he would have been hard and aching. Even in his mer form he was aware of his arousal. His fever rose sharply and spots danced in front of his eyes, yet he couldn't bring himself to stop now.

"What do you need?" Lyon asked Dax as they rolled about on the sand.

"I need to be inside you. Is that okay?"

Lyon nodded. "Oh yes."

Kai saw, much to his surprise, that Dax was surprisingly gentle with his new lover, preparing him thoroughly with his tongue and fingers, before he even attempted to enter him with the thick length of his cock.

Lyon moaned beneath him, panting and gasping as Dax pleasured him with obvious expertise.

Kai shut off his vision abruptly. This wasn't helping his fever at all. If anything, spying on Dax made it worse. He had to try to meditate or concentrate on something else. Since he had already struggled to focus he decided to see what Delwyn was doing back in the sunken city. He had been checking on him regularly during the journey, but it had been some days since he had last watched him. Kai wasn't surprised to see Delwyn stretched out on his sleeping sponge, lost in a vision of his own. Ula, meanwhile, swam back and forth in her chambers, twisting and turning in an effort to ease the pain she could never entirely erase.

There wasn't much else happening in the city. Most of the merpeople were up on the island, breaking their fevers. The few who remained were mostly guards, and they would be swimming to the surface just as soon as they had been relieved of their duties by those who had already been to the island earlier in the night.

Watching other mermen have sex had never been something he enjoyed, especially on the night of the solstice, when he was forbidden to do the same.

Kai, you're an idiot! he told himself. *You could have been up on the island right now with Dax, if you weren't so inept at seduction. You should have been working on him since the day you left the city, instead of worrying about your lack of experience. What does it matter if he's had a hundred mermen and you've had none? If he's that desperate to come he won't care.*

Instead he had left things too late. Kai knew Medina was right in this. If he gave his body to Dax tonight, it would just be sex. They would be using each other rather than making love. Kai didn't want to be just another merman Dax shoved his cock into on the solstice. He wanted to be someone worth keeping around the rest of the year, too. He wanted what Medina had promised him, and that meant he had to wait until the time was right.

With his mind on Dax already, Kai wasn't surprised to find himself in the midst of another vision. Already tired from overusing his powers, Kai knew he should snap out of it as soon as he could, but what he saw halted him in his tracks.

Dax and his lover had moved on from their foreplay and were well into the main event. Lyon was on his hands and knees with his arse in the air. Dax knelt behind him, his cock buried inside his lover.

Kai couldn't take his eyes off the sight before him.

Dax rammed into Lyon, moaning incoherently as he pulled out and pushed in over and over again.

Lyon keened and whined, begging for more, though Kai couldn't see how he could possibly take any more from Dax. There wasn't an inch of Dax's length visible where their bodies were joined.

"Dax, oh fuck, Dax," Lyon cried. "Right there, that's it, right there. Oh fuck!"

Kai watched as Lyon started to come, his seed spilling onto the sand beneath him. All thoughts of reasons why he shouldn't be watching this flew out of his mind the second Dax began to climax.

"Kai!" Dax screamed into the night. "Oh fuck, Kai!"

Kai's breath came short as Dax's words registered in his mind. Dax had called out *his* name while he fucked a far more willing merman than Kai. Maybe his traveling companion wasn't quite as immune to Kai as he had thought.

The two mermen collapsed in a heap, gasping and panting as they struggled to catch their breath. Kai was similarly breathless as he watched them recover their senses.

Lyon spoke first. "What is it between you and Kai then?"

"Nothing. We're just traveling together."

"Why didn't he want to come up here with the rest of us?"

Dax shrugged rather than reply. Kai felt a surge of gratitude for him for not betraying his confidence.

"You don't think he's a bit odd?" Lyon continued. "Doesn't he get a fever like the rest of us?"

"Yes, but he handles it in his own way."

Lyon sat up and stretched. "Anyone who handles the mating fever without a bit of fucking can't be right in the head if you ask me."

Dax frowned as he stood and brushed the sand from his body. "I don't believe I did ask you," he snapped, before running into the surf and diving into the water. Lyon's jaw dropped as he watched his lover transform and disappear under the waves without a backward glance. Kai pulled out of the vision and returned to his body, waiting for Dax to come back to the cave.

He wondered whether Dax would invite him to come back up to the island with him, or whether he no longer had any interest in him now he had broken his fever. He guessed he would have to wait and see.

* * * *

Dax swam into the cavern and found Kai right where he had left him. The merman looked to be in some considerable pain, if his position was anything to judge by. So much for the meditation technique. Dax was glad he had not resorted to such a method himself.

"Are you awake?" he asked, quietly, so his thoughts would not disturb Kai if he were asleep.

"Yes. Did you have a good time on the island?"

"It was fine. You should have come up there with us. There were plenty of mermen there who would have been happy to help you break your fever."

Kai didn't move from his position or open his eyes.

"You could probably still catch someone if you swim up there quickly," Dax continued. *"There are quite a few mermen who share partners and wait their turn in the group."*

That at least got a reaction from Kai. He sat up, grabbed a nearby shell and threw it at him. It floated through the water, stopping well before it reached Dax. Ah, so his prickly little merman was still in a temper. He wondered how far he could push him. It could be interesting to find out.

"Lyon was a good fuck," he stated with a grin as he swam closer to Kai. *"He begged for my cock."*

"How nice for you," Kai replied, and even Dax could hear the sarcasm in his tone.

"I may have to see if I can meet up with him again some time."

"Maybe next time you can get his name right when you're buried in his arse," Kai said. *"Though I found it quite flattering to hear you shouting out mine, I doubt he thought the same."*

Dax's grin froze on his face. *"What are you talking about?"*

"You called out my *name when you climaxed, instead of his."*

"No, I didn't."

"Why don't you go back and ask him? From the expression on his face I'm pretty sure he heard you. That's probably why he asked about me right after you were done."

Dax wasn't sure what to say, at least until he realized what Kai had done. *"You spied on me and Lyon?"*

"Er."

"You went up to the island?"

"No. I didn't have to, you know that."

"You fucking hypocrite!" Dax yelled. *"You go on about*

meditation and focus, and riding out the fever without the need for sex, while at the same time you use your powers to spy on me with another merman."

Dax regretted shouting when Kai cringed. *"It wasn't like that."*

"Then how was it exactly?"

"Er."

"I see you don't have an answer, do you? Well, just for the record, you might have been able to see what we were doing, but your hearing is a little bit off. It wasn't your name I called out, it was Kyle's."

"I know what I heard."

"And I know what I said. You thought you heard your name because that's what you wanted to hear. You want me, but you're too stubborn to admit the truth."

Dax knew he was right, but the look on Kai's face told him everything he needed to know. The Oracle who had used his powers to engage in a little voyeurism would never admit he wanted him.

* * * *

Kai wondered whether he had made the biggest mistake of his life in leaving the city with Dax. He knew the reason for the uneasiness was his own fault, and he only had himself to blame for Dax's temper. He should have known better than to spy on people during moments of intimacy. He didn't have the right to use his powers in such a way, and Dax had every reason to be angry with him for what he had done.

"I'm sorry," Kai offered when the silence had become too much for him to bear.

Dax grunted but didn't turn round. Kai guessed he wanted something more before he returned to the relatively easy-going merman he had been before.

They swam a little farther, and the whole time Dax refused to look at him.

"What more do you want?" Kai asked. *"I said I'm sorry for spying on you. And it's not like there weren't half a dozen other mer on the beach with you, watching you fuck Lyon."*

"It's not about the spying, though the fact you did it after all your talk about meditation makes you a damned hypocrite."

"What is it about then?" Kai pressed on, when it seemed Dax wasn't going to elaborate.

"It doesn't matter."

"Then why are you still in a temper?"

"I'm not."

"You haven't said a word since we left the cavern."

"Maybe I have a lot on my mind, thinking about Lyon."

Kai didn't believe him for a moment. He had witnessed Dax and Lyon's goodbye, and there was nothing between them to even suggest the two of them had had sex the night before. *"Fine. Don't tell me. But if you don't stop being such a misery I may just swim back to the city and leave you to it."*

"No you won't."

Kai glared at Dax. He was right, of course, but he didn't have to sound so sure of himself. *"You don't know me as well as you think you do. I can use my powers to get me safely back. I don't need you to guide me there."*

"It's nothing to do with you being blind," Dax replied. *"You won't go back because you want to stay with me."*

"Not while you're in such a temper, I don't."

"Well, you know what you need to do."

"No, I don't. I've already said I'm sorry."

Dax spun round and Kai, blind for the moment, banged into him. *"Sorry,"* Dax offered. *"I forgot you can't always see."*

"How can you forget?"

"Because you're so capable, obviously. You barely need to hold onto me to be guided at all."

"Would you prefer I cling to you like a bloody limpet?"

"Yes, no, I mean…"

"What?"

"Maybe I kind of like the idea of you holding my hand while we're swimming. I know you like to be seen as independent, but

sometimes it's as if you can't even ask for help when you do *need it."*

"I don't need your help to swim. I'm as much a merman as you."

"I never said you weren't. Damn, you're way too sensitive. I meant I want to hold your hand because I just want *to."*

Kai wasn't sure what to make of that. Dax didn't exactly seem the hand-holding type.

Dax sighed, and when Kai used his powers to see his expression, he realized he wasn't so much angry as sad.

"So, what you're saying is you're grumpy because you want to hold hands and I don't?"

"No! I want you to bloody well admit you want me. Is that too much to ask?"

Kai laughed. *"Don't you think you're being a little arrogant? Not every merman who sees you wants you to fuck them."*

"But you do."

"What makes you so sure?"

Dax's response was to take Kai in his arms and kiss him hard. They could have been set upon by a family of sharks and Kai wouldn't have noticed until it was too late. He didn't want to give Dax the satisfaction of knowing he was right, but he couldn't stop himself from kissing him back. He thrust his tongue into Dax's mouth and wrapped his arms around his back.

"Eager little bugger, aren't you?" Dax said, as they ravaged each other's mouths.

"You don't seem to mind."

"Definitely not."

"We shouldn't really be doing this out in the open."

"There aren't any laws against it," Dax reminded him. *"You aren't in the sunken city now."*

"I was thinking more along the lines of other predators who might think we're lunch."

"Good idea, we should keep moving."

Kai almost took Dax at his word, but the moment he tried to break the kiss, Dax made it clear he had no intention of stopping just yet. Kai stroked Dax's back, tracing the length of his spine right down to where his waist transformed from skin to scales.

"Lower," Dax encouraged.

Kai knew exactly where Dax wanted to be touched. It was the same place he, Delwyn, and all other mermen were extra-sensitive. The spot right where his fins spread out from his tail. In mer form it was impossible for either of them to achieve an orgasm, but sometimes, when he was stroked in just the right spot, he thought he just might manage it.

"Lower," Dax repeated. *"Touch me there."*

Kai did as Dax asked. He ran his fingers over the scales, brushing them lightly, until he reached the fins. When he touched Dax in *that* spot, Dax shivered in his arms and their tail fins tangled together as they sought a closeness they couldn't quite achieve under the water.

"We need to go to land, right now," Dax said, when he finally ended the kiss.

Kai shook his head. *"Not yet."*

"What? Why not?"

Kai didn't know why he wasn't taking Dax up on the offer to go to land with him. It wasn't as if he didn't want to be with him, he just didn't believe now was the right time. He had a feeling if they had sex now — that would be it. Dax would have got what he wanted and Kai would be the one wanting more. Dax had said himself he had been with a number of other mermen. Was Kai simply convenient?

"We should get to the land of humans."

"Stop changing the subject. Why are you being so contradictory? You kiss me like you want me to fuck you, but now you want to stay underwater instead of having some fun."

Kai yanked himself out of Dax's arms. *"I don't want to have 'some fun' with you."*

"It didn't seem that way when you were kissing me just now."

"I want more than fun from you!" Kai shouted. *"I don't want to be just another merman you stick your cock in on the solstice."*

137

Dax swam up into his face. *"It's not the solstice right now."*

"It's close enough."

"My fever has broken. The mating season's over for me."

"Oh." Kai's fever still raged, and would do for at least another day. It made it rather hard to tell when the season was over when you never broke your fever.

"Come to land with me," Dax whispered into his ear. *"I'll fuck that fever right out of you."*

Kai was nearly convinced. Then Dax spoke again.

"We'll get each other out of our systems and that will be it."

Kai shook his head and backed away from Dax. *"I think I'll pass."*

"Are you insane?"

"No. It's just I don't think we want the same things. I'd rather wait until I find a merman whose idea of sex is a little closer to my own."

"And what's your idea of sex?" Dax asked in a huffy tone. *"Moonlight picnics and whispered words of love?"*

"What's wrong with that?"

"It's a load of rubbish. We're mermen, we're half fish and we have needs we have to take care of, just like every other animal that goes into heat."

"We're half human too, and I'd rather think with my human brain and listen to my human heart, than be ruled by animal instincts."

Dax snorted. He obviously thought Kai was being an idiot. Kai didn't care what he thought about his choice. He had gone this long without breaking his mating fever, one more solstice wouldn't make much difference. Though he did wonder if being in close proximity to Dax was making the season even more painful than usual.

They swam on again, though at least this time, the unpleasant atmosphere had lifted.

"How long have you been in love with Delwyn?" Dax asked.

"I'm not," Kai replied immediately.

"Really?"

"Yes, really."

"There's something you should know."

"What's that?"

"You aren't the only one to have visions," Dax said. *"Thanks to Medina, the Goddess of Love, I had one of my own before I came to the city. At least I think I did, though it could have been a vivid dream."*

"What did you see?"

"You and Delwyn, touching and kissing each other. You certainly appeared to be very much in love."

"We're close, and I care for him a great deal, but I'm not in love with him, nor he with me."

"You sound sure about that."

"I'm not in love with him," Kai insisted.

"I meant about him. You don't think maybe he has feelings for you that you aren't aware of?"

"No."

"Why are you so sure?"

Kai smiled. *"Because we confide in each other and he gave his heart to another a long time ago."*

"Does his love know of Delwyn's affections?"

"Yes. They grew up together and were the best of friends. If it weren't for the curse of being an Oracle they would have been lovers a long time ago, or at least I think they would have. Of course, King Nereus might have had something to say about it too."

"What does it have to do with him?"

"Delwyn was in love with Prince Finn. He probably still is, though we don't talk about him much, not since he left for a new life on land. Delwyn had me checking up on him now and then, just to make sure he was happy. But after a while he stopped asking and I stopped looking. I think it hurt him too much to hear about the merman he loved being with someone else."

"Can't Delwyn use his own powers to see him?"

"Yes, but he sees the past. While he can see the recent past — anything that has already happened — he finds his powers far more unsettling than I do. The knowledge that what he is seeing has already happened, and can never be changed, is a strain for

him. Would you want to see the merman you love being intimate with another?"

"I guess not. It sounds like he has a raw deal with these powers of yours."

"Yes, though I personally think Ula has the worst. She doesn't talk about it much, but I know she finds seeing the future hard."

"Are all the visions set in stone, or can you change things once you've seen them? Can you alter destiny or are we stuck on a course we can't deviate from no matter how hard we try?"

"My visions and those of Delwyn are firmly set," Kai explained. "Delwyn can't change what happened in the past and I can't alter what events are happening in the here and now, other than by anticipating what is to come, like I did with the shark attack."

"And Ula's visions of the future?"

"They're a different matter entirely. Some things she sees seem to be changeable, particularly the small stuff. Sometimes she alters her own actions to try to prove her point, but it's open to debate as to whether that's what she's doing."

"What do you mean?"

"Well, she might see a vision of the future to tell her what is being served for dinner, with her present at the meal just like usual. Then she'll refuse to eat what's on offer and snack on something else instead. She says it means she has altered her fate."

"You disagree?"

"Our diet isn't exactly varied. Who is to say she was seeing that particular evening? It could have been another occasion two seasons from now where the same food was served."

"What about visions that are more specific? Can she change those?"

"We don't know. Some things are out of our control, maybe out of anyone's control. I don't have all the answers. We're still learning about the powers we carry."

Dax didn't press Kai any further about Ula's abilities, not that Kai could have told him much more. Ula was a private mermaid, and although she did open up to Kai and Delwyn occasionally, she was far more likely to keep her worries to herself.

"Can I ask you a personal question?" Dax asked.

"If you like."

"Why didn't you ever sneak out of the city to the island to get fucked?"

Kai sighed and shook his head at Dax's question. Even after all he had told him, he still didn't understand what Kai wanted from a lover. *"You keep assuming I want another merman to shove his cock up my arse. Did it ever occur to you maybe I want it to be the other way round?"*

"Are you deliberately avoiding answering my question?" Dax asked, in what Kai considered to be a perfect example of him doing the exact same thing.

"The Oracles are guarded at all times. We are forbidden to leave the city to go to land. If it weren't for the earthquakes, and your help, I'd still be there right now."

"Surely there have been opportunities for you to sneak out before?"

"We are watched whenever we leave the temple. We are always accompanied by at least one servant whenever we need to go anywhere. Our servants are also our guards."

"You could give a guard or two the slip."

"I wouldn't want to get one or more of the guards into trouble just to go to land and have sex."

"Maybe if you'd experienced sex you'd have considered it worth the risk."

Kai smacked Dax hard with his tail. *"I would never risk another just for my own pleasure."*

"What about for your freedom?"

"What do you mean?"

"Is there a law that says you have to live in the sunken city? What's to stop the three of you leaving and finding somewhere to live on land?"

"The sunken city is the safest place for us. It's dangerous for any merman to live amongst humans. For a blind merman it's even more so. Each time we take our mer form we are risking exposure of our kind. We wouldn't be able to tell if a human is coming upon us until it's too late."

"I suppose so," Dax conceded. "So, we've still got a long way to go. Tell me about what you do in that temple of yours. It doesn't sound like you have much fun if you're prisoners."

"Mostly we study the old Atlantean texts."

"That doesn't sound much fun."

"It's not. Delwyn loves looking into the past, but I find it boring."

"And you wanted to be a warrior, right?"

"Yes. In fact, I still do, even though it's impossible now."

Dax chuckled. "I knew you'd held a spear before when you disarmed me so easily that first time. Who taught you how to fight dirty?"

"I had two older brothers. I learned to defend myself pretty fast."

"What happened to them? Do they live in the sunken city?"

"No. My clan prefers the colder waters in the far southern oceans. When I came into my powers they delivered me to the sunken city, but few wanted to stay there for good."

"Your family just dumped you there?" Dax sounded appalled.

"My parents stayed with me. I was the baby of the family and my mother was reluctant to leave me alone in such a strange place."

"Where are they now?"

"They returned to our clan a few years later. They come and visit me every couple of years and tell me all the news about my brothers."

"Your brothers don't visit you?"

"Yes, but not as often."

"What about the other Oracles?"

"Delwyn was born in the city, and he sees his family every few days. Ula hasn't seen her family since she arrived in the city. They really did just abandon her. She was even younger than I was as well."

"Why would they do that?"

"Because of the curse."

"What curse?"

Kai wondered whether Dax would believe in the curse or not. From what he had said about gods and goddesses, he didn't seem to be the fanciful type. *"Some mer believe the inhabitants of the city have been cursed. Our numbers are falling every year, and our mermaids find it hard to conceive."*

"Do you think there's a curse?"

"I don't know. Sometimes I think it's ridiculous to believe in such things, yet at other times it makes a lot of sense."

Dax laughed and shook his head. *"Curses sound like a lot of nonsense to me."*

Kai chuckled alongside him and let his thoughts wander as they continued on their way. At least the air had been cleared between them.

Only later did Kai remember how deftly Dax had avoided his question about mating triggers. The truth was Kai had no idea what triggered a break in his fever. He had never been given the opportunity to find out. He wondered whether the next solstice would be the one during which he finally discovered his most intimate desire. Even more, he pondered whether Dax would be the one to help him in his search.

Chapter Ten

Dax recognized a nearby rock formation Lucas had told him about. He tapped Kai's arm, and they changed course once more. They began the steady climb to the surface, hoping to see land ahead.

"There it is, just where Lucas said it would be," Dax said after they emerged into the open air. "Do you know which way we have to go when we get to land?"

Kai shook his head. He had used his powers to see Kyle and Prince Finn on several occasions during their journey, but he hadn't seen anything even remotely useful. From his brief glimpses into their life, they seemed to spend most of the time in bed, sometimes in the company of their human lover, a handsome blond man who clearly had no trouble keeping his two lovers satisfied. The rest of the time they spent in some kind of indoor body of water, again with the human, who seemed to be quite accepting of his mermen lovers.

Unfortunately, knowing who did what to whom in the throes of passion didn't help Kai figure out where to find them.

"Lucas said Caspian sent him to Kyle's house, but he doesn't recall the exact location. Maybe Caspian will appear and do the same for us?"

"Let's store our spears underwater and swim to land while the beach is deserted," Dax said. "Maybe we'll get lucky."

Kai agreed. "I want to check on Delwyn one more time before we go to land, as well as having one more look at Kyle and Finn to see if I can see anything useful."

Dax waited patiently while Kai used his powers. From what Kai had told him, once the Oracle took human form he would be unable to use his powers. This might be their last opportunity for quite some time to observe them and discover their location.

"Anything?" he asked when Kai seemed to come out of his reverie.

Kai sighed with obvious frustration. "Delwyn seems to be well, if a little unhappy."

"You miss him, don't you?" Dax asked, even though he already knew the answer.

"Yes."

"Once we find Kyle, you'll be able to return to him, if you want."

Kyle shrugged and glanced away.

"What about Kyle? Did you see anything that might help us find him?"

Kai shook his head. "Kyle is asleep and Prince Finn is in a strange room with their other lover while water rains down on them."

"Rain falling inside a building?" Dax asked. "I've never heard of such a thing."

"Me neither, but that's what I saw." Kai blushed as he spoke.

"And what else did you see?" Dax whispered. "I know you saw something. I can tell from your face."

"Prince Finn's other lover is called Jake. I heard him shout his name out this time."

"Why was he shouting? Are they in some sort of trouble?"

Kai rubbed his nose and refused to meet Dax's gaze. "No trouble that I could see. His shouting probably had something to do with being fucked up against the wall."

"What? Again? It's not even the solstice." Dax had never heard of mermen who had sex as much as Kyle and Finn seemed to these days. What had happened to Kyle to turn him into this sex-crazed maniac?

"You do realize it doesn't have to be the solstice to have

sex?" Kai asked. Dax thought he could trace a hint of sarcasm in his tone.

"Of course I do," he replied as he flipped round and began the final stretch toward the shore. He checked behind him once to see Kai following him, just as he knew he would be.

They arrived on the deserted beach a short while later. Dax dragged himself out of the surf, and when Kai seemed to struggle, he helped him too.

"Sorry," Kai said. "I'm still not used to coming to land."

"I know. You did good. Now let's dry off before any humans spot us."

It didn't take long to change from their half-fish forms. Dax shivered from the chill in the air. Although the mer were quite good at adapting to colder climates, Dax truly did prefer to bask in the warmth of the sun.

Kai gave Dax a huge grin.

"What is it?" Dax asked.

"We made it."

"Of course. Did you doubt it?"

"Maybe a little. Now that we're here in the land of humans, I can't wait to see everything."

"I'm enjoying the view from right here," Dax teased as he gave Kai a sweeping glance.

Kai blushed a dark shade of scarlet, but didn't lower his eyes.

Someone coughed behind them and Dax twisted round to see who had crept up on them. A handsome man in strange human garments watched them with a faint smile.

"Would you like me to leave you alone while you gaze into each other's eyes like lovesick puppies for a little longer?" the man asked with a quirk of his eyebrow.

"Who are you?" Dax asked.

"What's a puppy?" Kai added.

"My name is Caspian. I'm here to tell you both to return to the ocean and for Kai to swim back to Atlantis as quickly as he can."

"We only just got here," Kai pointed out.

Dax guessed help from Caspian was out of the question.

"Yes, I know. I'm sorry you've had a wasted trip, but unfortunately we weren't aware you had left the city until you arrived on land. It would appear someone has been cloaking you from us."

"Us?"

"My sister and I," Caspian clarified as he turned to Kai. "You would know my sister as the Goddess of Prophecy. I'm fairly certain she will have told you when you came into your powers your home from that day forward would be Atlantis."

Kai scowled up at the god. "She didn't tell me I'd be a prisoner there."

"You have everything you could want for in Atlantis."

"Except my freedom."

"Nevertheless, you must go back to the city immediately."

Kai got to his feet so he could look Caspian in the eye. Dax could tell he was annoyed to find the god still towered over him by several inches. "You want me to go back there, you'll have to make me."

"That's easily done," Caspian replied with a smirk of satisfaction.

Dax and Kai waited for him to do his worst, but nothing happened. Caspian's smug smile vanished, replaced by a scowl of his own.

"Damn it," he muttered.

A moment later Cari appeared on the beach alongside her brother. "What is it?" she asked.

"I can't send them back," Caspian explained with a wave of his hand toward Kai and Dax.

"Just banish them back to my temple," Cari replied.

"I've already tried. I can't send them to your temple or mine either. Can you try?"

Cari closed her eyes in apparent concentration. When she opened them again she shook her head. "We're being blocked."

"Medina," Caspian muttered. "It has to be."

Cari nodded. "No one else has the power to block you and…"

"And what?"

"She did stop by and visit me a little while ago. She was quite vocal in her annoyance about the virgin status of my Oracles."

"Why didn't you tell me?"

Kai's blush flared up again. "Does *everyone* have to know I've never had sex?" he muttered.

Caspian pointed at Kai. "He refuses to return to the ocean."

Cari glared at Kai. "You must go back to Atlantis immediately."

Kai snorted. "Your orders are far less intimidating than your brother's, and if he can't make me go back, there's no way you can."

"Maybe a compromise," Dax suggested. "Kai stays here on land until we find Kyle, then I'll escort him back to the city."

"Don't make my decisions for me," Kai snapped.

"I'm only trying to help."

"There will be no compromise," Cari interrupted, before they could get into a full-blown argument. "You will both return to the city immediately."

"I'm not going anywhere," Dax argued. "I've come all this way to make sure Kyle is okay. I'm not going to turn back now."

"Kyle is perfectly well," Caspian replied. "Something I'm sure you already know, since Kai no doubt used his powers to see him during your journey."

"I want to speak to him myself. I've a message from his sister."

Caspian sighed. "If you insist on seeing him, I won't try to stop you. But Kai needs to leave right now."

"Kai comes with me," Dax stated.

"The Oracles must stay in Atlantis," Cari said. "You don't understand, but it's imperative Kai returns."

148

"Why?" Kai asked.

"The three Oracles are at their most powerful when they are together."

"Your powers make ours pale in comparison. I don't see why you even need Oracles, let alone why we need to live in the sunken city."

Cari looked at her brother, who gave a small shake of his head. "You have your powers for a reason."

"I don't care. I never wanted them, I don't like them, and I wish you'd chosen someone else to inflict them on. I hate living in the sunken city. Come on, Dax, let's go find Kyle."

"There are over sixty million people living in England," Caspian told them. "Do you think you'll find him without our help?"

"I have my powers," Kai replied. "We'll manage. We weren't even sure he was still in this place, but thanks to you at least we won't have to travel to other human lands."

"Your powers won't work while you're in human form," Cari said. "This is as far as your quest takes you."

"I don't think so. I'll just take mer form to look for him until I find the information we need to track him down."

Caspian sighed with obvious frustration. "Clearly there's going to be no reasoning with them. We might as well send them to Kyle's home and get this over with."

"Absolutely not," Cari replied. "And you aren't to help them either."

"I'm sworn to help all mer who come to the land of humans."

"I forbid it," Cari snapped. "No languages or knowledge of this world, nothing."

"Cari, I made a vow."

"The bigger picture is far more important than your personal penance. You are *not* to help them."

Caspian looked Kai and Dax up and down. "At least let me give them some clothes."

"No help at all," Cari repeated. "And I'll know if you disobey me."

"Cari, be reasonable! I can't let them run around town naked. They'll end up in jail in no time."

Dax didn't know what jail was, though he expected it might be something similar to the palace dungeons. Caspian's tone didn't make it sound too pleasant.

"Maybe spending a little time in a human prison will be enough to make them see sense," Cari replied as she vanished into thin air, her last words lingering on the winter breeze.

Dax took Kai's hand and tugged him away from the ocean. "Come on, let's start our search."

"You can't just walk around town with no clothes on," Caspian called after them.

"Then give us some clothes, if it bothers you so much," Dax shouted back without bothering to stop.

"You know I can't help you."

"We didn't ask for your help," Dax pointed out. "And we don't need it. We're not stupid. We'll figure out this world on our own."

Dax glanced back over his shoulder just in time to see Caspian disappear.

"They didn't seem happy about me staying on land," Kai said.

Dax wrapped his arm around Kai's shoulders and gave him a quick hug. "You're not a pawn of the gods. You're a merman with free will. If you don't want to go back to the ocean, you don't have to."

"But they're gods," Kai reminded him. "They have powers. What if they try to make me?"

"They already did," Dax said. "They couldn't send you back with their powers."

"Caspian mentioned Medina. Do you think she's protecting us from their powers?"

"Maybe. And if my guess is correct, Medina is more powerful than either Caspian or Cari, which means we can stay here as long as we want."

"What if I want it to be the rest of my life?" Kai asked

quietly.

"Then you better find some clothes," Dax teased.

Kai laughed as they approached the edge of the beach. The ground under their feet changed from sand to a strange material he had never seen before. It was hard, not soft and giving like the sand. Some of the stones were sharp and painful on the soles. The horrible surface stretched off to both the left and the right. There was nothing to tell them the best way to go.

There were several human buildings nearby, but no one seemed to be about.

"What's that noise?" Dax cocked his head, listening to something Kai hadn't yet heard. "It's coming from over there."

Kai looked in the direction Dax pointed and saw the strange human vehicle heading in their direction. "It's what humans use for traveling," he said, vaguely recalling seeing one in a vision. Kyle had been sitting in one with Jake. Kai had no idea how they worked, but he had figured out Jake was the one controlling the machine.

"It's coming in our direction," Dax said as he tugged Kai back onto the sand and yanked him out of sight. It passed by at a speed Kai didn't realize humans could travel at. Kai clapped his hands over his ears to shut out the noise it made.

"Maybe the human inside would have helped us," Kai said as he lowered his hands.

"Or maybe they would take us to the jail Cari talked about," Dax countered. "I'm not taking any chances. We need to find some human garments to cover ourselves with."

Kai agreed. He studied one of the nearby houses, but quickly discarded the idea of approaching it. The humans living there might have them arrested too. "What do you suggest?"

"I don't know," Dax admitted. "It's a pity Medina isn't

showing up to help us now that we need her."

"So, you believe in the gods now?" Kai teased.

"Like you said, it's a bit hard not to when they're right in front you."

"Maybe we could make up a story about how we lost our clothes?" Kai suggested. "Surely if we explain it was an accident or not our fault we won't be sent to this jail?"

"Maybe." Dax rose slowly, checked no more vehicles were in sight, and pulled Kai to his feet once more. "Let's see if we can find some garments by ourselves first."

Dax set a fast pace down the hard surface, and Kai hurried to keep up with him. The steps became increasingly painful, and before long, he was limping. Dax didn't seem to be troubled by the ground, but Kai suspected he had spent far more time on land. The soles of his feet had probably hardened years ago, unlike Kai, who, until leaving Atlantis, hadn't seen his toes since he hit puberty.

As they walked, Kai scanned the area for both humans or for spare clothes someone might have just left lying around, waiting for them to find. Unfortunately, the only item of clothing they came across was a small hand warmer with holes for each finger. Kai suspected it had belonged to a human child. He left it where it was, beneath the hedge.

"Medina!" Dax shouted.

Kai raised an eyebrow.

"I thought it might be worth a try. Caspian obviously knew as soon as we arrived on land. Surely she can tell we're here and need help too?"

"Maybe she thinks we'll do all right on our own," Kai said. He wasn't so sure they would, but right now they didn't have any choice.

They continued to wander away from the ocean. Although Kai had been used to cooler waters growing up, he shivered a little in the chilly air. Dax seemed to be suffering in the cold too. He rubbed his arms and continually quickened his pace, perhaps thinking the strenuousness of running would help to keep him warm.

A couple more vehicles passed them. When the first approached, the two mermen ducked into some nearby bushes until it had gone. Unfortunately, when the second one appeared on the horizon they were on a stretch of land where there was nothing to hide behind.

"Shit," Kai muttered as the two of them ducked down, hoping the humans wouldn't see them.

The loud honking noise made it clear they had been spotted, as did the raucous laughter and fingers pointed at them.

"At least we didn't get taken to jail," Kai said after the group in the vehicle had continued on their way.

Dax glared after the disappearing hecklers. "I think we need to make finding clothes a priority."

Kai snorted. "I thought it already was. In case you haven't noticed, they don't exactly leave piles of them on the ground for naked mermen to find."

Dax flinched and Kai wished he could take back his harsh words. "I'm sorry," he offered. "I know it's not your fault."

"Don't worry," Dax assured him as he wrapped him up in a warm embrace. "We'll manage."

Kai's human body reacted immediately and his cock hardened. "You should probably let me go," he said, though he made no effort to step out of Dax's arms.

Dax didn't release him either. If anything, he pulled him closer. Dax's hardness brushed against his own and Kai couldn't stop the whimper of desire.

"I don't think humans have public sex," Kai whispered.

Dax chuckled. "Considering how they cover up their bodies, I think you're probably right."

Kai shivered as Dax caressed his back and arse, stroking him with purpose. Kai bit down on his lip to stifle a whimper of desire. Dax licked at his ear and sucked the lobe into his mouth. Kai had never thought of his ears as particularly sensitive, but right now his left ear seemed to be directly connected to his cock. Each time Dax nipped on his ear a wave of longing shot through Kai.

Dax clamped his lips down on Kai's neck hard enough to leave a mark on Kai's skin. Kai didn't care. The sensation of Dax sucking on his neck was something he had never experienced before and he wanted more. He tilted his head to give Dax better access.

"Anyone who sees this will know you're mine," Dax told him before he licked across the place he had marked.

"Yours?" Kai asked. He felt the first glimmer of hope that he might mean something more to Dax than just another merman to fuck during the mating season.

Dax grabbed his arse and squeezed it tightly. "Oh yes. I want you, Kai. Right now."

"Humans don't do public sex, remember?"

Dax leaned down to murmur into Kai's ear. "I remember, but there's one thing you're forgetting. We're not humans. We're mermen, and right now I want you too badly to wait."

Kai clung to Dax as he kissed him hard on the lips. Kai moaned as he rubbed against Dax. It wasn't the mating season, yet he felt as though his body was on fire everywhere Dax touched him. Was Dax's desire for him now, outside of the mating season, a sign he had given Kai his heart? Kai hoped so, because right now he didn't know if he had the strength of will to push Dax away.

Kai suddenly felt a hand on his body that wasn't Dax's. He jumped and faced the two angry humans who had interrupted them.

The two men were dressed in nearly identical clothing, and their vehicle wasn't plain like the others they had seen. It was bright yellow and blue, had human writing on it and some kind of blue light on the top. From the harsh expressions on the faces of the humans Kai had a feeling they were in trouble. They should have been more careful to stay out of sight until they had found some clothing. Unfortunately, it was too late now.

The bigger of the men said something, but since he used the language of humans Kai had no idea what.

"I don't understand you," Kai said. He didn't expect either of them to understand mer, but he thought it worth a try. He and Dax weren't the first mermen to come to land. They were certainly overdue some luck. Unfortunately, it still wasn't with them and neither of the humans appeared to speak mer.

The man who had spoken said something else. This time the words he used sounded slightly different, more clipped and sharper. Kai suspected it might be another language, but since it still wasn't mer he had no clue what he said.

The two strangers conversed quietly with each other. The one who hadn't spoken shook his head at something the first man had said.

Dax grabbed hold of Kai's hand and gave it a quick squeeze. He leaned in to whisper in his ear. "Run."

Before Kai could say anything in reply Dax was moving, dragging him along with him. Kai stumbled a little at the sudden movement, but he quickly recovered and they ran as fast as they could towards some trees in the distance. Kai knew instinctively Dax's plan was to lose the humans in the trees. He chanced a quick look over his shoulder and saw the men were already giving chase. They were far too close for Kai's liking and he let go of Dax's hand and picked up his speed, overtaking Dax momentarily.

One of the humans shouted something. Even without knowing the language, Kai had a pretty good idea whatever it was meant stop. He ignored the command and raced toward the tree line.

Kai realized Dax was no longer beside him. He glanced back and saw Dax was tiring. While both mermen could swim at speeds that could outstrip some of the fastest creatures in the sea, neither of them was used to running.

"They're gaining on us," Kai called, trying to encourage Dax to hurry.

Dax looked back and as he did he stumbled again. Kai raced back to Dax. Whatever the humans had in store for them, they were in this together. Kai had no intention of leaving Dax behind.

When Dax saw Kai heading back to him he waved him on. "Run, Kai."

"Not without you," Kai replied between pants. He wasn't sure how much farther he would have made it, but he wasn't going anywhere without Dax at his side.

The humans were upon them within a few seconds. The head start they had managed while the men were talking hadn't been long enough to gain them any real advantage.

Kai may not have been a warrior himself, but he recognized the stance of human warriors when he saw it. These men were ready and willing to fight. Kai took hold of Dax's hand and pulled him away from the threat.

"It's not our fault we've got no clothes," he told them. Neither of the humans appeared to understand his words. So much for them being sympathetic to their predicament.

The men reached out to take hold of Dax, and Kai's anger flared at the rough way they grabbed him. He clenched his hand into a fist and swung at the smaller of the men, hitting him squarely in the jaw.

They turned on him so fast he barely had time to register what was happening. He wished they hadn't decided to leave their weapons in the sea before coming to land. It seemed there were predators here as well as under the waves.

Kai struggled against the men and he could see Dax doing the same. They might have had a chance if a second vehicle, this one making a horrendous wailing noise, hadn't arrived, bringing more humans for them to fight. Outnumbered as they now were, Kai knew they didn't have any real chance of escaping, but they gave it a damn good try. He got several good blows in, and he saw from the corner of his eye Dax held his own as well.

Instead of keeping his attention on his opponents, Kai found his gaze wandering to Dax, worrying about how he fared. Because his attention lapsed, he missed the man with the restraints until it was too late to stop him.

Kai struggled against the strange things the man had put round his wrists, but they seemed to tighten the more he yanked against them. He elbowed the human behind him, but trussed up as he was, he couldn't get the angle quite right.

Dax appeared to realize the fight was over and they couldn't win against so many humans. He didn't struggle as they restrained him too. The men were still talking to them.

"We don't understand you!" Kai yelled at them. "We don't speak your language."

None of the newcomers understood mer either. They stopped speaking to them and pulled them towards the nearest of the vehicles, manhandling Kai inside the machine.

Kai felt sick when he realized they were taking Dax to the other one. "No!" he shouted as they slammed the door on him. He pushed against it, but it wasn't so easy to open as it appeared. He banged against the window with his bound fists until one of the men climbed into the seat in front and turned to shout at him. Again, his meaning was pretty obvious. Shut up and stop being difficult came through loud and clear.

Kai twisted in his seat and looked to see where they were taking Dax. Dax continued to struggle against his captors, trying to get to Kai, but they were having none of it. The humans bundled him into the back of the second vehicle.

One of the men in the front spoke and Kai heard a strange-sounding voice respond. It wasn't either of the men who were with him, but there was no one else there. He wondered what sort of magic it was that someone could be there, talking to them, but remaining invisible. He had never heard of humans being able to do such things, but then again, he had never had any contact with them save through his visions, and if a human was invisible, how would he see one in his vision any easier than he could here?

Kai returned to staring out of the window, focusing on

the vehicle following behind them. The one thing that held his panic at bay was that they were, at least for the moment, going in the same direction. He wasn't sure what he would do if he lost sight of Dax. He didn't think he could do this alone. He wished their telepathic powers worked on land. More than anything he wanted to hear Dax's strong and sure voice in his head.

Chapter Eleven

It wasn't long before the vehicle drew up in front of a large building. Dax breathed a sigh of relief when he saw he and Kai were being taken to the same place. He was also glad the contraption had stopped moving, since he felt rather queasy from the twists and turns the short journey had required.

"Kai!" he called as the humans pulled him from the vehicle.

Kai heard his call, but when he tried to walk over to him, one of the men took his arm and stopped him in his tracks.

The man nearest to Dax chuckled and said something to cause his companion to snicker into his hand. Dax had no idea what his comment had been, but he had a feeling he and Kai were being laughed at again. He snarled at the two men, neither of whom seemed particularly bothered. They nudged Dax toward the same doorway Kai had gone through, and a few moments later, Dax found himself standing inside a real, human building for the first time.

There were a lot of people inside, many of them dressed in the same way as the men who had brought them here. Everyone seemed to be staring at him and Kai.

"Have you never seen a naked man before?" Dax shouted out to the room in general. No one replied, not in mer anyway.

"They can't understand you," Caspian said. Dax jumped, startled to see the god appear at the side of him.

"I figured that out for myself."

"Then why do you keep talking to them in mer?"

"Because it's the only language I know and I thought

maybe some humans might know it. We aren't the first to come to land."

Caspian nodded. "There are a few humans who, thanks to me, can understand and speak mer. But you won't find any of them in this place."

"I didn't see any harm in trying." Dax glared at the god. "Are you going to help us now?"

"No, he's not," Cari replied from Dax's other side.

Even though Cari was clothed, she seemed out of place compared with the other humans. Caspian appeared to fit in perfectly well, but his sister's attire was as incongruous as his and Kai's nakedness. Dax found it odd that no one stared at her, until he realized the goddess and her brother were invisible to the humans. This was quickly followed by the comprehension that it must appear as though he were talking to himself.

"Cari, we can't just leave them here in jail," Caspian said.

"They shouldn't have got themselves arrested," Cari replied. "It's not as if you didn't warn them about wandering around naked."

"It's not like they had any other option," Caspian countered.

"Some time in a human prison might encourage them to do as they are told," Cari stated. "Let me see, there's resisting arrest, assaulting police officers and, my personal favorite, indecent exposure."

"Cari…" Dax could hear the warning in Caspian's voice. "This isn't fair and you know it."

"They should have gone back to the ocean when I told them to."

Caspian stepped closer to his sister, getting right into her face. "Don't make me lock you down."

"You wouldn't dare."

"Watch me."

Dax wanted to back away from the two battling gods, but there wasn't anywhere he could go.

Suddenly the room shook. An earthquake, much like the

ones to hit the sunken city not so long ago, made everything shudder and shake.

"Grandfather," Caspian said, just loud enough for Dax to hear.

Dax watched as another god, for surely he had to be such a being, materialized in the middle of the room. Like Cari, his clothes were somewhat inappropriate. He wore a gray robe with gold trim, wrapped around his body.

"Grandfather," Cari greeted him with a small curtsy. "You've woken at last."

The new god stared around the room with a frown of apparent confusion. "What is this strange place?"

"The modern world," Caspian replied with a bow. "This is a police station."

"A what?"

Dax stayed quiet, wanting to know the answer to that question himself. He was thankful at least he could understand the gods, even if he couldn't understand the humans. He wondered why that was.

"A place where they bring humans who have broken the law," Caspian explained.

"And why are you here?"

"I want to help these two mermen who have come to land and got themselves into a little trouble."

"More mermen?" Caspian's grandfather asked. "Haven't you learnt your lesson in that regard yet?"

Caspian visibly bristled.

Cari pointed at Kai. "That one is an Oracle. He has no business being on land."

"Then send him back to the ocean," the new god replied with a fair amount of impatience.

"I can't."

"Why not?"

"Because they're under the protection of Medina. I tried to send them back before, but couldn't do it."

"Can you help?" Caspian asked.

Dax fidgeted under the god's steely gaze. "I don't want to

go back to the ocean yet."

The god gestured to the room around them. "You would prefer to stay here?"

"No." Dax ignored the staring humans. He knew it must appear as if he was talking to himself, but he didn't care.

"Grandfather, you *have* to send them back to Atlantis," Cari insisted.

Her grandfather turned to her with a withering glare. "I am Antar, God of Time and Space. Do not presume to tell me what I must do. Granddaughter or not, I won't take orders from you or any other goddess."

"Times have changed," Cari snapped back. "Women are far more powerful in this time and I think I can hold my own against a god who has been sleeping for hundreds of years."

"Do you?" Antar replied icily.

Cari buckled, falling to her knees with a cry of pain.

"I trust you recall your place now?" Antar asked her.

"Yes, Grandfather," Cari whispered.

Antar faced Dax again. He stared at him for several long minutes. "Yes, this one is protected by Medina. No magic will work on him if it is contrary to what he desires himself."

"What do you mean?" Dax asked. "Is there other magic?"

"Of course. There are many types. Magic that would assist you in your quest, giving you the language of humans for example, would be quite effective."

"Can you do that?"

"Yes."

"Please," Dax begged. "We don't know what anyone here is saying to us and they can't understand us either."

"I said I could, not that I would," Antar replied. "I will, however, turn back time to when you first came to land. Perhaps this time you will make better choices."

With a flash of lightning the world around him changed and Dax found himself back on the beach. Kai sat beside him staring at him with wide eyes.

"Do you remember what happened?" Dax asked him.

Kai nodded. "I think we need to get out of here, right now, before those gods turn up again."

"I don't think they will this time," Dax said. "They know we aren't going back into the ocean and they aren't going to help us find Kyle. We're on our own."

"Not quite," Caspian announced from behind them once more. "I won't give you the human language, but I'll risk the wrath of my darling sister by at least giving you some clothes."

"Why would you do that and not help us in any other way?"

"Because any other way would involve using magic," Caspian explained. "Clothes I can provide without my powers. Cari need never know."

"How is it we can understand you and the other gods?" Dax asked. "I thought you might be speaking mer, but now I'm not so sure."

"We speak Atlantean, but it doesn't matter what we speak — whoever is in our presence will always hear our words in their own language, except such words that have no translation — jail and police station, for example."

Dax didn't know how that worked exactly, but he didn't question it.

"Don't concern yourself with language barriers," Caspian said. "You've more pressing things to worry about. Here, cover yourselves up." With a grin he tossed a strange sack onto the sand and vanished.

Dax opened the bag and saw the human garments inside. "Come on, quickly," he said as he pulled the clothing out and tossed some of them to Kai. "Let's get covered up before any more humans see us."

The clothes felt strange against his skin and Dax soon realized the leg coverings were tight and restrictive. The partial erection he had gotten the moment he looked at Kai's naked body got in the way of doing up the fastenings. A glance at Kai revealed he had similar difficulties.

Dax was about to suggest they help each other out, but

the sound of some kind of animal approaching them halted his words on his tongue. The creature was followed by a human woman, who thankfully hadn't seen them yet. The thought of being taken prisoner again killed his erection. He swiftly covered himself up. Kai did likewise, and they hurried inland once more.

This time they didn't bother to hide from the vehicles when they passed them. The humans continued on their journeys without taking any notice. There were no shouts or jeers, and when the two of them passed other people walking they were greeted with nods and smiles or ignored completely.

"Quite a difference clothes make," Kai said.

Dax agreed. "Let's ask the next person we see if they can help us find Kyle."

"We still can't speak their language," Kai reminded him.

"Do you have any other suggestions?"

"No."

"Then the next person we meet, we'll try to ask."

They continued walking for another ten minutes or so, until a woman pushing a strange contraption with a human baby inside approached in the opposite direction. She didn't appear threatening in any way, so Dax raised his hand to draw her to a halt. The young mother looked at them with clear apprehension.

"We need help," Dax said.

The woman frowned and shook her head. She said something in the human language which Dax guessed was something along the lines of not understanding them. She began to walk away, but Kai moved into her path.

"Kyle," he said clearly and slowly. "Kyle."

"Kyle?" the woman repeated.

Kai nodded. He raised his hand to what he hoped was Kyle's height. Having never seen him on land he wasn't entirely sure it was right, but he gave his best guess. With more gestures, Kai tried to explain Kyle had dark hair like hers, but Dax wasn't sure he was getting his point across.

Eventually they gave up and let her continue on her way. She clearly didn't know the name Kyle.

"Maybe someone else will have heard of him," Dax said. "That's just one human."

"Perhaps."

"We just have to keep searching for him. Hopefully someone will recognize his name and point us in the right direction."

As they carried on walking Dax noticed more and more buildings around them. He shivered when he saw the human jail they had been taken to before. He quickly tugged Kai in another direction rather than approach it.

They stopped several people, but no one seemed able to help them. One old man pointed them in the direction of a building where people purchased various strange objects, but while one of the men working in there answered to the name of Kyle, he wasn't the merman they searched for, just a human who happened to share his name.

All day they wandered the area without success.

"I'm hungry," Kai complained as they watched a group of people eating some strange yellow things the size of fingers.

They had soon discovered human food cost money and since they didn't have any currency, they had no way of buying anything.

Even though they had been approaching people in the community all day, they hadn't traveled far from the beach where they had arrived. Dax could still taste the salt in the air.

"Let's go back to the ocean for the night," he suggested. "We can find some food there."

Kai didn't argue with him and they set off back in the direction they had come. Maybe tomorrow they would head away from the beach and have better luck finding Kyle there.

Chapter Twelve

By the time they arrived back at the beach, the air had become bitterly cold. The sun had almost disappeared below the horizon, and the wind had picked up quite a lot.

More worrying than the weather was the group of young men and women who had gathered on the shore. Strange music played, getting louder the nearer they approached. The noise didn't sound anything like music Ula created with her shell instruments. It appeared to be some sort of party. Several of the revelers moved rhythmically to the music coming from the box, while others ate and drank as they congregated round a large fire.

"Damn it," Dax muttered as he realized they couldn't enter the ocean from this part of the beach without being seen.

"Maybe they'll let us warm up by the fire," Kai suggested as he rubbed his arms. The clothing Caspian had provided them with covered them up, but did little else. The garments worn by the party-goers appeared far thicker and much more suitable for the climate.

Dax wasn't entirely sure about approaching such a large group of humans, but when he saw Kai shivering he nodded.

The humans greeted them with wide smiles as they joined them. They didn't seem to mind the two of them warming up by the fire. Kai held out his hands toward the flames, enjoying the heat.

When Kai's stomach growl loudly, one of the girls held out a box with some kind of circular-shaped food inside, cut into segments. Dax had no idea what it was, but it smelled delicious. Apparently a rumbling stomach didn't need a translation. Several people around the fire were eating the segments, so Dax and Kai helped themselves to a slice each.

Dax hissed when the food burned his fingers. He had never eaten anything that had been heated up before. There were, of course, no fires underwater, and even on the islands it was rare to have one. On the coldest nights of the year the mer tended to stay beneath the waves. The only real exception was the night of the winter solstice, and since on that night every merman and mermaid suffered with the mating fever, they didn't bother with lighting fires for warmth. Dax had never heard of warming food to eat.

"It doesn't seem to be doing the humans any harm," Kai said before he took a large bite out of his slice. "Hmm, try it Dax, it's *really* good."

"What do you think it is?" he asked, still hesitant to take a bite.

"I've no idea."

"What does it taste of?"

Kai rolled his eyes. "Like nothing I've ever eaten before. I can't describe it, just try some for yourself."

Dax squinted at his own portion dubiously.

"Coward," Kai teased as he quickly polished off his slice.

The human holding the box with the slices in laughed and pushed it toward Kai, who helped himself to a second piece. He offered a thank you, even though they couldn't understand what he said.

Dax gingerly bit into his slice and found Kai was right. He had never tasted anything so delicious. He tried speaking to them in mer, to ask what it was, but unsurprisingly he received blank expressions and shakes of the head in response.

As the evening turned to night it became clear the group didn't intend to go home any time soon. Some of the humans stumbled in the sand as they struggled to keep their balance.

Across the other side of the fire a young man and woman

were locked at the lips and the youth had his hand firmly on the breast of the female. He slipped his hand inside her garment, and Dax could see her pawing at his groin.

One of the revelers shouted something at the couple and threw an empty drink container at them. Everyone laughed, and even though Dax couldn't understand the joke, he smiled at the way everyone was having such a good time. These people were far more like the mer than the other humans they had encountered. They didn't mind showing affection for each other in public.

A dark-haired youth passed Dax and Kai a drink, and they each took a long swallow of the liquid. Dax wasn't sure he liked the taste much, but it was better than nothing. Under the ocean they didn't need to drink to survive, but the longer they stayed in their human forms the more dehydrated they would become.

Kai seemed to enjoy the drink, and quickly finished off his bottle. Their new friends passed him another and he took a long swig of that one too.

The humans cheered him loudly, apparently impressed with Kai for some reason. Dax wasn't sure why and he couldn't ask, but as long as they weren't being taken prisoner he didn't care.

Dax watched one of the girls pull Kai to his feet and drag him over to the humans jumping around to the music box. Kai wove unsteadily, and Dax wondered if something might be wrong with him. He seemed to set himself to rights and joined the girl, trying to mimic her movements. Dax squashed down the jealousy at the sight of the human female's hands on Kai's arse. Kai didn't push her away. Dax gritted his teeth and wished several horrible fates on the unsuspecting girl.

A giggling blonde dropped down beside him. She said something, but Dax could only shrug and shake his head.

"Vicky," the girl said, pointing to herself. "Vicky."

Dax repeated the word and pointed at himself. She chuckled and shook her head. She pointed at one of the others. "Liam."

When she got to the fourth person Dax realized she was telling him their names. He nodded and pointed at himself. "Dax."

"Dax," she repeated. She looked over at Kai and gestured in his direction.

"Kai," Dax told her.

Vicky smiled and repeated their names again. Then she picked up her drink. "Beer," she said as she took a swallow.

Dax had no idea what the name meant, but repeating the word back made her smile.

She pointed over to Kai and said something Dax didn't understand.

Kai continued to move clumsily with the girl Vicky told him was named Madeline. Kai either didn't notice or didn't mind she was practically throwing herself at him. She pushed her hands under his clothes and dragged him close against her. Dax shot her a black look.

Vicky said something to him, but the only word he understood was Kai's name.

Then Madeline tried to kiss Kai. Dax jumped up and immediately fell back to the ground. The world swayed about him and he felt strange and disoriented. He wanted to drag Kai away from the girl, but he suddenly felt ill and it he didn't think his queasiness was because of the sight of Madeline trying to shove her tongue into *his* Kai's mouth.

Vicky pushed a bottle into his hand and encouraged him to take another drink.

Kai pushed Madeline away. "No," he told her firmly, though to Dax's ears his voice sounded strangely slurred.

Madeline didn't seem to understand Kai any more than they understood the humans, but something did seem to register when Kai pointed over to Dax. He wasn't sure if it was Kai's gesture or his own glare that got the message across that she shouldn't be touching Kai. Either way, she stepped back and let Kai make his way back to Dax.

Kai flopped down beside Dax and wrapped his arm

around Dax's shoulders. "Want you," he slurred into his ear.

Dax took another drink rather than respond. Even if Kai had forgotten what had happened the last time they had got intimate in public, he hadn't. Although the group here seemed far more relaxed and open than the others, he didn't want to take any chances.

He patted Kai's knee and handed him a bottle of beer. "Drink this. You must be thirsty after all that hopping about."

"Were you jealous?" Kai whispered.

"No," Dax lied.

"Did you enjoy seeing her touch me?"

"Of course not."

"Then you *were* jealous."

Dax scowled at Kai. "Maybe a little," he admitted.

Kai leaned into him and rested his head on his shoulder. "I like these humans."

"Me too," Dax replied with a laugh. "But I don't think they'd be agreeable to us having sex in front of them."

"Those two over there are practically having sex already," Kai muttered. "Look at them. His cock is nearly poking out of his clothes."

"Stop staring at other men's cocks," Dax scolded. "Isn't mine enough for you?"

"I don't know," Kai whispered. "You've not put it in me yet, have you?"

Dax, who had chosen that moment to take another drink, spat it out in surprise.

Even though Vicky had no idea what they were talking about, she must have got some sort of gist of the conversation because she blushed and focused her attention on speaking to a young man on the far side of the fire. A moment later Dax realized what she had seen. Kai slipped his hand closer to Dax's crotch than propriety allowed.

"Let me see it again," Kai begged as he shoved his hand into Dax's clothes. Dax hardened instantly to Kai's touch and he couldn't stop his loud groan of pleasure at the way Kai's fingers wrapped around his dick.

Feeling a little self-conscious — a new experience for the merman — Dax grabbed Kai's wrist and stopped his play. "Let's move away from the fire," he suggested. Maybe if they moved to somewhere darker they would be safe from the others noticing what they were doing.

Although the couple on the other side of the fire had been groping each other for some time, they hadn't gone anywhere near as far as Dax wanted to go with Kai right now. Touching and stroking wasn't going to be enough for him. He wanted to be inside the younger merman. He wanted to take Kai's erection between his lips and drink down his seed. Vicky's beer just didn't have the same appeal.

With some difficulty, since Kai wouldn't take his hand off of Dax's cock, they moved out of the light, slightly away from the rest of the group.

Dax eased Kai down onto the sand again and pressed their lips together. Kai's lips were warm and soft, yet unmoving against his own. Dax drew back, wondering what could be wrong. The answer soon became obvious.

Kai snored loudly, passed out on the beach, and was clearly not going to be taking part in any sexual activity any time soon. Dax shook his head and sighed. Apparently his kisses had put Kai to sleep, leaving Dax hard, aching, and in for a long night.

Vicky glanced in his direction and he caught the flicker of amusement on her face. She held up a bottle and waggled it enticingly. Dax nodded, and after checking Kai was comfortable, left him to sleep and crawled back over to the fire. He took the bottle from Vicky and drank deeply.

She pointed to the humans swaying to the noise box. "Dancing."

Dax tested the word, not sure whether she referred to the humans, what they were doing, or the noise. Either way he had difficulty wrapping his tongue around the new word.

His voice sounded strange to his own ears. "Danshing."

Vicky passed him a slice of the strange food they had been eating earlier. "Pizza," she explained.

A spark of a memory came to him. Justin talking about the foods he missed. Now Dax understood what one of them was. But again, Dax had trouble saying the word. Things seemed to spin out of focus a little and he felt a bit light-headed. He tried not to let it bother him and took a bite of the pizza. It was lukewarm now, rather than piping hot.

They passed the rest of the night in much the same fashion. Eating cold pizza, drinking beer, and with Vicky pointing out things around them and telling him the names. Dax tried to tell her his words for the same things, but just as he had having trouble speaking the human language, Vicky's ability to speak was similarly impaired. She gave it her best effort, before quickly dissolving into giggles.

The world swam in and out of focus. The couple on the other side of the fire disappeared into one of the vehicles near the edge of the beach.

"Car," Vicky said.

Again, Dax was confused. Did she mean the vehicle was called a car, or did she refer to what the couple was no doubt doing inside it?

He decided it probably didn't matter.

One of the men joined them for a while. He spoke to Vicky and pointed at Dax. Vicky shook her head and said something in response while gesturing between Dax and Kai. He couldn't understand anything, other than his name and Kai's.

The man, Vicky called him Eric, pointed at Dax and said a new word. "Gay?"

It sounded like a question, but Dax didn't know what he meant. Had he got his name wrong? He shook his head and patted his chest. "Dax."

Vicky laughed and pointed to him, then Kai. "Gay," she repeated.

Dax didn't know what she meant.

Eric laughed, pointed at Dax and Kai, and made a familiar gesture with his hands. *That* Dax understood. While the mer didn't have any real form of sign language, a few chose to communicate underwater with their hands and body language, rather than telepathy. Every young merman quickly picked up the universal sign for fucking. Dax found it amusing humans apparently had the same gesture.

He nodded to confirm he had understood what he meant.

"Gay," Vicky repeated with more points at him and Kai.

Guessing the word meant sex and they were asking if he and Kai had sex together, Dax nodded again. It wasn't strictly true, but he was sure it soon would be. The last thing he wanted was for some human to come between the two of them, before he had been given the chance to make Kai his own.

In twos and threes the humans left the beach in their vehicles. They took the music machine with them, as well as most of the remaining bottles of beer. They left a couple behind for Dax and Kai.

Finally, the beach was quiet and only the two mermen were left on the sand.

Kai still snored away and Dax didn't want to disturb him. They didn't need to return to the ocean for food now. They had both eaten enough to stave off the hunger pangs. A trip under the waves for Kai to use his powers could wait until morning.

Dax drank another bottle of beer. He had lost count of how many he'd had during the course of the night. He felt a little sick, and when he crawled over to Kai his stomach rolled. He didn't even try to walk.

Tired and ill, he dropped his head onto Kai's chest. The younger merman didn't stir.

Dax watched the waves rolling in. The tide was going out, so at least they wouldn't be woken any time soon by a soaking from the incoming waves.

Closing his eyes, he listened to Kai's heartbeat against his ear. Tomorrow they would take a quick swim in the ocean, and if Kai's vision didn't help them locate Kyle, they would search in the opposite direction to the one they had traveled today. If Kyle had come ashore here, surely he couldn't have strayed too far from the beach. He was a merman and the ocean was in his blood. To go so far inland that he couldn't dive into the surf whenever he wanted would be unthinkable.

Chapter Thirteen

Kai groaned loudly as he opened his eyes. His head pounded and he could hear a loud, obnoxious crashing noise coming from somewhere to his left. "What's that dreadful sound?" he whispered.

"Not so loud," Dax replied with a moan of discomfort of his own.

Kai risked a look toward the noise. "Have the waves always been this loud?"

"Is that what it is?" Dax asked. "I thought a hammerhead shark had taken up residence in my skull."

"Do you remember what happened last night?" Kai questioned. He had only vague recollections of the party on the beach. There was strange music, and a girl, and Dax. Oh *fuck* he had tried to shove his hand into Dax's clothes to touch him intimately. When there were *humans* watching them. *What* in the world had he been thinking?

"Not a damn thing after our new friends gave us some food."

Kai took a moment to savor the relief that Dax didn't recall his inappropriate behavior of the night before. He glanced slowly around the beach. "Where's everyone gone?" The shore was deserted, save for a man walking toward them with a black sack.

"I don't know and right now I don't care," Dax muttered. "I think I've been poisoned."

Kai sat up and the world spun out of control. His stomach rolled and he thought he might vomit. "Me too."

The man approaching them called out something in the strange human language. Kai didn't bother to reply. He didn't see the point when neither of them would be able to understand what the other said.

Kai eased himself back down onto the sand, closed his eyes, and flung his arm across his face. "I think I'm dying."

"Then do it quietly," Dax mumbled back.

Kai would have laughed, except he thought his head might explode if he made a sound louder than a whisper.

The man with the sack arrived at their spot and greeted them with a toe to Kai's leg. He said something, but again Kai had no idea what message he was trying to convey.

Kai moaned and struggled to sit up again. The man continued to speak to him and although Kai could tell he wasn't pleased with them, he still had no clue what he actually wanted.

"I wonder what go away is in the language of humans," Dax said without bothering to sit up. "I just want to die in peace."

"You're mer?" the man asked in their own language.

Dax shot up—something his stomach immediately protested—and stared at him in horror. "What did you say?"

"I asked if you were mer," the man repeated. "Since it's the language of the mer you're speaking, I drew the logical conclusion."

"You know about the mer?" Kai asked. "I thought humans weren't aware of our existence."

"Most aren't, but a few of us have been lucky enough to meet your people before."

"Oh."

"Normally when mermen wash up on this beach they're naked, but I see you've managed to find yourself some clothes."

"Caspian dressed us to keep us out of jail," Kai explained.

"Caspian?"

"He's one of the Atlantean gods."

"I know, but I wonder why he didn't give you the knowledge of the English language. He usually does when a merman or mermaid comes to land, just like he gave me your language."

Dax frowned and rubbed his forehead. "He probably didn't give us English because Cari, his sister, wants us to go back to the sea and giving us your language will make it easier for us to stay. He wouldn't have given us clothes except we were taken to something he called a police station when we walked around without them."

The man quickly smothered his smile. "I see. Well, actually I don't, but I can't leave you laying out here on the beach. Give me a hand to pick up the rubbish left by the rest of your party buddies and I'll take you back to my house for some breakfast."

"Who are you?" Kai asked.

"My name's Malcolm."

"And how do you know about the mer?"

"I'm married to a mermaid, and our two sons take after her. When you're outnumbered by the mer in your own family, it's rather hard to keep those fins a secret."

Kai staggered to his feet and looked at the rubbish left on the sand. He had a feeling if he bent down to pick anything up he would be sick, yet Malcolm seemed to expect him to help clean up the mess.

Malcolm picked up an empty bottle. "You had some of this last night?"

Kai nodded.

"How many?"

"I don't know. Four or five that I can remember."

Malcolm gave a low whistle. "And you've never been to land before now?"

"No."

Malcolm chuckled. "For future reference, this is alcohol, and last night the two of you drank quite a bit of it. You might want to stick to non-alcoholic drinks from now on. Neither of my sons has a particularly high tolerance for alcohol, and I seem to recall my wife being in a similar state the first time she went to a beach party."

"It's poison," Dax moaned as he buried his face in his hands.

"It is indeed," Malcolm agreed. "Why don't you leave me to clean up and go along the beach to my place?" He pointed to a house farther down the shore. "It's locked up, but you can wait on the steps until I get back. I won't be long. Then you can tell me who you are and what you're doing here."

"I'm Kai and this is Dax," Kai said. He reached down and helped Dax up. Dax swayed on his feet and clutched his head, moaning the entire time.

"Once you've had a full English breakfast you'll both feel much better," Malcolm told them with a chuckle.

Kai's stomach lurched at the mere thought of food. He wondered if he'd ever be able to eat anything again. Even his favorite sea fruits didn't sound appetizing right now. He looked at Dax, taking in the strange green tinge to his face.

"I think I'm dying," Dax moaned.

Malcolm chuckled again. "Don't worry, we've all been there, me more times than most in my younger days. I don't remember most of the Sundays after I turned eighteen until I was around twenty three. It'll pass, and I promise, you're not dying."

Kai wasn't so sure, but Malcolm seemed to be a friendly face in this strange land, and he hoped the man might be able to assist in tracking down Kyle. Maybe he could even help Kai and Dax find a way to live on land as well. He said he had mer in his family, so it wasn't an impossible dream.

Malcolm quickly finished cleaning up the debris left on the beach and returned to his house to let Kai and Dax inside. Kai helped Dax to his feet from his seat on the worn, wooden steps. Dax continued to moan softly and Kai wondered if he might be really ill, or whether he was simply making more fuss than necessary. Kai himself was starting to feel a little better, though he still didn't think he would manage to eat anything for a while.

"Come on then, let's see what I can rustle up for you two strays," Malcolm said as he hopped up the steps and unlocked the door.

"I'm not hungry," Kai said.

"Me neither," Dax added.

"Okay, how about you clean up and sleep a while in a bed instead?"

Kai nodded. "That would be good."

Malcolm guided them into the house. "I have the place to myself this morning. My wife's shopping and my son's over at his fiancée's house. Why he doesn't just move in there I don't know. He spends more time there than he does at home."

Malcolm pointed toward some pictures on the wall. Kai walked over to take a closer look.

"Prince Finn?" he asked, recognizing the blond merman immediately.

Malcolm chuckled. "No, that's Finn's twin brother, Alex. The one to the right there is of the two of them together."

Kai studied each of the pictures on the wall and soon recognized another face. "Queen Coral."

Malcolm smiled. "My wife."

"Shouldn't you know all this?" Dax asked. "You being an Oracle and all-seeing."

"I'm not all-seeing," Kai replied. "I had no idea the queen had come to land, nor that King Nereus isn't the father of Prince Finn."

"He's not?" Dax asked.

Kai shook his head. "You've never met Prince Finn, so you won't have spotted the resemblance between him and our host. If I wasn't so bleary-eyed I might have noticed the similarities myself."

Malcolm nodded. "You're quite correct."

Dax wandered over to take a look at the photos himself. He suddenly seemed to realize the implications of who they were talking to. "If you're the prince's father, you'll know where to find him."

"Finn doesn't like being called a prince," Malcolm warned him. "And his mother is no longer a queen. They are just Finn and Coral here in England, and that's exactly the way they like it."

"But you know where he is?" Dax stepped forward eagerly.

"Yes, but forgive me for asking why you wish to know." Malcolm had switched from friendly to outright suspicious, and Kai couldn't say he entirely blamed him.

Kai placed a hand on Dax's arm, tugging him back. "We mean him no harm," he assured Finn's father. "In fact we're not searching for Finn himself. We're hoping to track down a merman named Kyle, who we understand may be with him."

Malcolm folded his arms over his chest. "And what do you want with Kyle?"

"I want to ensure he's well," Dax explained as calmly as he could, "and to deliver a message from his sister."

"Lynna? How is she doing? Is she still in Atlantis?"

"You know Lynna?" Kai asked.

"No, not personally. Kyle speaks fondly of her and often wonders how she is. He'll be delighted to have any news of her. How do you two know Lynna?"

"I don't," Kai replied. "But Dax is from Kyle and Lynna's birth clan. He chose not to travel to the sunken city with the rest of his people."

"I visited there recently, hoping to see Kyle and his family. Instead I discovered Kyle had been banished, his mother left, and Lynna alone remaining from his family."

"Then Lynna still resides in Atlantis?" Malcolm asked.

"Yes, with her mate and their young daughter."

Malcolm grinned widely. "Oh Kyle will love to know he's an uncle. When he left Lynna had told him she believed she might be pregnant, but that was the last time he saw her. He'll be delighted."

Dax frowned at Malcolm. "If only someone could tell us where to find him, we'll be happy to pass on the glad tidings to him."

"Patience," Kai chided gently. "You've waited this long, surely a few more hours won't be so hard."

Dax agreed, albeit somewhat begrudgingly. "As long as Malcolm promises to take us to Kyle, I'll wait."

Malcolm directed the two of them to the staircase and shepherded them to the upper floor. "Bath first, then sleep, and afterwards we'll see about taking you to Kyle."

Malcolm showed them to the room he called the bathroom, but the items within it were a mystery to Kai.

"Didn't Caspian give you *any* knowledge of the modern world?" Malcolm asked after Kai jumped back, startled, when he turned on what he referred to as the taps.

"Not a thing," Dax said. "He doesn't want us here in England. Or at least he doesn't want Kai here."

"Why not?" Malcolm asked.

"Because the Oracles have traditionally stayed in the sunken city," Kai explained. "He doesn't think I should have left."

"Can you tell me why you did?" Malcolm asked. "Are you a friend of Kyle's too?"

"Not really, though I did meet him briefly. I left for reasons of my own, though forgive me for not explaining them to a stranger."

Malcolm frowned and his brow furrowed.

"Don't be offended," Dax said. "He hasn't exactly told me why he chose to leave either."

Kai bit his lip. "I guess it's long past time I told you everything. I'm sure you know I didn't just leave because I wanted to live as a free merman on land, rather than remain a prisoner under the water."

"Does that mean you'll confide in me soon?"

Kai nodded.

Malcolm made a non-committal noise, finished showing them how the bath and other amenities worked, and left them to wash up. "You can sleep in the bed across the hallway." He pointed to the door.

"Thank you," Kai said. "I think I'll wait through there until Dax has bathed, if that's okay?"

Malcolm's eyes widened and he grinned. "You're sure you don't want to share a bath?" he asked. "The tub's big enough for the two of you."

Kai's face heated.

Malcolm laughed. "I thought so. You don't have to mind my sensibilities if you want to share. With a son like Finn I've learnt to recognize the signs of young men who are smitten with each other."

"I'm not smitten with anyone," Dax replied shortly.

Malcolm chuckled again. "Of course not," he said as he wandered back down the stairs, shaking his head as he went. He called back up to them. "Though if that's the case, you might want to let go of Kai's hand or he might get the wrong impression."

Kai looked down at their joined hands and immediately tried to free himself from Dax's grip. Dax wouldn't let him go. Instead he shut the door and pushed Kai up against it.

"You just said you weren't smitten with anyone," Kai reminded him, wondering when he had become so breathless.

"I'm not," Dax insisted. "But I want you pretty badly."

"You do?" Kai asked.

Dax rested his forehead against Kai's. "Oh yes. And I'm telling you right now, you're not going back to that prison again. We'll find a way to live on land. Kyle will help us, I know he will."

"I don't want to go back to the sunken city. Not if it means being apart from you."

"Sexual relations are forbidden for you in the city, remember?"

"I've not forgotten."

"We're not in the city anymore," Dax whispered. "Last night, when you touched me, I felt it to the core of my soul."

"You remember me touching you?" So much for Dax not recalling anything.

Dax grimaced. "Vaguely. You put your hand into these strange human garments. I remember that, but not much afterwards."

"There wasn't much after that," Kai told him. "The others at the beach were watching us."

"There's no one here now." Dax took Kai's hand that he still held and placed it on his chest. "Touch me?"

Kai wondered whether he was doing the right thing. Dax wanting him and Dax loving him were two very different things. Dax wanted him in his life, surely that had to mean he had feelings for him that went a little beyond sexual attraction.

As he undid the top fastening of Dax's garment, Kai hoped he wasn't making the biggest mistake of his life. He couldn't resist Dax any longer. He *had* to take a chance. He undid the buttons and rested his palms on each side of Dax's chest. He rubbed at the smooth flesh as he pushed the material aside. With each stroke of skin, he inched his fingers lower. When Dax encouraged him, he slipped his right hand into the garment covering his legs and groin, and sought out his cock.

"Kai," Dax breathed.

Kai took his name to mean to carry on, and he ran his fingers along Dax's cock, tracing the flesh and delighting at the way his length hardened at even the slightest touch.

Dax stared at him as Kai explored. "I need to kiss you," he whispered. "I need…"

Kai used his left hand to grab Dax's head and draw him closer. He pressed his lips to Dax's, opening his mouth and pushing his tongue against Dax's lips, begging silently for entry. Dax responded to the kiss with enthusiasm, pushing Kai against the door and groaning into his mouth.

Kai released Dax's cock, and Dax took the opportunity to close the gap between them. Kai could feel the hard ridge of Dax's erection pressing against his own. He hated having two layers of fabric between them, yet he didn't want to break away from Dax long enough to remove them.

Lightning flashed and Kai wondered at the apparent sudden storm. Then Dax clawed at his clothes and thoughts of the weather flew from his mind.

"Stupid human clothes," Dax complained as they struggled to undress. "What do they need such ridiculous things for?"

"Don't rip them," Kai said. "We have no more if these are ruined. You heard what Caspian said. That was the only time he would help us."

Dax continued to grumble until finally he managed to undo the buttons on Kai's shirt and pushed it aside. With a strength Kai envied, Dax picked him up so his nipples were level with his mouth. He took one of the nubs between his teeth, alternately nipping and sucking at it. Kai shivered with desire. He whimpered as Dax moved from one nipple to the other, then back again. Kai's cock, still confined in his clothes, strained against the fabric.

"Have you ever come before?" Dax whispered into his ear.

Kai shook his head. "I've always been in mer form, remember?"

"Do you want to know what it feels like?"

Kai nodded. "Yes, oh, Dax, yes."

Dax grinned and knelt on the floor in front of him. "Let me see you hard and aching, before I take you into my mouth and drink down everything you have to give me."

"Drink?" Kai squeaked.

Dax's grin widened even farther. "You'll see."

Kai fumbled with the fastenings of the strange garment, but eventually managed to push it over his hips. Dax pulled it the rest of the way down his legs, and steadied Kai while he stepped out of it.

Dax stared at Kai's groin for several long minutes. Kai fidgeted under his scrutiny. Was there something wrong with him? "Is it normal?" he finally whispered, almost afraid of what the answer might be.

Dax blinked up at him as though he had forgotten he was

there, although since he stared at his cock so intently Kai wondered how that could possibly be the case. "Normal?" he asked.

"You're staring," Kai explained. The queasiness he had experienced on waking returned again in full force at the thought of Dax disliking what he saw.

"I'm sorry. I didn't mean to make you nervous."

"I'm not!" Kai lied.

Dax raised an eyebrow in question.

"Maybe a little," Kai amended. "But is there something wrong with me?"

"Not at all." Dax reached out and ran his finger gently along Kai's length. The digit barely brushed his skin, yet Kai shivered uncontrollably. He felt as though he might burst. He closed his eyes and drew in a shaky breath.

"That feels so good," he said.

Dax laughed. "You think *that* feels good? Wait until you see what I do next."

Kai stared down at him curiously.

"Do you want to come quickly or do you want this to last?" Dax asked.

"I don't know. Which will feel better?"

"Either would make you feel great, at least I hope they will. I guess it depends on my own skills and…"

"And what?" Kai prompted.

Dax ducked his head. "I haven't done this too often."

"You haven't? But you said you never go through a solstice without relief."

"I don't, but this isn't what I need to break my fever."

"You need to fuck someone, yes?"

Dax nodded. "I just find a merman, stick my cock up his arse until I come, and that's pretty much it."

"Do you want to fuck me now instead?"

"No. I, well, I guess I want to make sure your first time is about you, if that makes sense?"

"Not really." Kai had no idea what Dax meant by his words. Surely whatever they did would be enjoyable for both of them, else what would be the point?

Dax smiled and shook his head. "If I fuck you, it'll hurt because it's your first time, and nothing I can do will prevent the pain. If I suck you, then you get to come without the pain."

"Will you come when you suck me?" Kai asked.

"I can if I touch myself at the same time," Dax replied. "So, what do you think, quick or slow?"

Kai still didn't know which to choose. He wanted to come so badly, just to know what it felt like to lose himself in the pleasure of an orgasm, yet this might not happen again. Dax said himself he didn't do this often. "Make it last."

Dax took Kai's cock in a firm grip at the base. "Do this when you think you're close and it'll stop you from coming."

Kai didn't doubt it. The feeling that he was about to burst had receded with the pressure Dax had put on him.

Dax loosened his grasp and Kai breathed a sigh. Then Dax touched his low-hanging balls and he moaned with desire. As Dax stroked him Kai leaned back against the door, feeling unsteady on his feet and needing the solid wood at his back.

With slow and deliberate movements, Dax traced the length of his cock and teased the foreskin with his thumb.

"Oh, oh, oh," Kai gasped over and over as Dax touched every inch of his sensitive cock, following the thick vein with his index finger.

Even though he had asked for slow, Kai wondered whether he would be able to make this last. He knew what he needed to do by placing pressure at the base of his cock, yet he didn't think he could remember how to use his hands.

When Kai gazed down, Dax licked his lips. "Oh my," Kai whispered when he realized Dax was leaning toward him again.

Dax swiped his tongue around Kai's cockhead, pushing back the foreskin and licking at the slit. Kai gave a strangled moan as his knees buckled. He scrambled back into a standing position, mumbling apologies to Dax.

"It's okay," Dax assured him. "Just enjoy what I'm doing to you and hold on tight."

"Hold onto what?" Kai gasped.

"Anything you like," Dax replied. "But try not to pull all my hair out if you can help it."

Kai smiled at Dax's joke, but when he opened his mouth to respond no words came out. Instead he stood transfixed by what Dax seemed to be doing. Surely Dax wasn't going to...

"Oh fuck!" Kai cried, as Dax wrapped his lips around the tip of his cock and sucked on the head.

Kai couldn't take his eyes off Dax as he took more and more of his length into his mouth. Dax stroked him with his tongue as well as fondling with his hands the last couple of inches he couldn't quite take.

Spots floated in front of Kai's eyes. When Dax gave a particularly hard suck Kai wondered if he might be going blind again.

He wanted to make this last. He *really* did. He needed to remember these amazing feelings. Yet his control slipped away with every passing moment.

Dax may have said he didn't do this often, but Kai wasn't sure he believed him. How could anyone with no experience of such matters make him feel so good?

He couldn't help it. Kai bucked his hips a little, pushing into Dax's mouth. Dax didn't seem to mind. He made a humming noise deep in his throat that sent vibrations through Kai's entire body.

"I need..." Kai begged. "Please, Dax, please."

Dax didn't waste any time in obeying Kai's demands. Kai cried out as his balls drew up. He couldn't hold back any longer. With a final shout of ecstasy his orgasm crashed over him. He spilled into Dax's mouth, letting him drink down his seed, just as he had promised he would.

When he had finally given Dax all he had, Kai slid down the door. Dax held him between his lips for as long as he could, until Kai slid out of reach and he released him with one final lick.

"You enjoyed that?" Dax asked with a toothy grin.

Kai nodded mutely. He could see Dax hadn't come. His stiff erection jutted out from between his legs, poking Kai in the shin when he moved.

Dax looked down, clearly following Kai's gaze. He reached between his legs, but Kai quickly stopped him. "Let me?"

Kai eased Dax's hand aside and touched his lover's cock. The flesh was hot in his hand.

"I'm close," Dax said. His voice was breathless and a little raspy.

Kai stroked his length, noting the places which elicited the most delightful responses from Dax. When he found one, he touched it again, enjoying that he could give Dax the same pleasure he had just experienced. Fluid came from the tip of Dax's cock, and Kai used his free hand to gather it up.

"Taste me," Dax ordered.

Kai held Dax's gaze as he raised his fingers to his lips and licked them clean. Dax's pupils dilated as he watched.

The moment Kai finished, Dax launched himself forward and kissed him hard. Kai moaned into the kiss as he continued to hold Dax's stiff cock in his loose grip. He tightened his grasp as Dax plundered his mouth. They were still joined at the lips when he felt the warmth of Dax's release on his skin. Dax pulled out of the kiss and buried his face in Kai's shoulder. "Now we really need to bathe."

Kai chuckled. "We were already covered in sand. We needed to anyway."

"Sand I can live with," Dax replied. "I draw the line at our seed."

Neither merman made any effort to move toward the bathtub. They sat together for several minutes in comfortable silence, until Dax finally stood and held out his hand to Kai. "Join me?" he asked.

Kai took his hand and nodded. He had a feeling Dax

wasn't just asking him about the bath. His answer was the same, though. Whatever the gods had in store for them, Kai would be at Dax's side. At some point during their journey to land, the warrior had inserted himself into Kai's small family, and Kai had a feeling he might be there to stay.

Chapter Fourteen

Dax and Kai took their time in the bathroom. They decided against taking a bath when Kai recognized the room that rained from one of his visions. Stepping into the tiny enclosure together, they laughed and squealed as the water poured down on them. They had difficulty taking their hands off each other long enough to get clean. They kissed beneath the spray as they traced each other's bodies. Neither of them even attempted to pass their touches off as washing. In a stranger's bathroom, in an alien world, they set about the task of discovering each other in the most intimate of ways.

The longer they spent in the shower, the more aroused Dax became. His cock rose in anticipation of more attention. Dax could feel Kai's erection brushing against him too, but neither of them reached for the other.

Kai yawned loudly and Dax chuckled. "Tired?" he asked.

"No," Kai replied. His response was immediately followed by another wide yawn.

"Liar."

"I want to have sex with you," Kai blurted. "Proper sex, I mean."

Dax laughed. "We will, just not right now. I don't want you falling asleep when I'm balls-deep in your arse." He grabbed the rear in question and gave the buttocks a quick squeeze.

Kai moaned, but a third yawn made it clear he wasn't in a position to argue.

Dax stepped out of the shower and grabbed a couple of towels from the rack. He held one out to Kai, who turned off the shower and took it from him. They dried quickly and crossed the hall to the bedroom.

"Is that what humans sleep on?" Dax asked as he looked at the large bed.

"I think so." Kai walked over to the bed and sat on the edge. "Ooh, it's all soft and bouncy."

Dax quickly smothered his smile, but not quite fast enough to hide his mirth from Kai.

"What?" Kai asked.

"Soft and bouncy are two words no grown merman should utter."

"Why not, if those are the correct words to use?"

Dax didn't have an answer for that. Kai, despite what they had done in the bathroom just a short while before, was still an innocent in so many ways. Dax supposed when it came to the human world they were both equally clueless.

Kai crawled onto the bed, tossing aside the towel he had wrapped round his waist, and stretching out naked on top of the covers. Dax's erection returned in full force and he tried to will it away. It didn't work anymore than it would have on the night of the solstice. Kai gave a loud snore and Dax sighed. He hoped Kai didn't make a habit of falling asleep on him at such times.

Even though Dax wasn't particularly tired his head still felt somewhat fuzzy from the alcohol of the night before. Sleep would be the best thing for both of them. Then, when they awoke refreshed, they would ask Malcolm to lead them to Kyle and begin a new life together on land.

He joined Kai on the bed and closed his eyes. Beside him he heard Kai mutter a single word.

"Family."

Dax frowned. Did Kai refer to him, or was he mourning the absence of the other Oracles? They had been his family for a long time.

Even as he drifted off to sleep, Dax pondered just how committed Kai was to their relationship.

* * * *

From the position of the sun, Dax guessed it to be early afternoon when they woke and struggled back into their clothes. His head had cleared and his stomach growled, protesting the lack of food.

They found Malcolm downstairs, reading a book. "Ah, you're awake," he said, putting his book aside on the table. "I had a visitor shortly after I left you upstairs."

"You did?" Dax asked. "Was it Kyle?"

"No, I'm afraid not. It was Caspian."

Dax frowned. "What did he want? Other than to tell us to go back to the ocean, of course."

"He insisted I obey his orders not to help you by taking you to Kyle."

"And?"

"And I told him I would do as I pleased."

"Was that wise?" Kai asked. "He *is* a god and has a great many powers."

"Yes, I know. He threatened to put my house into lockdown so we couldn't leave. I pointed out to him it wouldn't work since Kyle would be visiting here for Sunday lunch in a couple of days anyway."

"What did he say to that?"

"Not a great deal. I'm surprised he doesn't just transport you back magically."

Dax was about to explain he couldn't when someone else answered the question for him.

"Caspian hasn't the power to send them back."

Dax jumped as a familiar figure appeared before them.

Medina smiled and gracefully sat on a nearby chair. "You have both been under my protection for quite some time," she explained. "Neither Caspian or Cari has the power to send you back while I'm shielding you from such magic. It's a pity they know you've arrived on land at all. Unfortunately it seems Caspian's vow to help all mer who travel to human lands overrode my own magic just enough for him to know you had arrived."

"Why would you protect us?" Dax questioned. "I've never prayed to you and I doubt Kai has either."

"Um, actually…" Kai began.

"Actually what?" Dax asked.

"I might have gone to Medina's temple to ask her for help."

"You did indeed," Medina agreed. "There are few who even remember my name these days, so I can't begin to tell you what a pleasure it was to hear you calling for me. Even after so long away I still feel the desire to bring love and happiness to those who need it. When I discovered Cari's Oracles had been denied love I made it my mission to rectify this."

Dax had little interest in Medina's words. He was far more interested in what Kai had to say about his visit to the goddess's temple. "Kai?"

Kai sighed and wandered over to gaze out of the window overlooking the beach. "I hate being an Oracle, not because of the powers and the blindness, but because we're denied love. When Medina awoke I decided to go to her to ask for help on behalf of the three of us."

Dax could sense there was more to the story. "And?"

"And she showed you to me and told me I could have you, but I'd have to leave the sunken city."

"Have me?" Dax frowned at the way Kai had phrased his words.

Medina seemed to sense his annoyance and rose to stand by his side. "You wanted him too, don't deny it. What does it matter if I helped bring things about? The result is the same as if you were in charge of your own destiny."

Dax still didn't like the sound of what he'd heard, yet he couldn't deny his attraction to Kai, and despite the goddess's interference, he still wanted the merman with a desperation he didn't know he could feel outside of the mating season. Had the goddess put him under some sort of love spell?

Kai didn't turn back to Dax, but continued to stare out of the window. The atmosphere had become strained and Dax didn't know what to say. Malcolm stepped in to break the silence.

"You say you're here to help, yes?" he asked the goddess.

Medina nodded. "In any way I can, so long as it is within my powers."

"Can you give these mermen knowledge of English and the world around them?" Malcolm asked. "They're struggling a little at the moment since Caspian refused to oblige."

Medina tapped her lower lip with a manicured finger. "I know little of this world myself, and while I could give them some knowledge of English, it wouldn't include modern phrases and sayings. Caspian has remained in this world over the centuries. He has learnt languages as they have been born and evolved. I have not had this luxury."

"Any English would be helpful," Malcolm insisted.

Medina sighed. "Very well, but don't expect too much."

Dax didn't feel any different after Medina had placed her hand on his shoulder. He supposed he would find out soon enough whether her magic had worked.

Kai remained quiet and Dax yearned to get him alone to talk things through. Before he could find a way to tactfully request to be alone with him, Kai spoke and revealed what was really bothering him.

"It doesn't seem fair that I'm here with Dax, while Delwyn and Ula are still stuck in the sunken city, forbidden from going to land."

Medina sighed. "I completely agree. I'm working on a plan to ensure all three of you are able to live as other mer do."

"There are reasons we're not allowed to have sexual relations," Kai reminded her. "While procreation isn't going to happen between myself and Dax, nor Delwyn and whatever merman he falls for, Ula is a different matter. For us to be allowed love and not her would be too cruel. All three of us desire the touch of a merman, yet for Ula it could result in a pregnancy and her powers would be inherited by any child."

Medina waved away his concerns. "I'm aware of the reasons why Cari has forbidden sexual relations. I'm searching for a solution."

Dax believed her, yet he wondered if one was even possible.

"If there were a solution, surely Cari would have found one by now?" Kai asked, giving voice to Dax's own question.

Medina frowned and vanished from the room. Her presence lingered a moment or two longer. "Cari isn't the most powerful goddess any longer. *I'm* the one who wears that particular crown. If there's a solution, I assure you I'll find it."

"If?" Dax asked.

Medina didn't reply. Dax couldn't tell if she had simply not heard, or she had chosen to ignore him. Either way, it was clear Kai was worried for Ula, if he and Delwyn were allowed to find love while she, by virtue of her sexual orientation, was denied the same.

* * * *

Despite Caspian's threats, Malcolm drove Kai and Dax in the strange human conveyance to a large house. The journey wasn't without its problems—the car had stalled several times for no apparent reason, and even though the tank was full, the machine seemed to think it had run out of something called petrol. When they finally got moving, each road they tried to travel down had been closed, and lengthy traffic diversions had been put in place. Malcolm commented there were no road works happening and no reason he could see for the closures. He confided in them his suspicions there might be some immortal interference happening to try to stop them.

Eventually, when the car had started billowing smoke

from the front, Malcolm pulled over to the side of the road and raised his eyes skyward.

"I'm not giving up, so you might as well stop with the delaying tactics. I waited over twenty years for Coral to come back to me. You know I'm a patient man and I *am* going to get these boys where they need to be. Nothing is going to stop me, so back off."

Dax cringed. "Are you sure you should speak to them like that? They have some pretty impressive powers."

Malcolm shrugged. "Caspian, bad tempered though he is, has sworn to protect all mer who come here. He won't hurt you, which means all he can do is slow us down."

"Cari hasn't made such a vow," Kai reminded him.

"Maybe not, but if she wanted to harm you, surely she would already have done so."

Malcolm climbed out of the car and went to check under the hood. "Just as I thought," he said as he got back into the driver's seat. "Nothing wrong with the car at all."

He started the engine again, and this time the car worked perfectly. It seemed Malcolm's demands to back off had had the desired effect, and they continued their journey without incident.

"Well, here we are. I must admit I didn't think we'd ever make it."

"Kyle is here?" Dax asked.

Kai frowned as Dax spoke the words he had been thinking. This seemed a strange place to find a merman, especially one who had lived most of his life in the ocean. The building was quite a distance from the water. Kai could barely taste the salt in the air. The house was large and intimidating. It didn't seem like the cozy dwellings in the sunken city at all.

Malcolm opened the door of the car and climbed out. "If he's not home at the moment, he won't have gone far. Like I said, there was no answer on their phone, but that doesn't mean anything. When they're in the pool they rarely hear the ringing."

Dax followed Malcolm onto the driveway and Kai stepped

out immediately after.

"Are you all right?" Kai asked.

"Yes, why wouldn't I be?"

"Well, we've come a long way to find him. I thought you might be nervous."

Dax grinned. "Does that mean you're worried about facing one of my former lovers?"

Kai shook his head. "No."

Dax quirked an eyebrow.

"Maybe a little. You and he were lovers for longer than we've been." Kai didn't bother to add that technically he was still a virgin.

Dax wrapped his arm round Kai's shoulders. "We've both moved on. He has a new life here on land, and I have you."

Kai's heart fluttered a little at Dax's declaration. Although he hadn't said he loved him, he spoke as though he planned on keeping him, and making their arrangement permanent.

Malcolm led them to the front door and hit a button that made a ringing noise inside the building. A few moments later Kai heard footsteps, and the door opened to reveal Prince Finn.

Kai's first instinct was to bow or drop to his knees, yet he knew the prince hadn't liked such displays back in the sunken city, and he doubted he would appreciate the gesture any more now. By leaving the city he had given up his claim on the throne and his right to the title.

"Kai?" Finn stared at him in shock. "How did you get here? Is Delwyn with you?"

Kai shook his head. "Delwyn's still in the sunken city."

"You left him there?" Finn didn't seem happy at the news. Belatedly, Kai recalled that the prince had adored Delwyn as much as his fellow Oracle had cared for Finn. Were it not for circumstances outside their control, Kai had no doubt the two men would have been lovers long ago.

"He's safe and well."

"And a prisoner while you walk free," Finn replied. "And who's this?"

"Now Finn," Malcolm interrupted, "you don't know the circumstances and I know your mother raised you better than to be so rude to guests."

Finn hung his head. "Sorry, Dad."

Malcolm waved behind Finn at another man who had come to see what was happening at the door. "Hello, Jake."

"Hi, Malcolm, what brings you here?"

"Delivering a couple of strays who want to see Kyle."

"What do you want with Kyle?" Finn asked.

"Is he here?" Malcolm replied. "I'm sure you know they've come a long way to find him."

"He's in the kitchen," Jake said. "Come on through."

Finn stepped aside and Kai and Dax followed Malcolm into the house. Kai gazed about him in wonder. The place was far grander than Malcolm's house or any of the other buildings they had seen since their arrival in the land of humans.

"Visitors for you, Kyle," Jake announced.

Although Kai had seen Kyle in his visions, nothing could prepare him for the smile of pure joy spreading across his face the moment he laid eyes on Dax. He jumped down from the counter he sat on and launched himself across the room and into Dax's arms.

Kai tried to squash the feeling of jealousy burning in his chest at the sight of Kyle in *his* lover's arms, kissing him as thoroughly as Kai ever had.

Jake coughed while Finn covered his smile.

Kyle pulled away and grinned. "You have no idea how much I missed you. The number of times I wondered if I had made the right decision in letting you swim away. I can't believe you're here, in England, in my kitchen."

Kyle finished rambling and kissed Dax again. Kai practically growled with annoyance.

Dax drew out of the kiss first and chuckled. "Did the mating season arrive without my noticing? You never used to enjoy kissing outside of the solstice."

"I was a fool. We could have been doing this every day

instead of waiting for the mating season."

"Maybe you should stick to kissing your own men," Kai muttered under his breath, yet loud enough for everyone in the room to hear.

Kyle took only a moment to realize what Kai's relationship to Dax was, and what he had just done. "I'm sorry. I didn't mean to encroach on your territory."

Jake laughed. "I love that you apologize to him, but not to your own men, who might not want to see you shoving your tongue into another man's mouth."

Kyle grinned over his shoulder at Jake. "Ah, but I know you and Finn like to watch as much as participate. Besides, you both know I love you."

Jake tugged Kyle into his arms. "Yes, we do, and it's a good thing too, especially when you throw yourself at another man. What *am* I going to do with you?"

"I'm sure you'll think of something," Kyle teased. "Or Finn will help you find some suitable way of keeping me in line."

"Kyle!" Finn exclaimed. "You do remember my dad's right here in the room?"

When Kai glanced at Malcolm, he saw his face was a shade of crimson, and he appeared to be studiously avoiding listening to the conversation.

Jake patted Kyle on the arse and shook his head. He turned back to Dax and Kai with a smile. "I'm Jake, and it appears you know Kyle and Finn."

"I know Kyle," Dax said.

"And I've met both Kyle and Finn," Kai added. "This is Dax, and I'm Kai."

"Ah, Dax." Finn grinned. "We get to put a face to the name at last. We've heard quite a bit about you."

"We were just about to eat," Jake said. "Do you want to join us?"

Kai looked to Dax for direction. Dax agreed and Jake guided them all into what he called the dining room.

"I think I'll have to decline," Malcolm said as the others

filed past him. "I've got a delivery coming at the new café soon. Will you be able to find your way back to the sea from here?"

"Yes," Kai replied. Although he was in no hurry to do so, they would have to find their way back there sooner or later. Even if he decided to remain on land, he would still have to take mer form to check on Delwyn and Ula.

"I hope the journey back is smoother than the one here," Dax said.

"I think it will be, after all, Cari was simply trying to stop us reaching our destination. Now we're here, what can obstructing us achieve?"

"Cari, the Goddess of Prophecy?" Jake asked. "She's been trying to stop you coming here?"

Kai nodded. "She didn't want me to leave the city. The Goddess of Love shielded us on our journey here, but as soon as we arrived on land Caspian, another god, arrived with Cari and told us we had to go back to the sunken city."

Finn sucked in a sharp breath. "Does anyone else think this means we might have some pissed off immortals on our hands?"

Jake leaned back in his seat, a thoughtful expression on his face. "Medina is more powerful than Cari and Caspian though, and if she's on your side, you may just get out of this unscathed."

"You know the Atlantean gods?" Kai asked.

"Jake's a descendant of Medina," Finn explained. "She visits from time to time. Jake's right, if she's on your side, you have a powerful goddess in your corner."

Kai didn't quite understand the terminology Finn used, but the general point wasn't lost on him. Medina had protected them so far — he had to trust she would continue to do so.

"Where are you staying here in England?" Kyle asked.

"We stayed on the beach near Malcolm's house last night," Dax replied.

"You can stay here until you decide to go home," Kyle

suggested. He belatedly turned to Jake and Finn as though to ask if this was okay with them, and both nodded and smiled.

"We've plenty of room here," Jake agreed.

Dax eagerly agreed, a little too enthusiastically for Kai's liking, but it wasn't as if Kai had any alternative ideas about where they would live.

Kyle seemed to pick up on Kai's reluctance and rolled his eyes. "I promise to keep my hands off your man."

"It's not your hands I'm worried about," Kai snapped.

Kyle threw his hands in the air in a gesture of surrender. "I'm sorry, okay? I shouldn't have kissed him."

"You don't have to apologize," Dax interrupted. "Kai, it was nothing more than an old lover saying hello, and if you can't handle that, perhaps we should re-think things. There are a lot of mermen out there who have shared themselves with me, and none of them deserve to be subjected to your jealousy and temper."

Kai's face heated and he pushed back from the table. Had he made a mistake when he had given his body to Dax? Medina had warned him not to have sex with Dax before he was sure he had his heart. For the first time he wondered if perhaps he had misjudged Dax's feelings and they had come together too soon. Had he simply been convenient?

"Maybe we should leave you two to talk in private." Jake stood and gestured for Kyle and Finn to do the same.

Kai waved him back down to his seat. "No, you don't have to disturb your meal. I'm going to go for a walk."

He didn't give anyone time to stop him. He left his barely touched plate of food and ran for the door.

Outside in the fresh air he scolded himself for his jealousy. He knew Dax had had other lovers, and he knew Kyle had been one of them. He had no right to act the way he had, but the cold fury he had felt when he saw Kyle kissing Dax had caught him completely off guard.

With a glance over his shoulder to confirm that no one had bothered to follow him, Kai left the house and headed down the road back toward the beach.

Chapter Fifteen

Dax watched Kai run from the room. His appetite vanished with the disappearance of the young merman.

"Quite a jealous little merman you have there," Kyle commented.

"Apparently so," Dax muttered.

"How long have you been fucking him?" Kyle questioned.

"We haven't even gotten that far yet," Dax admitted. "Though we came pretty close this morning."

Finn snorted. "Well, that explains why he's so unsure of your feelings for him."

"Does it?"

"Of course. You traveled here from the sunken city, spending a solstice together—if my calculations are correct—and only came close to having sex with him this morning. What did you do on the solstice?"

"He refused to come to land with me."

"So you both had a very painful solstice?" Kyle asked, his voice betraying his skepticism. Kyle knew him better than anyone.

"He did, I went to land with a small clan who were in the area at the time."

Kyle groaned. "You didn't?"

"What's wrong with that? You have no idea how painful the solstice is without someone to relieve the pressure."

"I know," Kyle said quietly. "When Finn and I couldn't be together in the sunken city I didn't take my pleasure on the solstice. The pain was dreadful, but I didn't want to be with anyone else when I had given him my heart."

Dax didn't understand why any merman would willingly

suffer through a painful solstice.

"Let me ask you a question," Finn said. "If you're here for the next solstice and Kai says he doesn't want to have sex with you, what will you do?"

Dax turned immediately to Kyle.

"And that's when you'll lose him," Finn continued without waiting for Dax to speak.

"If he doesn't want me, what harm is there in my seeking relief with someone else?" Dax asked.

Finn laughed loudly. "Of course he wants you. He's head over fins in love with you. Anyone can see *that*."

"Love?" Dax shook his head. "We haven't even had sex yet. No one can fall in love that fast."

"Love and sex are two different things," Kyle reminded him. "You've been on a long journey together, and somewhere along the way, your companion has fallen for you. He probably thinks of sex as the sealing of a bond between you. If you don't feel the same way, you have to tell him, and soon."

"I…" Dax didn't know what to say. Were Finn and Kyle right? Was the reason for Kai's jealousy because he had fallen in love with him? How in the world did that happen, and how had he failed to notice?

They finished their meal quietly. Dax barely tasted the strange human food. At any other time he would have been curious about what he was eating and asking a million questions, but his mind couldn't seem to process anything other than thoughts about Kai and his feelings for him.

Kyle finished his meal first and leaned back in his seat, staring at Dax until he began to feel a little uncomfortable under the scrutiny.

"What is it?" he asked.

Kyle shook his head and smiled.

"What?"

Finn chuckled.

"*What?*" Dax looked from one merman to the other, then over to Jake. "What has this pair so amused?"

Jake smirked at him and Dax glared back. *What was he missing?*

Kyle snorted with laughter. "I think you have it as bad as Kai does."

Dax frowned. "Have what?"

Kyle and Finn laughed again, tears running down the former's cheeks while the latter's mirth triggered a bout of hiccups.

Jake finally took pity on him. "You've been so lost in your thoughts you haven't heard any of our questions about your journey, the immortals mixed up in this, or anything else. Nor have you asked about the food, which is no doubt as strange to you as it was to Kyle and Finn when they first came to land. It's pretty obvious to everyone here you've spent the better part of the last hour thinking about your green-eyed Oracle. One might think your feelings for him are a little more than just those of a fuck buddy."

Dax hadn't heard of the term Jake used, but he could figure out the meaning with ease. He didn't get the chance to say anything before Kyle decided to add his opinion.

"And if you do happen to be here next solstice, I think maybe you should spend it with Kai, whether he wants to have sex or not."

"I can't go through a solstice without release," Dax complained.

"If you love him, you will. He needs to be sure of your feelings for him, and if you choose to fuck another man every time Kai isn't available or in the mood, he'll never know if you love him or whether you're just using him."

Kyle's words reminded him of the last solstice and Kai's anger at Dax's suggestion that they *use* each other. *Oh fuck.* Kai *was* in love with him and had been for a while now. How had he missed this? Even more worrying, how had he missed the realization that he had fallen in love with Kai?

* * * *

Kai didn't make it as far as the beach before the rain started. At first the drops were small, but they quickly became heavier, until he found himself caught in the middle of a total downpour. There seemed to be a small shelter at the side of the road and he ran to take cover. As a merman who had lived underwater for most of his life, he had forgotten how it felt to be caught in the rain. He only had a vague recollection of a rain shower on an island he had visited as a child, and the sprinkling of drops had been nothing like this torrent. He shivered in his damp clothes. He *hated* the rain.

He was still waiting for the shower to stop when Cari appeared beside him.

"Are you ready to go home yet?" the goddess asked. "Or are you going to insist on being stubborn?"

Kai folded his arms across his chest and ignored her. Hopefully she would get the message. He wasn't going to be bossed about by the goddess he considered to be the source of most of the misery in his life.

"I'm not trying to make you go back to punish you," Cari said. "Your powers are more potent in Atlantis. The mer will need to know of your visions."

"Why?" Kai snapped. "You're the Goddess of Prophecy. You see far more than I ever will. If the visions are so important, why don't you stay in the city and tell them what *you* see?"

Cari waved her hand airily. "My visions are far too numerous and varied. As a merman, your visions will always be more likely to be of your people and what lies ahead for them."

"You seem to have mistaken me for Ula. *She's* the one who sees the future, you know, the important stuff. I only see what's happening in the here and now. What use is that to anyone?"

"More than you know," Cari replied. "The three of you together are far more powerful than you are when you're apart. Ula's visions have already become vaguer since your departure. Delwyn is also struggling. He cannot see as far into the past without you there."

Kai felt another pang of guilt. If Delwyn couldn't see as far into the past as he had, did that mean he would suffer more on the solstices now Kai had left?

"The solstice is hard for all of you, but there is nothing I can do about it," Cari said.

"Would you get out of my head!"

Cari held up her hands in a universal gesture of surrender, and Kai sighed with annoyance.

"I gave up everything to take my place with the other Oracles," Kai whispered. "Why is it so wrong for me to want something for myself?"

"It isn't, but when you're bound to a goddess and have been gifted with powers, you *must* make sacrifices."

"Sacrifices are given freely. I had no choice."

"Do you *really* want to stay here on land? In this alien world you know so little about? You'll never be truly comfortable here. Your place is in the ocean."

"Kyle and Finn seem to be doing okay for themselves," Kai pointed out.

"They have had much help to become accustomed to this world, and yet they still find things overwhelming on occasions."

"If they can manage, so can I."

Cari sighed before trying a different tactic. "You think Dax is worthy of your devotion? How do you know you're not making a mistake by choosing him over your fellow Oracles?"

"I don't, but if being with Dax is wrong, it's my mistake to make."

"You have given him your body, haven't you?"

"Yes, not that it's any of your business."

"Have you given him your heart too?"

Kai shrugged. What did he know of matters of the heart?

"I cannot take back the gift I gave you," Cari said.

"I didn't ask you to."

"I know, but I thought you should know anyway. If I could gift another merman or mermaid with the power, I would. Unfortunately, my powers are not what they once were. As the other immortals awaken my powers grow, but right now if I were undo the magic that makes you an Oracle, it would wipe me out."

"What do you mean?"

"I would go into stasis, just as the ones that are waking now have been for so many centuries. I can't afford to let such a thing happen. The only way another Oracle can be appointed is if you die."

Kai shivered and stared at the goddess, for the first time feeling true fear at what she might do to him if he continued to defy her.

"Oh, I won't kill you," Cari said. "That's not my way, though I can't say the same for some of the other gods and goddesses of my pantheon."

"What do you mean?"

"There are those amongst my kindred who would do great harm to the merpeople who reside in Atlantis. As they waken from their long sleep, they will seek to reclaim their land and powers, by any means necessary. For some, such as me and Medina, we foster devotion from those who believe in us. Others instill fear in those who cross their paths, and get a power boost that way."

Suddenly Kai knew exactly why Cari appeared so eager for him to return to the sunken city. "If I go back, your powers increase, don't they?"

Cari blushed and wouldn't meet his eyes.

"I'm right, aren't I? You need me to live in your temple to increase your powers."

"Very well, yes," Cari snapped. "My powers diminish the longer you stay away from Atlantis."

"It seems to me you have plenty of powers already," Kai replied.

"If you had left the city a few years ago, I would probably have allowed it, but not now. You *must* return, and soon."

"Why? Give me one good reason why I should go back?"

"You mean besides the fact you're missing your family, missing Delwyn and Ula?"

"They could leave too, if you helped them."

"If they left my powers would decrease even more than they have already."

Kai rolled his eyes. "And again, it all comes back to you and your precious powers."

"I'm going to need every bit of power I can summon in the coming months," Cari said. "Only with all my powers at full potency will I be able to help protect the mer."

"Protect us from what?"

Cari looked as though she wouldn't answer, but after a few moments of contemplation she did. "The merpeople of Atlantis, simply because of where they live, are going to be on the front lines of the coming war."

"What war are you talking about?"

"The war for the city of Atlantis," Cari replied. "As my people wake, yours become ever more endangered. Each of the gods and goddesses will take sides, and for some, their whole focus will be on driving the mer out of the city."

"But the sunken city is the last safe colony for our people. It's the only one protected by the sea dragons. We're too vulnerable anywhere else."

"The sea dragons don't protect you because they want to. They are your prisoners, remember?"

"I know, but we couldn't move elsewhere and take them with us. The guards have a hard enough time keeping them under control where they are now."

"I'm not suggesting an evacuation of the city, though the idea does have some merit." Cari appeared thoughtful, chewing on her lower lip in a surprisingly human manner.

"The mer could come to land and live here." In Kai's mind it was the perfect solution. He wouldn't have to swim back to the city, Delwyn and Ula could join him here, and they would all be safe from the waking immortals.

Cari shook her head. "No, that wouldn't be wise. The

land of humans can be as dangerous as the ocean."

"We could find somewhere uninhabited by humans. An island somewhere."

Cari raised her hand to halt his words. "You are clutching at straws, my Oracle. Even if the mer were to leave Atlantis and found a new colony, you would still be you, and the law would still prevent you from being with Dax, or any other merman."

"It's not fair." The words sounded sulky even to his own ears. "Why can't I have what other mermen have?"

Cari sighed. "I'm not going to talk you into returning, am I?"

Kai gave a quick shake of his head, even though he already wondered whether he had made the right choice. Dax didn't seem to harbor any strong feelings for him, and he hadn't made any effort to come after him. Then, there was his family, Delwyn and Ula. If Cari was right, and a war was about to start, how could he leave them there? If anything happened to either of them, he wouldn't be able to live with himself.

He breathed in the smell of the sea and sighed with contentment. A vehicle full of humans sped past, noisy and churning out some kind of smoke that caused him to cough and gasp. The land of humans wasn't what he had expected. The truth was, he didn't like England much. The drink he had tried the night before was some kind of poison, the towns were crowded and smelly, and he still shivered at the recollection of his arrest.

The sunken city was home. If he could just find a way to live there and have love as well, he would go back in a heartbeat.

Cari patted him on the arm. He had forgotten she was even there. "I'll think more about the problem," she said, before vanishing into thin air. Kai didn't even have time to tell her again to stop poking around in his head.

Kai hoped she did a bit more than just think about it, not just for his sake, but for that of Ula and Delwyn too.

Kai lingered in the shelter for a long time after Cari had disappeared. Several times one of the strange human conveyances drew up beside him before leaving again. Sometimes people stepped on or off the contraption. Kai ignored them and eventually began walking toward the sea. He felt so lost and alone. It had been too long since he had checked in on Delwyn, and even though he couldn't be there with him, perhaps it might help to at least see how he fared.

The bad weather seemed to keep humans away from the beach, so Kai had no difficulties entering the water and transforming. A calm came over him and he accepted that this was where he belonged. Now he was back in the water, he had come home. He didn't like the strange land of humans. Even though Kyle and Finn were clearly happy there, it would never be for him. His place was in the ocean, though he would much rather it was not as a prisoner.

The farther away from the city he had traveled, the more energy it took to see those he had left behind. He found a spot on the ocean bed and closed his eyes, concentrating on Delwyn. He found it harder to focus his vision, and wondered whether this was what Cari had meant when she talked about their powers being stronger in Atlantis. It took him several minutes to see Delwyn with any clarity, but there he was, talking to Ula.

Kai could tell the two Oracles were communicating from their gestures, but once again he could not tell what they said. Their expressions were a little more revealing. Ula appeared impatient and there was a stubborn frown on Delwyn's face. He had his lower lip stuck out and his arms folded across his chest. Kai recognized the expression from numerous squabbles they'd had between the two of them. Normally Kai would have been acting as peacekeeper during such arguments. Eventually, Ula waved Delwyn away.

Kai pulled back from the vision and let the darkness wash over him once more. He wondered what they had been arguing about. He hated to see two of the people he loved the most at odds with each other.

Even though he knew it would be tiring he concentrated on Delwyn once more. This time it was even harder to focus on him. Eventually, the vision came into focus and he saw Delwyn had retreated to his chambers — no, he was in Kai's chambers — curled up on a sleeping sponge, an expression of utter misery on his face.

Kai ached to take Delwyn in his arms and comfort him, as he had so many times before. He reached toward the merman, but he could no more touch him than he could touch the stars.

Too soon, Kai had to end the vision. He simply didn't have the strength to sustain it.

When Kai went back to the surface, the biting chill in the air told him night had fallen. He wondered whether he should return to land, but he wasn't sure he could find his way back to Finn's house without help. Chances were they wouldn't miss him anyway, he thought with rare bitterness. Dax was probably fucking Kyle right now. He didn't need Kai getting in the way. Kai was tempted to use his powers to see them, but his visions of Delwyn had taken a lot out of him, or at least that's what he told himself. If he were truly honest he would admit he didn't want to see Dax and Kyle kissing — or doing even more — again.

Still, he didn't want anyone worrying about him, and Finn had always been a friend of the Oracles. Kai swam back to the beach. He used his powers as much as he could to make sure the coast was clear for him to swim ashore and transform. He found his discarded clothes and walked barefoot down the sand towards Malcolm's house. He hoped he hadn't gone out, and that he didn't mind Kai imposing on him once again.

Malcolm was home and he let Kai in without any questions. "Come on, lad, let's get you something to eat and some dry clothes."

Kai nodded and let Malcolm take care of him.

"I'll give Jake a call and let them know you're here," Malcolm said after he had sat Kai down at the table with a bowl of something he told him was vegetable soup. "He phoned here earlier asking if you'd stopped by. They're quite worried about you."

"They are?" Kai couldn't keep the doubt out of his voice.

Malcolm sighed and took a seat beside him. "I don't know why you ran off from the boys' house, but I assure you, when you didn't return they were most concerned indeed. They've been out searching for you. Dax was frantic, thinking you'd been arrested again."

"Frantic? Dax?" Kai couldn't imagine such a thing.

"Oh yes." Malcolm picked up a strange thing he called a phone, tapped at it several times and began talking.

Kai listened to Malcolm's end of the conversation, but he had no idea who he was talking to.

"Yes, he's perfectly fine. He's eating. I think he's going to stay here for the night. I'll bring him round to your place in the morning."

Kai shook his head rapidly.

"Hold on a minute." Malcolm turned to Kai. "What is it? Do you want me to drive you over there tonight?"

"No," Kai replied. "But I think it's best for me to go home in the morning. There's no need to trouble your family any more than I already have."

Malcolm frowned. "It's a dangerous journey to make on your own. I don't like that idea at all."

Kai wasn't sure how much Malcolm knew about the Oracles. He decided not to mention his blindness when in merman form. He had a feeling Malcolm might insist on him staying on land if he found out just how dangerous an undertaking the swim would be.

Malcolm turned his attention to the phone again. "No, he's not leaving right away," he said. "I think he wants to leave in the morning, though."

Kai took another sip of his soup. His stomach growled as a result of skipping the earlier meal. Kai knew he would need all his strength for the swim back to the sunken city. He wondered if he could impose on Malcolm for another meal in the morning before he left.

Malcolm continued to listen to the other person. Kai finished his meal, his attention drifting to the long journey ahead of him. When he had emptied the bowl he gestured towards the stairs, silently asking Malcolm's permission to go up to the room he had stayed in before. Malcolm waved him away with a smile.

Kai made his way to the bedroom he had slept in earlier and took off the irritating human clothes. The sooner he was on his way back to his family, the better. Now that he had made the decision, he didn't find the human world quite so daunting. By the time he arrived back in the sunken city, England would be nothing more than a memory, soon to be forgotten.

Chapter Sixteen

"He's what?" Dax couldn't believe his ears.

Jake repeated his words. "Malcolm says Kai is going to stay at his place tonight and intends to swim back to Atlantis in the morning."

"That's what I thought you said. Is he out of his mind?"

No one replied. Finn and Kyle knew exactly how dangerous the journey could be, and while Jake had never swum it himself, he was an intelligent man and had no doubt been told of the perils by his lovers.

"I need to go over there, right now," Dax said.

Jake didn't argue. He steered Dax out of the door and into his car.

"What are you going to do?" Jake asked, as they pulled up outside Malcolm's house a short while later.

"I'm going to stop Kai from doing anything stupid."

"And how do you plan on doing that?"

"By making him see sense."

"How?"

Dax had no idea. He couldn't imagine why Kai would consider voluntarily returning to his prison, even less why he would go alone. He had seemed amenable to the idea of them making a life together on land. What could have happened to change his mind?

Jake chuckled. "Tell him how you feel about him. If you don't, you'll lose him whether he stays here or goes."

"What if I've already lost him?"

"I doubt that. Now, I'm going to leave you here and hurry back to my men. I'm sure they're having far too much fun without me."

Dax thanked Jake for his help and watched him drive off.

Malcolm, who appeared to have been expecting him, opened the door with a smile. "Come in then, don't stand lingering on doorsteps. Kai's upstairs."

Dax hurried inside and rushed up to see Kai.

He found the merman curled up on top of the bed, fast asleep.

His first instinct was to wake Kai so he could tell him how much he loved him, but he appeared so peaceful, Dax didn't have the heart to disturb him.

Instead he carefully climbed onto the bed and wrapped himself around the sleeping merman.

Kai murmured in his sleep and snuggled closer. Dax smiled and closed his eyes. There would be time enough in the morning for them to talk, and hopefully to do a lot more too.

* * * *

Kai woke feeling far warmer than he had expected. It took a few moments before he realized the reason for the heat was Dax.

"Good morning," Dax whispered. "I hear you're thinking about running out on me."

Kai closed his eyes rather than meet Dax's gaze. "You don't need me now. You've found Kyle and he's obviously safe and well. You can make a new life here in England."

"Yes, I found Kyle, but that's not all I've found, is it?"

Kai didn't say a word.

"Look at me, Kai." Dax nudged Kai's chin and he opened his eyes. "You were right."

"About what?"

Dax leaned closer to whisper in his ear. "It *was* your name I called out on the night of the solstice."

Kai flushed in embarrassment at the reminder of his voyeurism.

"It was *you* I imagined when I took that other merman,"

Dax continued, his breath warm against Kai's ear.

"Lyon," Kai reminded him, his own voice catching slightly.

"Was that his name? I'd forgotten."

Kai wasn't sure he believed him, but he appreciated the gesture. "What are you doing here?"

"Waiting for you to wake up."

"You know what I mean. Why aren't you with Kyle and the others?"

"As huge as their bed is — and you should see it, it's enormous — I think there are plenty of men in it already."

"I guess." Did that mean they had refused Dax? Had he come here because he had no other option?

Dax's kiss took him by surprise. It was soft, gentle, and far too short. "You weren't really going to leave me, were you?"

"I don't know," Kai admitted. "The thought of making the journey alone is daunting."

"Well, don't you worry, I'm not letting you go anywhere without me."

"You mean that?"

"Yes, of course I do. Haven't you figured it out yet?"

"Figured what out?"

Dax smiled and pressed their lips together again. Kai sighed into the kiss. He let Dax take control for a moment before he pulled away.

"What haven't I figured out?" Kai asked again, hardly daring to hope. He had never seen Dax like this before. He seemed both tender and playful, and maybe just a little nervous.

"You knew before I did," Dax said. "I can't believe I didn't see it."

"See what?"

Dax frowned, but there was a twinkle in his eye. "You're going to make me say the words, aren't you?"

"Say what?"

"I love you, you infuriating merman."

"Infuriating?" Kai shot off the bed and glared down at Dax. "Why am *I* infuriating?"

Dax laughed as he held out a hand to Kai. "Come here, Kai. You're too far away from me."

"I'm not infuriating," Kai snapped. "You're the one who, who, who — wait — you're, did you say you're in love with me?"

"Oh, so you did hear something else besides infuriating?" Dax teased. "Yes, I did."

"Oh."

Kai stared at Dax for several long seconds.

"You know, Kai," Dax finally said, "this would be the perfect moment for you to tell me how you feel about me."

"I…"

When Kai hesitated, Dax's face fell. With his words deserting him, Kai did the only thing he could. He launched himself at Dax and threw himself into his arms.

"Does this mean you love me too?" Dax asked.

Kai nodded, still mute.

That was good enough for Dax. At least Kai guessed so from the way the merman held him and coaxed him gently onto his back.

"May I?" Dax asked.

Kai knew exactly what he meant without being told, and he opened his legs so Dax could see what he wanted. He expected Dax to eagerly push his way inside him, yet just as he had during their previous encounter, he surprised him by taking things slowly.

Dax rubbed his fingers between Kai's legs, touching him lightly at first, but growing firmer with each stroke. Kai quivered and moaned. When Dax inserted one of his fingers into Kai's arse, Kai groaned and gripped the sheets until his knuckles turned white. He stared down his body to where Dax worked magic between his legs.

"Fuck me," Kai whispered. "Please, Dax, I've wanted you for so long."

"How long?" Dax asked.

"Since I first saw you. Since I watched you with Lyon, wishing you were inside me instead of him. Please, please."

Dax pushed a second finger inside, and Kai gasped at the burn. "Do you want me to stop?"

"No, I need you. Please Dax."

Dax twisted his fingers and Kai bore down on his hand. "That's it, Kai. Now moan for me. Tell me how much you want this."

"So badly," Kai replied, with a loud groan of pleasure. "Need you in me."

Kai whimpered when Dax removed his fingers, but when he replaced them with his tongue he thought he might just die from sheer pleasure.

Dax lapped at him, over and over, licking around his arse and pushing his tongue into his tight hole.

Somewhere in the back of his mind, amid the jumble of knowledge Medina had given them, Kai remembered lube. While the goddess appeared to know little about modern technology and local colloquialisms she was a wealth of knowledge about all things relating to sex.

"Lube," Kai managed to say.

Dax nodded to indicate that he knew what he meant.

Unfortunately for Kai, even though they knew what lube was, and that right now they could do with some, they didn't know where they would find it, especially at such an early hour.

Dax sat up and crawled to the bedside table, opening one drawer after another, each as empty as the last.

"Try the bathroom," Kai suggested. "And hurry, please hurry."

Dax kissed him swiftly and ran for the bathroom. When he didn't reappear after several minutes, Kai went to find him. He found Dax searching through the cabinet, muttering in annoyance.

"Anything?" Kai asked.

"Not a damn thing. How can Malcolm have a gay son with two lovers and not have any lube in the house?"

"Because Finn doesn't live here," Kai pointed out. "Come on back to bed, we'll make do without."

Dax ignored him and continued his search.

Kai put his hand on Dax's shoulder. "If we were anywhere but the land of humans, there would be no lube for us to even know about."

"But we *do* know about it, and it'll make your first time so much easier."

Kai tugged Dax out of the bathroom and back into the bedroom. He drew him down onto the bed and back into the position they had been in before. He spread his legs and guided Dax between them. "We're not humans, we're mer. Ready me as you would have if I'd come with you to the island the night of the solstice."

"Are you sure?" Dax asked, glancing round the room at the other pieces of furniture, perhaps wondering if it might be worth searching them too.

"I'm sure," Kai said. He turned Dax's face back to him. "Finger me, lick me, make me wet. Then when I'm slick and ready for you, give me your cock."

"Oh fuck," Dax gasped.

"Unless you want me to prepare myself," Kai suggested with a grin. He put his index finger into his mouth and sucked on it noisily. When he had Dax's undivided attention he released the digit with a pop and slid his hand between his legs. He found his hole and thanks to Dax's earlier efforts his finger slipped inside with ease.

Dax's breathing became ragged and Kai could see his attention was fixated on the spot where Kai touched himself.

Kai pushed a second finger inside and Dax lowered his head. Dax's hair brushed against Kai's inner thighs as he licked around Kai's hole. Kai shivered as Dax slicked him with his saliva.

The sight of Dax's head between his legs and the feel of his tongue sliding over his sensitive flesh as he fingered himself was too much for Kai and he cried out as he lost control, spilling his seed over his belly.

Dax moved his attention from Kai's arse to his cock, licking lightly at the pulsating flesh as Kai's orgasm sent him spiraling into a place he had never dreamed existed. He floated, even though he wasn't anywhere near the water. He could see stars, yet the only thing above him was an off-white ceiling. His entire body felt as though a single feather-light touch would be enough to send him over the edge again.

Somewhere deep in Kai's soul, he knew this is what he would need on the solstice. Dax's tongue, warm and wet, as he licked him intimately, exploring him with his mouth, tasting him and readying him for what Dax himself would need to break his mating fever.

When Kai came back to his senses, Dax was licking at his seed, cleaning him up.

Kai's fingers were still inside his own arse, yet he felt fuller now, like there was something else there too. He moved one of his fingers and realized Dax had pushed a digit of his own inside him, stretching him even more than he had been before. Kai had been so lost in his pleasure he hadn't even noticed.

"Are you ready for me?" Dax asked.

Kai nodded and slid his fingers free. Dax did the same as he sat up on his knees. Kai let Dax pull him closer and push his legs farther apart. Dax gazed at his arse for several long minutes before he finally lined up his hard shaft with Kai's aching hole.

"Do it," Kai said. "Fuck me, Dax."

Dax didn't waste any time in obeying Kai's order. He pushed inside him with one swift thrust.

Kai cried out, this time not entirely in pleasure. Maybe they should have hunted longer for some lube, or asked Malcolm for some. It was too late now, though. Dax was inside him, the heat of his erection filling him so completely, he wondered how he had ever been satisfied with a couple of fingers.

"How are you doing?" Dax asked. "Good?"

"Yes," Kai groaned. The burn receded, and instead he felt full. When Dax gave the smallest nudge inside, Kai gasped. "Do that again."

Dax began to move in earnest, and all thoughts flew from Kai's mind. He could do nothing except hold on as Dax pumped his hips over and over, pushing Kai back toward the edge once more.

"Touch yourself," Dax commanded.

Kai wrapped his fingers around his cock. Even though he had so recently spent, the flesh was already hardening again. All mermen were very sexual creatures, with a lot of stamina and voracious sexual appetites. Kai, for the first time in his life, was able to bask in his nature, and feel like a normal merman.

As Dax thrust into him, faster and harder, Kai stroked himself with increasing speed.

Dax stiffened as he climaxed. Kai felt a new type of heat in his arse as Dax spilled into him, filling him with his seed as he screamed his release. Kai cried out in unison as he came for the second time.

Kai panted as Dax collapsed on top of him. He wondered whether he would ever be able to catch his breath again. Dax sounded similarly exhausted, but he finally managed to move. Kai winced as Dax withdrew from him.

"Sorry," Dax managed to say as he shifted to the side and rolled onto his back. "Are you all right?"

"Yes," Kai replied, once he had found his voice again.

"You're not hurting, are you?"

Kai considered the question carefully before he answered. He felt sore, but he wouldn't say he was hurting. "I feel fine."

"You're sure?"

Kai nodded. "I think maybe we better not do that again for a few hours, but yes, I'm sure."

Dax chuckled. "I suspect it'll take more than a few hours before the soreness in your arse is gone."

"I don't care," Kai said. "I like feeling sore. It means I'm a man now."

Dax laughed loudly.

"What's so funny?" Kai asked, feeling a little unsure in the face of Dax's obvious mirth.

"You've always been a man, at least as far as I could see."

"You know what I meant," Kai said. "Before I felt like a eunuch. Only I had all the right parts, but no way of using them."

Dax tilted Kai's face towards him. "Being untouched didn't make you less of a man."

"I know. It just felt that way sometimes." Kai rested his head on Dax's chest and closed his eyes. "I love you too," he whispered.

Dax didn't reply, other than to wrap an arm around Kai's shoulders. It was enough. Kai had no doubt he had waited long enough before giving himself to Dax. For the first time he was certain of his affections, and he sent a silent thank you to Medina for her part in bringing them together.

Kai had nearly drifted off to sleep when Dax spoke again. "We'll build a new life here, or anywhere you want," he said. "Just not in that prison of a city under the ocean."

It sounded a wonderful idea, yet Kai knew it was an impossible dream. His family were in the sunken city, and Delwyn, especially, needed him to return.

Dax had told him he loved him, but were his feelings strong enough for him to come back to the sunken city with him, knowing as soon as they crossed the boundary, they might never be able to experience the pleasure of sharing their bodies again?

* * * *

The next morning Kai slipped out of bed, hoping not to wake Dax. Unfortunately, he wasn't as stealthy as he would have wished and Dax stirred within moments of Kai leaving him.

"Where are you going?"

"For a swim," Kai replied.

"I'll come with you," Dax said. He hopped out of bed and pulled Kai into his arms for a lingering kiss. "It's been too long since I stretched my fins."

Kai pried himself away from Dax and checked the window. "There's no one on the beach. It's pouring with rain."

"Then let's go." Dax grabbed Kai's hand, and without bothering to dress, he shooed him out of the door.

Downstairs, Malcolm and Coral sat talking in the living room, but neither raised an eyebrow at the two naked mermen hurrying through the house.

"Just be careful no one spots you," Malcolm called after them.

Kai gave him a wave and a nod.

The two of them ran through the surf, dove beneath the waves and transformed into their half-fish forms. They swam on the surface of the water, splashing and playing like children in the sea.

When the vision came upon him, it took Kai completely by surprise. Because he had not triggered the vision himself he had no idea who or what he would see.

The stone columns toppled as the ground shook. The palace seemed to be the epicenter of the latest earthquake.

Mermen and mermaids swam out of the building. Kai caught sight of Ula's long aquamarine hair as the two guards at her sides steered her away from the danger. He searched for Delwyn amongst the chaos. Finally, he spotted him with his guard, directly in the shadow of a column swaying dangerously before tumbling towards the two mermen.

"No!" Kai screamed. "Delwyn!"

The dark shadow of a sea dragon swooped down. His guard appeared panicked, with no idea which way to go.

Then the vision ended and Kai could see only darkness. He tried to trigger another, but he was too weak and it was too soon.

"What is it?" Dax asked. "A vision? What did you see?"

"The sunken city," Kai replied. "I saw another earthquake."

"You called Delwyn's name?"

"He's in danger. I saw a sea dragon heading for him and the columns near him were collapsing."

"I thought the guards kept the sea dragons under control?"

"They do, but in the chaos I guess one broke loose."

"Is he okay?"

"I don't know. The vision ended before I saw the conclusion. I tried to trigger another one, but I'm too far away and my powers are too weak."

"You need to return to the sunken city, don't you?" Dax said.

Kai nodded. "I needed to anyway. Finn was right. I should never have left Delwyn behind, or Ula. They're my family. I have to go back and check that he's safe. If anything has happened to him, I'll never forgive myself."

"This isn't your fault," Dax assured him. "You can't blame yourself."

"Cari told me all our powers are weakened by my leaving. If I had stayed in the city, Ula might have been powerful enough to see the danger."

"We should at least let Malcolm and Coral know we're leaving."

Kai agreed. "You go and speak to them and I'll go find our spears."

"Are you sure you're up to using your powers that much?" Dax asked.

Kai smiled. "It's like I told you before, seeing things right in front of me takes a lot less effort. Now hurry up. I want to start back as soon as possible."

Dax swam back to the beach and Kai dove under the waves searching for the place they had hidden their spears before coming to shore. He wished they had taken the time to eat before going for their swim, but he wasn't hungry enough to waste time going back to land. They would find something to eat on the way, as unappetizing as the food in the immediate area was.

The sooner they returned to the sunken city, the happier Kai would be.

* * * *

Dax hurriedly relayed the details of Kai's vision to Malcolm and Coral. They understood immediately the urgency of the situation.

"I'm sure Delwyn will be fine," Coral said. "He's quite a resourceful young merman, from what I recall. He and Finn were good friends."

"So I've heard," Dax said. "But Kai's worried for him all the same."

"I'm sure he is. They were very close."

An unfamiliar stab of jealousy hit Dax in the gut. Even though he knew the two mermen had never been together sexually, the irrational part of his brain managed to provide him with plenty of mental images of them, bodies entwined. If this was jealousy, no wonder Kai had reacted so badly to Kyle kissing him.

Once he had thanked Malcolm for his hospitality, and accepted the use of his phone to speak to Kyle one last time, Dax raced back into the water. He found Kai with ease, and they began their long journey back to the sunken city.

Chapter Seventeen

Kai grabbed hold of Dax's arm as they swam away from the shore. The vision of the sunken city, rocked by another quake, came on so suddenly it took him by surprise. It didn't last long, and they swam on.

Less than an hour later, Kai stopped again.

"Another?" Dax asked when they were once more underway.

"Yes."

"Is that normal? To have two visions you haven't instigated, so close together?"

"It's happened before, but not very often," Kai replied. He didn't add that when it had, the visions weren't of events so far away. He hoped there wouldn't be any more for a while. He needed time to recover.

Too tired to see his surroundings, Kai let Dax guide him as they continued their journey.

A third vision, later that same day, made it obvious they weren't going to stop.

Kai watched a dozen mer flee from the marketplace, as one of the columns marking the entrance swayed dangerously. He searched for Delwyn, yet couldn't see his distinctive silver fins. He thought he saw Ula in the distance, but the vision ended before he could be sure.

"It's going to take us a long time to reach the sunken city if your visions keep coming at this frequency," Dax said.

"I know, but there's nothing I can do about them. I think I'm going to have to rely on you to guide me back. I can't keep using my powers to see where we're going. It's getting too tiring."

"Just hang onto my back," Dax suggested. *"We'll follow the*

currents as much as we can. Let me know when you need to rest."

Kai passed his spear to Dax and wrapped his arms around Dax's chest. They swam in tandem as Dax steered them on their way.

Kai hoped by preserving his strength he might be able to see Delwyn, and put his mind at ease.

* * * *

"You need to rest," Kai said as he tapped Dax on the shoulder.

Dax could see an island ahead of them and realized Kai must have been using his powers to see their surroundings. *"I'm good. I can go for a few more hours yet."*

"You've barely stopped for the last six days."

"I've rested a little when we caught the current."

"That's not enough. You need to sleep properly."

"I'm fine, really."

Kai smacked him on the chest. *"Well, I'm not. I need a break from these visions and I'm not going to get any while I'm in mer form."*

Dax hadn't even considered that. *"I'm sorry, I didn't realize. We'll head to land for a while."*

"Thank you." Kai rested his head between Dax's shoulder blades and let him carry him upward.

It was dusk when they reached the beach and Kai could barely keep his eyes open long enough to appreciate his restored vision. Dax wrapped him in his arms and let him sleep. Even though he was exhausted himself, he couldn't sleep right away. He wondered what awaited them on their arrival in the sunken city. Would he be thrown in the palace dungeons for kidnapping one of the Oracles, or would King Nereus be sympathetic to their situation? From what Finn and Kyle had told him, he had little hope of any forthcoming sympathy.

Finally, he slept, his dreams haunted by a green-eyed merman and an ache he could not assuage.

He woke grumpy and ill-tempered. Kai slept on, and Dax tried to shake off his bad mood before his lover rose. The thought of another solstice without release lingered in his mind. Dax wasn't sure he could handle going through the pain again, yet the thought of leaving Kai to participate in the city's mating rituals made him feel sick to his stomach.

Dax glanced at Kai and realized he had woken while Dax pondered their problem. Kai smiled up at him and stretched his arms above his head.

"Ah, you're awake," Dax said.

"I am indeed. Nice of you to finally notice." Kai's teasing smile brought an answering grin to Dax's own lips.

"Hungry?" Dax asked.

"Starving," Kai replied.

Dax pointed to the tree line behind them. "I'm sure we can find something to eat back there. Come on."

He made to stand up, but Kai pushed him back down before he had even fully found his feet.

"I'm not hungry for food right now."

Dax didn't believe him. His own stomach had been growling for hours. "We should eat first."

Kai ignored his advice and climbed on top of him. "I need you inside me."

Dax groaned as Kai rubbed up against him. His cock rose, hard and ready for Kai to ride him.

"We should probably get moving," Dax said, without any real conviction.

"My last few visions have shown no more quakes, just the mer putting things back together."

"Have you seen Delwyn?"

Kai shook his head. "No, but I think he must be safe."

"Why do you believe that?"

"Because I've seen Ula several times, and if he were..." Kai closed his eyes and shook his head. "He has to be safe or she would be mourning him. She doesn't act like someone who has lost her brother."

"Then why can't you see him?" Dax asked.

"I don't know. He might be in a temple where his presence is shielded from me, or he could be hidden by one of the immortals — Cari maybe — so I'm forced to return to check he is safe."

"If you're so sure he's safe because of Ula's demeanor, why go back?"

"Because I have to," Kai said. "Delwyn and Ula are my family. I could never have left them forever. I need to hold Delwyn in my arms, only then will I be sure he's well."

It had been so long since he'd had a real family, Dax wasn't quite sure he understood the connection between Kai and the other Oracles. He didn't need to understand the bond to respect Kai's wishes. His lover needed to go home, and prison or not, the sunken city *was* his home. Dax could do nothing else except deliver him safely back.

They made love on the beach. Kai straddled Dax and sank down on his stiff member. Dax could tell, from how loose he was, that Kai had been awake for longer than he had thought. The merman had prepared himself to take him, all while Dax had been gazing out over the waves. Kai set a slow and languid pace as he rocked back and forth.

Dax moaned as he reached out to touch Kai, stroking his lover's erection and coaxing him to full, aching, hardness. He fingered the tip of Kai's cock, each touch on the slit causing Kai to shiver and cry out.

When Kai clenched around him, Dax lost control completely. They came together and Kai fell forward onto Dax's chest. Dax cradled Kai in his arms as he rode out his orgasm.

"What are we going to do when we get there?" Dax asked, as he stroked Kai's back and arse. "I don't want this to be our last time together."

"There'll be other islands between here and the sunken city."

"You *know* what I mean."

Kai sighed. "Yes, I know, and I've no idea what'll happen when we return. I wish I did."

Kai eased himself out of Dax's embrace and nodded over at the trees. "I think I see some berries over there. We should eat before we get swimming."

Dax knew a change of subject when he heard one and didn't try to press the issue. He hoped today wouldn't be the last time they were together, but as he stepped into the surf, he couldn't quite shake the feeling of dread.

* * * *

Kai gazed up at the clear blue sky from his position on the last beach they would visit before they reached the islands used by the mer inhabitants of the sunken city.

He rested his head on Dax's shoulder as he traced his fingers along the now familiar scar on Dax's chest.

"How did you get this?" Kai asked. "Was it a shark?"

Dax chuckled. "A shark would have left a bigger mark than that. Nah, that was from a spear."

"You got in a fight with another merman?"

"No, we were training and I was distracted by a handsome set of fins."

Kai laughed. "I guess some things never change."

They rested quietly, their bodies sated and bellies full. Time was running out and Kai accepted he had to raise the subject they had both been avoiding. "We need to talk."

"I know," Dax replied. "So, have you had any thoughts about what we're going to do when we get to the city?"

"Have you?" Kai asked, hoping Dax had been hit with some inspiration, because he had nothing.

"Not really. I guess the first thing we need to decide is whether we sneak in the way we left."

"We can't," Kai said. "The tunnel collapsed behind us, and from what I've seen, no efforts have been made to fix the damage. The other repairs are more essential."

"Do you know of any other way to sneak in?"

"No, and the city is invisible until you pass the sea dragons anyway. The sea dragons hide the city from everyone, even those like us, who know where to search for the place. With guards on every dragon, it would be impossible to sneak in unless we know of any more tunnels leading outside the boundaries."

"Then we'll have to turn ourselves in as soon as we arrive?"

"I will, you don't have to."

"What do you mean?"

Kai studied his feet as he made grooves in the sand with his toes. "You don't have to come with me once we're in sight of the city."

Dax shook his head and drew Kai into his arms. "If you think I'm leaving you for even a day, you can think again. Whatever waits for us in the sunken city, we're going to face it together."

Kai breathed a sigh of relief. "I just wanted to give you the option, you understand?"

"Yes, I know, but it's not necessary. I'm coming with you."

"You do realize you might end up in the dungeons?"

"I know, but I'm trusting you'll visit me."

"Every day," Kai promised. "Though I hope it doesn't come to that."

"Me too."

Kai patted Dax on the back and eased away slightly. "We should probably get going."

Dax nodded, but neither of them made any effort to return to the ocean.

"It'll be okay," Kai said. "It has to be. Medina is protecting us, and she's the most powerful goddess around right now. I have to believe she'll find a solution that will allow us to be together, just like the rest of the merpeople."

The two mermen stood at the edge of the surf for a long time watching the sun sink past the horizon. They hadn't seen Medina since England. Kai would have a lot more faith in the goddess if she put in an appearance once in a while.

* * * *

The first sign of the sunken city was the solitary merman situated just outside the boundaries, waiting to guide in any visitors.

Kai had hoped to see Calder, who was often the guard on duty for such tasks, but his heart sank when he recognized Otus. Kai had never liked the arrogant merman and he silently cursed the bad luck that meant he would be the one to bring them in.

"Oh this is perfect," Otus crowed as they approached. *"The runaway Oracle and the merman who kidnapped him. I can't wait to see what King Nereus does to you when I bring you before him. I think a few decades in the dungeons for the pair of you would be a good thing."*

"King Nereus would never put one of the Oracles in the dungeons," Kai replied. *"He's always treated us well."*

"That's before you went swimming off, defying his orders," Otus pointed out. *"I think you'll find him less inclined to pander to your needs, now you've finally decided to return."*

"Won't he be relieved to see Kai's returned?" Dax asked.

"I'm sure he will, but he'll want to make sure the same thing doesn't happen again. You shouldn't worry about Kai, you have enough problems of your own. If you're lucky, he'll only banish you. I'd chain you up in the dungeons for the rest of your life, or feed you to the sea dragons."

"The sea dragons don't eat mer," Kai pointed out.

"Only because they never get the chance. They'd have a banquet with your friend *here."*

Kai cringed at the way Otus said the word friend. The inference — correct though it was — that they were lovers, sounded dirty and sordid when it came from Otus.

"One of them nearly took a bite out of your other little friend," Otus continued. *"A few more inches and we'd have had a new Oracle to babysit."*

Kai had heard enough. He did his best to ignore Otus as they continued on their way.

"Thank goodness he isn't in charge," Dax commented to Kai privately as they approached the palace.

Kai snickered to himself and took Dax's hand in his own.

King Nereus was holding audience, as he did every day, when they entered the building. Although it was normal practice for those who wished to see the king to queue, Otus shoved his way to the head of the line, pushing Kai and Dax ahead of him with his spear.

Thanks to Otus and his bad manners, they didn't have to wait long to be seen.

"King Nereus," Otus said in a voice that must have carried to everyone in the palace. *"I return to you our missing Oracle."*

Otus nudged him with his spear and Kai rubbed his arm where the tip of the weapon had caught him.

"Kai," King Nereus said. *"I'm glad to see you safe and sound. We feared for you when it was discovered you had left the city."*

Kai frowned. *"As you can see, I'm perfectly well, save for the scratch caused by this clumsy guard a moment ago."*

Otus began to protest, but King Nereus halted his words almost at once. *"You can return to your duties now."*

"But — "

"Now," King Nereus repeated.

Kai used his powers briefly and caught the furious expression on Otus' face as he swam out of the chamber.

"Come forward, Kai," King Nereus said, when only Kai, Dax, and Justin, sitting in his usual spot at the king's side, remained in the room.

Kai swam toward the throne, Dax at his side.

"I won't pretend I don't know why you left the city," King Nereus said. *"But you have to understand that now you've returned, it cannot happen again."*

Kai hung his head. *"What about Dax?"*

"Dax won't be punished. I spoke with Delwyn not long after you were discovered missing. It was clear from what he said, as well as what he didn't, you left of your own free will and the plan was largely of your own making."

"It was," Kai agreed. *"But what about in the future? Can I be*

with Dax?"

King Nereus was quiet as he considered the question. *"Dax can live in your quarters with you, and he can come and go to the island as he pleases."*

"What about the mating rituals?" Dax asked. *"I would wish to be with Kai on the solstice."*

"I'm sorry, but if I bent the rules for Kai, it would be unfair on the other Oracles. You can, however, benefit from the recent change in our law which means you can choose not to participate in the mating rituals if you so desire."

"I thought the law about the Oracles was so they can't have children," Dax said. *"Forgive me if I'm pointing out the obvious, but Kai and myself are both mermen. Procreation would be something of a miracle."*

"It would, but the law is for all of the Oracles, including Ula, who is female and desires men. If she should conceive we would run the risk of finding ourselves in the same situation we were in when the law was first made."

"But – "

"The law will not be changed," King Nereus interrupted. *"Now I suggest Kai take you to his quarters in the palace. I know there are a couple of mer there who'll be delighted to see him."*

They left the king and Kai guided Dax through the palace.

"At least you aren't being thrown in the dungeons," Kai said.

"I guess."

Kai didn't think Dax sounded particularly pleased about their lucky escape. King Nereus had been surprisingly lenient with them. Kai suspected Justin's influence had something to do with his change of heart. The king's son had definitely brought out his softer side.

Kai wondered what Dax would do when the next mating season arrived. He had avoided bringing up the subject with Dax because he knew how much his lover hated the idea of going without release on the solstice. Kai didn't want to admit *he* hated the idea of being stuck under the ocean while Dax went to land and found another merman to fuck.

He pushed the thought from his mind as he entered their chambers. Delwyn and Ula sat on two of the sponges, a board game between them. Ula was using her fingers to count out her moves by the ridges round the squares. Kai watched them for a few moments, knowing, thanks to his powers, that he had an advantage and neither of them had noticed him there.

"Missed me?" he asked.

Delwyn spun round and Kai swam into his arms, hugging him tightly. *"You came back? Why in the world would you do that? Didn't things work out with Dax? Did you make it to land? Did you find Kyle? What about Finn? Did you see him? Is he well? Did he ask about me?"*

Kai laughed at the barrage of questions. *"And here I thought the first question you'd ask would be whether I've had sex or not?"*

"Have you?" Delwyn asked. *"You have to tell me all about it, so I can live vicariously through your adventures."*

"From what I saw, you've been having a few adventures of your own," Kai said. *"The last vision I saw you in had a sea dragon diving at you in the middle of an earthquake."*

"You saw that?"

"Yes, it scared me half to death. Since then, no matter how hard I've tried, I've not been able to see you in a vision."

"How strange. I wonder why."

"I don't know. I wondered if perhaps Cari might be stopping me seeing you. So the only way I would know for sure you were safe would be to come back here, just as she wanted."

Kai could see Ula was eager to have her say as well, though she hesitated behind Delwyn. Kai pulled her into an embrace and was rewarded with a hard smack from her tail.

"That's for not even telling me what you planned on doing," Ula scolded. *"The first I knew about your plotting was when I had a vision of you sneaking down a tunnel in the middle of a quake."*

"You saw me leaving? Why didn't you say anything?"

Ula snorted. *"Unfortunately my vision didn't come early enough to stop you. The vision had barely ended before the quake hit. And don't even get me started on the fact you didn't take Delwyn with you when you took off."*

"I didn't want to go," Delwyn argued. *"I told Kai to leave me behind and if he found love, to stay away from this prison."*

"Since when did Kai ever take your advice?" Ula asked. *"He shouldn't have left you behind."*

"I'm right here," Kai reminded her.

"I know, that's why I'm saying this now, so you can hear me."

"I'm sorry," Kai said. *"I should never have left."*

"Yes, you should," Ula replied. *"But you should have taken Delwyn with you. He would have loved to see Finn again."*

"No, I wouldn't," Delwyn argued quietly. *"Not when seeing him means watching him happy and madly in love with someone else."*

Kai interrupted them with a nudge back toward the sponges. *"Let's sit down and you can let me and Dax know what's been happening while I've been away. I've seen lots of movements of the earth in my visions. How bad has it been?"*

"Dax is with you?" Delwyn asked.

"Yes," Kai replied. *"He's seen Kyle and now he's come back here with me. Now, tell me everything I've missed."*

They sat on the sponges with Dax taking a seat close to Kai. Neither of the other Oracles questioned his presence there. From Kai's point of view, Dax was part of their family now. It might take the others a little time to become accustomed to having him around, but they would welcome him.

"The immortals are waking up," Ula said. *"The God of Space and Time is already walking around, as is the God of the Earth and the Goddess of the Moon."*

"Has there been any trouble from them?" Kai asked. He would fill them in on his own meeting with the god who had the power to reset time later.

"Not yet, but this is just the start. I have been looking into the future as much as I can and things don't appear good for the mer."

"What do you mean?"

"There are some immortals who don't want us here. They never did, not even when the city of Atlantis first sank beneath the ocean. They see this as their place and the home of the Atlanteans, and they want the mer gone."

"Do they have that sort of power?" Dax asked.

"Not yet, but they will. Haven't you noticed your own powers growing in recent weeks? My visions are more than daily now and so are Delwyn's. As the gods awaken, our powers increase."

"My visions have increased in number too," Kai admitted. "What can we do to save our people?"

Ula shrugged. "I don't know. We've spoken with the king, but he won't entertain the idea of evacuation of the city. He believes we're safer here with the sea dragons and their power of invisibility protecting us from prying eyes."

"Will the sea dragons protect the mer from the gods?" Dax asked.

Delwyn shook his head. "No, they're prisoners of the mer. We can't control them and should they ever escape we'll be in as much danger from them as we are from the gods."

"What are we going to do?" Kai asked.

No one seemed to have any answers. When the room shook with another quake Kai grabbed hold of Dax and held on tightly. He wondered who was waking up now and whether they would be friend or foe.

Chapter Eighteen

Kai and Dax settled into the Oracles' quarters, and Kai wasn't surprised to see extra guards stationed on the door.

Dax glared at them, obviously unhappy at their presence.

"Come sit down," Kai urged. *"You must be as exhausted as I am."*

Dax swam to his side, yet sat a little farther away, compared to usual. *"Are they going to be with us all the time?"*

"For the moment, yes. Maybe in time King Nereus will agree to relax the guard on us."

"How much time?"

"A few years, maybe."

"Years!"

"You'll get used to them," Kai assured him. *"After a few months, you won't even notice they're here."*

Dax growled and pulled Kai through to the sleeping chamber off the main room. Kai didn't need to use his powers to know the guard followed right behind them.

"You aren't coming in here with us," Dax said. *"We're entitled to some privacy."*

"We have our orders," the largest of the two guards replied. *"The Oracle is not to be left alone for any reason."*

With one deft move, Dax grabbed the guard's spear and turned it on its owner.

"Get out," he snarled. *"I want to have some private time with my lover, and that means without the audience."*

Kai sighed. *"Just ignore them and come over here to me."*

Dax prodded the nearest guard with the spear. *"Get out,"* he repeated.

"We have orders not to leave the presence of the Oracle," the

guard argued.

"Kai. His name is Kai. He's more than just his powers. He's a fellow merman who wants some privacy."

"Dax, you're wasting your time. They aren't going to let me out of their sight, not after I left the city the way I did."

Dax swore and tossed the spear aside. Kai was right. The guards had no intention of leaving them alone together. *"Can you at least turn your backs?"*

Kai laughed. *"Since when have you been so shy?"*

"It's different when you're on a beach and everyone around you is having sex. These guards aren't busy finding their release, they're just watching us."

"You have to learn to ignore them," Kai said. *"Now, come over here and kiss me."*

Dax grumbled to himself, but with Kai appearing so tempting, stretched out on the sponge, licking his lips enticingly, he couldn't do anything other than obey.

"After a few years, you'll barely notice them," Kai promised as they kissed and touched.

"Easy for you to say," Dax complained. *"You don't have to see them staring if you don't use your powers."*

Kai chuckled in his mind and when he kissed him again, Dax nearly forgot they had company. *Nearly.*

* * * *

Within a few months, Dax had, mostly, managed to push the ever-present guards from his mind. It wasn't so easy when the guard was the extremely unpleasant Otus, who sent snide remarks to Dax whenever he got the chance, but most simply stood by and let the Oracles get on with their lives.

Dax curled on up the sleeping sponge with Kai, their kisses becoming increasingly urgent. *"I want you so badly, Kai."*

"I know, Dax. I need you too, and I'm sorry it's only going to get worse."

"What do you mean?"

"The mating season is almost here," Kai explained. "Haven't you noticed your temperature rising?"

Now Kai mentioned it, Dax had been feeling a little warm the last couple of days. He was surprised he hadn't noticed, but then again, his temperature rose every time he was in Kai's presence anyway, and they had barely spent a moment apart since their return to the city.

"What are you going to do tomorrow night?" Kai asked. He pulled out of the kiss and Dax could tell he was using his powers to study his expression.

"What do you mean?" Dax tried to avoid Kai's question by drawing him into another kiss, but the stubborn merman wouldn't let him distract him.

"You know what I'm asking," Kai replied.

Dax did, and the truth was he wasn't sure what he intended do when the time came. He knew the answer Kai wanted to hear. He wanted Dax to stay with him on the solstice. Yet, as the time drew near, Dax couldn't bring himself to agree, even though he knew going to the island would hurt Kai. He could already feel the sharp pain in his gut, and past experience told him the stabbing sensation would only worsen if he didn't have sex during the mating season.

He had gone through this before, when he'd lived in a clan with few mermen who desired their own gender. He hadn't imagined there would come a time when he'd be suffering without release again, and certainly not voluntarily.

Dax truly wanted to stay with Kai, but he couldn't bring himself to commit, not when every movement of his body sent another shot of pain through him, and he knew it would worsen over the coming days.

Kai pushed him away slightly and sighed. "You're going to go to the island, aren't you?"

"I don't know. I saw Gilad earlier, and I know he would be happy to let me join him and Keshet."

"Are you going to?"

"I don't know. I don't want to hurt you, but I don't want to go through the solstice without finding release either. I've done it before and I hate the pain."

"So do I, but I manage it."

Dax could tell he was handling the conversation badly, but he couldn't give Kai the answer he wanted. *"Sometimes sex is just that. Even if I went to the island with another merman, it wouldn't change how I feel about you. I love you more than I've ever loved anyone in my life."*

Kai rolled away and turned his back to Dax. *"If you feel you have to go to the island, I won't stop you."*

Dax groaned and ran his hands through his hair, tugging at the strands. *"Are you going to sulk if I go there?"*

"Sulk?" Kai swam off the sponge and flippered back and forth across the room. *"You're asking me to be happy about you going to land and having sex with another merman."*

"It's just sex."

"Not for me, it's not," Kai said. *"When I gave you my body, I gave you my heart too."*

Dax didn't know what to say. He didn't know how to make Kai understand what he meant about the difference between sex and making love. While his birth clan had mostly comprised committed couples, Dax's time, since leaving them, had been vastly different. He'd had sex with many mermen, and while some, like Gilad and Keshet, had become good friends, most disappeared from his thoughts as soon as they'd parted company. They didn't mean anything to him, and even those who had become friends didn't mean half as much to him as Kai did.

Kai swam over to another sponge and curled up. He kept his back to Dax and made it clear he wasn't welcome to join him right now.

Dax watched Delwyn swim in later and head straight for the sponge Kai was on, the place Delwyn had taken to sleeping. Dax knew the two male Oracles had often shared a sponge, he had seen them together himself. Yet he felt a twinge of jealousy as he watched Delwyn curl up next to

Kai.

"*Dax, are you in here?*" Delwyn asked.

"*Yes. I'm over here.*"

"*Had a fight?*"

"*How did you know?*"

"*Because Kai's on my sponge instead of his own. Is it because of the solstice?*"

"*What else?*"

"*I know you'll make the right decision,*" Delwyn said. He nudged Kai over to the other side of the sponge and made more room for himself.

Dax wondered why Delwyn had such faith in him.

Dax needed some advice and knew exactly where to go to find it. He searched the sunken city for Keshet and Gilad, but to no avail. He eventually found them outside the city at one of the gathering grounds. Gilad was picking fruits, while Keshet and his fellow guards kept their eyes open for predators.

"*Dax, what brings you here?*" Keshet asked.

"*I'm looking for you and Gilad, of course.*"

Keshet waved Gilad over. "*Have you changed your mind about tomorrow?*"

"*No, at least not yet. I don't know what to do and I was hoping you two might have some advice for me.*"

"*You know we'd welcome you to join us,*" Gilad said. "*You only have to ask.*"

"*I know, but Kai doesn't want me to.*"

"*He'd rather see you suffer?*"

Dax sighed. "*No, he says I can come with you if I want to.*"

"*Then what's the problem?*"

"*He doesn't* want *me to,*" Dax repeated. "*His words might say he understands, but his eyes tell me different. I don't know what to do.*"

"*He loves you,*" Keshet said. "*He's giving you permission to seek out what you need, even though it hurts him to do so.*"

Gilad nodded. "*What you need to ask yourself is whether you love him enough to give him what* he *needs.*"

"What would you do?" Dax asked. "If Keshet was imprisoned down here, would you go to land with another?"

"No."

"Are you sure about that? Have you ever been through a mating season without release?"

"Yes, we both have."

Dax blinked in surprise.

Gilad laughed. "We both went without before we met, and there have been a few seasons since when we've been too far from land."

"That's not the same thing as this."

"No, but it means we do understand the pain involved."

"So does Kai," Dax reminded them. "But he still wants me to suffer through it."

Gilad smacked him with his tail. "No, he doesn't, that's why he said you could go to the island."

Dax hit him back, but without much feeling. "If Keshet was locked up in the dungeons tomorrow, would you go to the island without him?"

"No."

"You sound very sure about that."

"That's because I am."

Dax faced Keshet. "What about you, if Gilad couldn't come to land?"

"I'd stay down here with him."

"Even if he told you it was okay to be with another merman?"

"I wouldn't tell him that," Gilad replied.

"And I wouldn't leave him to suffer alone," Keshet added. "If it were us, this wouldn't even be a discussion."

Gilad nodded. "We've been committed to each other for years now. Neither of us would leave the other behind during the mating season."

"You think I should stay with Kai, don't you?" Dax said.

"We're not going to tell you what to do," Keshet replied. "This is your decision. You have to make the choice for yourself."

"That's what I've been trying to do. But if I stay with him this solstice, he'll expect me to stay underwater every mating season.

The pain will get worse every time and the thought of going through that every solstice for the rest of my life terrifies me."

Gilad and Keshet exchanged a look Dax couldn't interpret. He had a feeling they were speaking privately and didn't wish to interrupt.

"Dax," Keshet said, *"ask yourself what scares you more, the pain of the mating season or losing Kai forever?"*

"Kai wouldn't end things with me if I went to the island tomorrow."

"Maybe not, but in time I think he'd start to resent it."

"Kai isn't that selfish."

Keshet raised a brow, but didn't say a word. He didn't have to, Dax understood. Kai wasn't selfish, but Dax was. He should have been putting Kai's feelings before his own. Dax thought it was about time he started to do that. He just hoped he had the courage to follow through.

* * * *

When Dax woke the next morning Kai and Delwyn had both already risen, leaving him alone in the chamber.

Not knowing what else to do, he went for a swim around the city, mulling over his thoughts and considering his options.

Keshet and Gilad had made their feelings clear. While they were happy for him to join them, they believed he would be selfish for doing so. Dax, though he hated to admit it, agreed with them.

Dax saw Malka at one of the market stalls, studying some large shells. Since losing her mate, Malka voluntarily chose to ride out the mating fever and suffer through the pain. Dax had never heard her complain. She had loved her mate and even though he was gone, she respected his memory. Dax admired her a great deal.

In the end it came down to one thing. He loved Kai, and if he wanted to be true to that love, he wouldn't — couldn't — do anything to hurt him.

Dax swam back to their chambers and saw Delwyn stretched out on a sponge, lost in a trance. Two guards lingered in the entrance and Kai sat eating a fruit. He didn't seem to be enjoying his meal.

"Delwyn's having a vision?" Dax asked.

Kai nodded. *"He retreated to the past a while ago."*

"Are you going to start meditating?"

"Not tonight."

"Why not?"

"My concentration isn't so good today. I can't focus."

"Because of me?"

"Yes."

Dax flinched and swam to Kai, taking him into his arms. *"I'm not going to go to the island. I've decided to stay here with you tonight."*

"You have?" Kai's unseeing eyes widened.

"Yes. I don't want *another merman. If loving you means I have to live a life of celibacy, so be it. We'll suffer through the solstices together."*

Kai hugged him tightly. *"I'm so selfish. I know how painful it is to go through the mating season without release, and yet I'm forcing you to do it because I'm such a jealous merman. You should go and find someone else who'll treat you better."*

"I don't want another merman. I have you and you're not selfish. Nor are you forcing me to stay down here. This is my choice. If our roles were reversed I wouldn't want you going up there with another merman and I would hate it if you went anyway."

Dax guided Kai to the sleeping sponge and held him in his arms. The ache to bury himself inside Kai was already a constant presence in his daily life. Now that the solstice had arrived it was becoming increasingly painful. Yet somehow the ordeal didn't seem quite as bad with Kai in his arms. He also reminded himself that as much as it pained him to go without release, Kai had been through this many times during the course of his life and if he had survived, so could Dax.

He didn't want to be selfish any longer. Kai made him

wish to be a better merman, one who put other's needs before his own. Staying with Kai instead of seeking his release would be the first step toward that.

His love for Kai would see him through the coming days. Together they would get through the solstice and all those to come.

Chapter Nineteen

A few days after the solstice, Cari appeared unexpectedly in the Oracles' living chamber.

One of the guards spotted her first.

"Calm yourself," Cari said. *"I mean my Oracles no harm. I'm here with good news."*

"You are?" Kai asked.

"Yes," Cari answered with a bright smile. *"I'm just sorry it didn't occur to me sooner. I believe we have found a solution to the problem of Oracles and their powers passing down to any child they may have. Medina gave me the idea with her constant reminders that I'm not the most powerful goddess awake any more. There are many gods and goddesses whose powers far exceed my own, and they are waking even now. I believe there is one among them who can help."*

All three Oracles sat up straighter, and Dax could see the hope on their faces. He took Kai's hand and gave it a squeeze.

"Come with me," Cari said. *"We're going to pay my mother a visit."*

The Oracles and their guards followed Cari out of the door. Dax was surprised to find their first stop was the chambers of Justin and Lucas. The goddess added the two mermen to their party, and they continued on their way.

Cari didn't seem to walk through the waters so much as disappear from one place and reappear in another a little farther down the way. They swam downward into the darkness as they followed her.

"Have you been down here before?" Dax asked Lucas.

"No." Lucas guided Justin round the corner. Dax followed

him, leading his chain of Oracles behind him.

They hadn't seen another merman or mermaid for at least ten minutes of swimming when Cari finally came to a halt.

"*Here we are,*" the goddess announced, waving them into the room ahead of her. "*This is the last surviving temple of my mother, and the best place from which to summon her.*"

The chamber was dark and gloomy. Dax could barely see a hand in front of his face. Suddenly lights emanated from the torches on the walls. He didn't know how the flames survived under the water, but since he could now see where they were, he wasn't going to question it.

"*You need to call out to my mother,*" Cari explained. She pointed to the worn stone statue at the far side of the room. "*No one has prayed to her in centuries. She sleeps, but your prayers may be enough to wake her, at least long enough for what we need her for.*"

"Who is your mother?" Dax asked.

"*She's the Goddess of Fertility, Family and the Home,*" Delwyn replied. "*She was most beautiful and known to be fair in all she did.*"

"*That's right,*" Cari said. "*Her family always came first.*"

"*How do we call her?*" Kai questioned.

Cari swam to the side and gestured for the mermen to move closer to the statue. Dax and Lucas guided the Oracles and Justin closer. "*You'll need to call her by her given name,*" she explained. "*Only that will have enough power to wake her at the present time.*"

"*What do you mean?*"

"*The Oracles have always known me as the Goddess of Prophecy and calling out to me in such a manner will ensure I hear their call. This is because I'm still a part of this world. My mother, unfortunately, has been in stasis for a long time. To bring her forth today will require more, and using her given name should be enough.*"

"*And what is her name?*"

"*Odessa.*"

Dax repeated the unfamiliar name several times in his

head. He wasn't entirely sure this would work, but what else could they do? It wasn't as if they had anything to lose.

"Call out to her together," Cari advised. *"Repeat your entreaty over and over. It's the only way to make her hear us."*

All the mermen began the chant, doing as the goddess instructed. They kept up their prayers for a long time, until Dax wondered whether they were wasting their efforts.

The tiny glowing lights in front of him flickered in and out of sight so fast he couldn't be sure he had seen them. The more he concentrated on the spot in front of the statue, the more convinced he became that something was there. The glow intensified and grew larger, until Dax was sure the goddess had heard them and was even now coming to her temple.

It took quite a while, the lights fading before brightening again, until eventually the goddess stood before them. She didn't seem solid, like Cari, but she was definitely there. She shimmered in and out of existence, and when she first opened her mouth to speak Dax couldn't hear her.

"Mother, thank you for coming to us," Cari said.

The goddess stared around her chamber with a frown of confusion. *"What has happened to my temple?"* Her voice seemed to come from a great distance, echoing in his mind as though from the far end of a tunnel.

"I'm afraid it has fallen into disrepair over the centuries," Cari replied.

"Centuries?" Odessa asked. *"How long have I been sleeping? Where's Caspian?"*

"Caspian's on land at the moment," Cari told her. *"He sends his love."*

Odessa appeared doubtful. Justin gave a small snort beside him. Dax had a feeling he didn't believe Cari's words either. He couldn't imagine the bad-tempered god sending anyone his love.

The newly woken goddess shimmered out of sight for a moment. *"I feel quite weak. What have you summoned me for, my daughter?"*

"My Oracles are in need of your assistance," Cari explained.

"They need me to bless them?"

Cari shook her head. "No, they need you to curse them."

"What have they done to upset you?" Odessa asked. "And why can't you simply remove their powers to punish them?"

"My powers have diminished a great deal since we last spoke. I don't have the strength to take away powers I have gifted and give them to another in their stead."

"There are other ways of punishing them."

"They have done nothing to offend me, and don't need punishing."

"Then why do you wish me to curse them?"

"My Oracles have been forced to live lives of celibacy for many centuries, because their gifts of sight transfer down from parent to child."

"That didn't used to happen," Odessa commented.

"No, only since that day."

Odessa gave Cari a speculative look. "Are you saying I caused this?"

"I'm not sure if you caused it, but many things happened that day and this seems to be one of them."

"I don't know how to undo whatever magic has caused this, not without causing repercussions for Caspian."

"I'm not asking you to," Cari assured her. "I'm hoping you might have enough power to curse my Oracles with infertility."

"Ah, I see. You wish for them to never have children at all."

"Yes. At the moment they are unable to take lovers, though as you can see, it doesn't stop them falling in love. If you were to curse them, they would be able to live and love, as other mer do."

"And they would agree to such a curse?" Odessa looked them over speculatively.

"Yes," Dax said.

Odessa stared at him, her eyes cold. "You are not an Oracle. Do you seek to be cursed as well?"

"Yes," Dax replied. "If that's the price I have to pay for a relationship with Kai, then yes, curse me as well."

Odessa raised her hand. "Such a curse will be unbreakable.

251

There will be no turning back, no changing of minds. Do you understand?"

The Oracles all nodded, as did Justin.

"What of you?" Odessa asked Lucas. *"Do you wish to be infertile too?"*

"Like Dax, I'll pay that price if you wish."

"Then step forward, all of you, and let me touch you."

One by one each of the mermen swam forward, with Lucas and Dax helping those who were blind. Odessa touched her hand to each merman, leaving on their skin a tattoo of a trident. For the Oracles it was the second mark of that kind. *"A sign you have been touched, or in this case cursed,"* she explained when Dax rubbed at the mark. *"It is permanent and will remain until the end of your life."*

Dax didn't mind. As long as he could be with Kai, he would put up with a simple tattoo. It was a small price to pay.

"What of you, child?" Odessa asked when Ula took her turn. *"Unlike these mermen who desire their own gender, you appear to be different. If I curse you, you will be giving up any chance of children when you find the merman you wish to spend the rest of your life with."*

"As a prisoner here, my chances of having children are equally remote. At least this way I will be able to spend the mating seasons with the merman I love, instead of the way it is now."

Odessa placed her hand on Ula's shoulder and a second trident appeared on her skin too. *"It is done. Now I must rest. This task has taken a lot of energy."*

"Thank you, Mother," Cari said.

Odessa smiled as she faded out of view. *"It won't be long now until I'm able to walk among you once more."*

The goddess vanished from the chamber, leaving no trace of her presence.

Kai clung to Dax's arm. *"Does this mean we can be together properly now?"*

Dax turned to Justin. *"Will your father change the law? Will he let them go to land with the rest of us?"*

"I'll speak to him immediately," Justin promised. *"With the mark of the trident upon each of us, he should believe what we tell him."*

"I'll go with you," Cari said. *"With me at your side to confirm what you're saying, he cannot deny your request. Besides, it was myself who insisted on the law being introduced in the first place. I have every right to request it be changed now. I only wish I had considered this option sooner."*

Dax smiled at Kai and squeezed his hand. He could tell what Kai was thinking without communicating with him. As soon as King Nereus repealed the law, Dax had every intention of taking Kai to land and making up for lost time.

Finally, they had a future together.

Epilogue

Delwyn looked around the island, his eyes wide as he shielded them from the sun.

Kai and Dax watched him as he took in his surroundings. He wobbled unsteadily on his feet, but they stayed at his side, ready to catch him if he began to fall.

Ula and the merman she had been in love with for so long had already disappeared into the trees. Even though it wasn't the solstice, the Oracles acted as if it were.

Kai raised his eyebrows in Dax's direction, and his lover nodded. They had talked about Delwyn and the fact he was the only Oracle who didn't have someone to be with.

"Delwyn, I made you a promise once," Kai said.

Delwyn glanced up from studying his toes. "Hmm?"

"I said I'd never leave you to suffer through a solstice alone."

"It's not the solstice," Delwyn reminded him.

"No, but my offer still stands."

Delwyn gaze flickered momentarily to Dax. "And what do you think about that?"

"I love Kai, and I know he loves me. I also know he loves you."

"Dax understands we come as a pair, at least for so long as you don't have a merman of your own to be with."

Kai took Delwyn's hand and guided him down to sit on the sand. Dax sat beside them on the other side of Delwyn.

Delwyn smiled back and forth between them. "You don't have to worry about me. I'm sure the love of my life is just around the corner."

"But until he turns that corner, you have us," Kai assured

him.

Delwyn kissed Kai, thrusting his tongue into his mouth and moaning. He ended the kiss sooner than Kai would have anticipated. "I love you, Kai, but I'm not *in love* with you. You have Dax now, and I won't come between you."

"You wouldn't be," Dax assured him.

Delwyn shook his head. "You're kind and I know you'll take care of Kai, but I promise I'll be perfectly fine."

Delwyn stood and brushed the sand from his legs and buttocks. "I'm going to take a walk along the beach. I'll be back in an hour or so, will that be long enough for you two?"

"More than long enough," Kai said. "And if you want to join us, you know where to find us."

Delwyn smiled. "Call me a fool, but I think I'd rather wait for the man of my dreams, even if I have to go through a few more painful solstices."

"If you change your mind..."

"I won't."

Delwyn wandered off down the beach, leaving Kai and Dax sitting on the sand.

"I can't believe he doesn't want to join us," Dax said.

"I can," Kai replied with a smile. "Delwyn is a romantic. He has read the stories of heroes and heroines on the walls of the city and he believes in true love and soulmates."

"Are you saying you don't?" Dax teased as he trailed kisses down Kai's neck and chest.

"I'm becoming convinced," Kai replied as Dax slipped his hand between Kai's legs, stroking him with feather light touches.

It had been a few months since they had last come together and for Kai it was too long. He couldn't wait for Dax to enter him. He pulled Dax down on top of him and wrapped his legs around Dax's thighs, trapping their erections between their bodies.

They rubbed against each other, keening and moaning, until they spilled together, crying out their pleasure for everyone on the island to hear.

"Too fast," Kai gasped. "Way too fast."

"It's fine," Dax replied, equally breathless. "We can stay here all night if we want. You're no longer a prisoner, which means we can come here whenever we like, for as long as we wish."

They still had guards, because the Oracles were still the most protected mer in the sunken city, but for the first time Kai felt as if the guards really did just watch over them, keeping them safe, rather than holding him prisoner against his will.

Life was good. Kai basked in the knowledge he was safe in his lover's arms with his family close by. This life was more than he had ever hoped to have and he had never been happier.

"Make love to me," he said as he stared into Dax's eyes.

Dax kissed him deeply and did exactly as Kai asked, taking him to the stars and beyond as they came together with a passion that left Kai shaking, breathless, and thoroughly sated.

They slept on the beach, secure in each other's arms and in their love for each other.

He has no choice except to go where most angels fear to tread.

HEAVENLY SINS

BETWEEN LIFE & DEATH

Between Life & Death

Excerpt

Chapter One

In the exact center of the entire Underworld the throne room of the king of all demons could be found. Easy to find from any direction, the audience chamber drew demons in like moths to a flame. Escaping the large cavern was another matter entirely. For many demons—particularly those who had incurred the wrath of the Demon King—the only way out was via flames that shot out from the cracks of the floor, sucking the miscreant down into the torture chambers, known as The Pit.

For one demon, there was no way to leave the Underworld at all.

At the back of the throne, hidden behind a stone wall, the chambers of the Demon King were located.

Tristan's new quarters were not at all what he'd expected. Luxurious and well lit, they were nothing like the rest of the Underworld. He had expected to find a dingy and dirty cave, something similar to the catacombs he had stayed in with Alastor not so long ago. Instead, the chamber seemed more like a swanky hotel room, though one without windows. The wall sconces were not naked flames as he had seen throughout the Underworld. Instead they appeared to be electric, although he could see no obvious light switches on the walls. Tristan cringed at the brightness of the nearest of the lamps and as soon as the thought formed in his mind, the light dimmed to a more bearable level.

Thick rugs covered most of the highly polished marble floor.

Every item of furniture seemed to be modern and expensive. The glass coffee table held current magazines and newspapers, including the ones Tristan liked to read on a regular basis. The bookshelves showcased his favorite books, all of which were in mint condition.

A bowl of fruit sat on an end table and even from a distance, Tristan could see the bowl was made of silver. He sighed and shook his head.

All the luxury in the world made no difference to the fact he had been imprisoned.

How had he gone from a regular human with a job and a life to king of the Underworld?

The bed, large enough to accommodate him and his lovers with ease, looked comfortable and tempting. Like his bed at the penthouse flat he shared with Mac and Alastor, the headboard comprised of iron bars, perfect for holding onto while being taken by one of his men. Tristan wanted to take a torch to the sheets and set the whole thing alight. Had the sconces been actual flames, he may have done just that.

"Your quarters really aren't so bad."

Tristan spun round at the sound of his jailer's voice.

"You think I want to sleep in the bed of the monster who put me here?"

"This bed wasn't his," Lucifer replied. He walked to the object in question and ran his hand lovingly over the surface.

"This room is new and created by your own subconscious mind."

"It is?"

Lucifer smiled and pointed to the bookshelf at the far side of the room. "Take a look and tell me what you see there."

Tristan shrugged. He had already seen the shelves. "They contain my favorite books. So what? I'm still your prisoner."

Lucifer ignored his comment. "I must say…this room is a vast improvement on your predecessor's quarters. He had no taste at all. Did you know the candle holders he used had been made from human skulls?"

"No I didn't know that, nor did I wish to."

"There's no need to be rude," Lucifer chided. "I'm merely making conversation and paying you a compliment on your superior taste in decorating."

"What are you doing here?" Tristan asked impatiently. "I thought you intended to give me time to celebrate my new status with Alastor?"

"And were he here with you, I'd leave my visit until later, but you haven't bothered to summon him, have you? Instead, you're wallowing in self-pity in a manner unbecoming of the new king."

"Are you avoiding my question?" Tristan snapped. "Why are you here?"

"Idle curiosity as to what makes our new king tick," Lucifer replied. "This room only generated when you crossed the threshold, so I couldn't snoop earlier."

"But now you can."

"Yes. I make no apologies for my actions. If you don't like my being here, tough luck."

"Charming."

"I can be extremely charming when the occasion warrants it," Lucifer purred as he continued to poke around the room, checking cupboards and alcoves as he did. "My lover has always said my smooth tongue and way with words are my greatest talents. After all, I am the First Demon, and were I not so tempting, I would be the only one."

Tristan crossed his arms and waited for Lucifer to finish wandering.

"Ah, yes, I think you'll settle in here quite well."

"I don't want to stay here."

Lucifer gave him an annoyed look. "You can sulk, complain and rage until hell freezes over, it makes no difference."

"Maybe I'll turn the heating off," Tristan suggested.

Lucifer chuckled. "Oh, I suspect the heat will be rising in here before too much longer."

"What do you mean?"

"The Underworld will be opening again soon, which means regardless of whether you summon him or not, Alastor will be running down here in search of his missing 'baby'. I suspect it will only be a matter of time before he's in here helping you to break in your new bed."

Tristan sighed. "I think we have a lot of talking to do before we jump into bed again."

"You're an incubus. You'll be fucking him through the mattress before the end of the week."

Tristan didn't see the point of arguing with Lucifer. If he and Alastor did manage to sort through their problems, it would have nothing to do with the demon standing before him.

Lucifer continued to poke around the room while Tristan did his best to ignore him. Eventually he stepped into the path of the demon and glared at him. "Are you done?"

"You really shouldn't be so rude to me," Lucifer chided. "I'm here to help you."

"Help me?" Tristan shook his head and rolled his eyes. "Help me, he says."

"Who else is suitably qualified to guide you through your first days as our new king?"

"What makes you think I need your help?"

Lucifer smiled, clearly unfazed by Tristan's attitude. "Even now the throne room is filling up with the leaders of each of the factions of demons, all here to bow down before you and swear their loyalty."

"You're joking."

"Well, most of them will probably want to kill you and take your place, if truth be told, but they generally wait until after the banquet is over."

Tristan dropped into one of the soft leather chairs. "This is going to be a disaster."

"Not if you let me guide you."

"Why are you so keen to help me? What difference does it make to you who's king?"

"I don't care who sits on the throne, but I do like to ensure our new kings are settled in as soon as possible. That way I can turn my attention back to more pleasurable activities."

Tristan cast a glance toward the wall where the entrance to his rooms had been. "How do I even get out into the throne room again?"

"Just walk toward the entrance and imagine the doorway opening for you."

Tristan took a step forward and the entrance began to form. The most powerful demons in the Underworld congregated just on the other side of the wall. Shit!

"Wait a moment," Lucifer called. "You aren't ready to go out there yet."

Tristan looked down and groaned when he realized what Lucifer meant. He couldn't go out there in his human form. Reluctantly he took on his golden demon persona.

"You should be wearing something more appropriate than that dirty tunic too," Lucifer advised. With a snap of his fingers, the tunic transformed into a silken black one with gold braiding. Tristan hated the garment on principle.

"We'll be invisible when we first go out there," Lucifer said. "You'll appear before the crowd when you sit down on the throne."

"Why?"

"Because that's how it's done. I'll remain at your side, invisible to all others. I'll speak to you only in your mind and tell you what you need to know."

"Terrific."

"I'm glad you think so, because you'll need me there."

Without any further ado, Lucifer swept past Tristan and out through the entrance. Tristan dawdled after him with a sigh of annoyance.

The throne room appeared packed to the brim with demons, many of them jostling their way to the front of the room. Some openly fought with others, while still more watched the displays of aggression. Tristan could tell instinctively which demons fed on the hatred and which merely looked on in idle interest. He had a feeling this might be one of his new powers, though he didn't bother to ask Lucifer to confirm his suspicion.

More books from
L.M. Brown

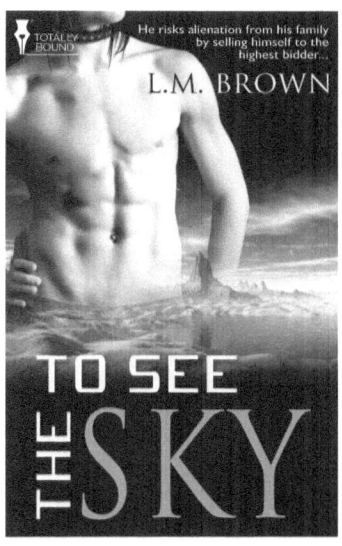

Can a lab rat whore find love with the servant of his master, or will their different backgrounds and prejudices keep them apart?

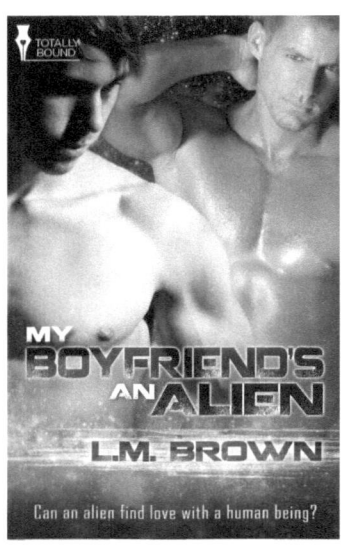

Can an alien with no knowledge of humans or concept of sex find lasting love with a human man?

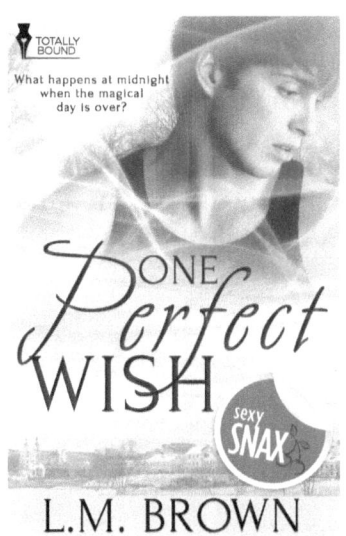

ONE
Perfect
WISH

sexy
SNAX

L.M. BROWN

Playing the part of another man's husband to fulfil a wish
is easy, but what happens at midnight when the magical
day is over?

About the Author

L.M. Brown

I live in England, in a quaint little village that time doesn't seem to have touched. No, wait a minute—that's the retirement biography. Right now I am in England in a medium sized town that no one has ever heard of, so I won't bore you with the details. Keeping me company are numerous sexy men. I just wish that they weren't all inside my head.I love hearing from readers so don't be shy.

L.M. Brown loves to hear from readers. You can find contact information, website details and an author profile page at https://www.pride-publishing.com/